D0727152

Please return/renew this item by the last date shown on this label, or on your self-service receipt.

To renew this item, visit **www.librarieswest.org.uk** or contact your library

Your borrower number and PIN are required.

Libraries**West**

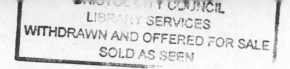
PARASITE POSITIVE

By Scott Westerfeld

Midnighters
THE SECRET HOUR
TOUCHING DARKNESS
BLUE NOON

PARASITE POSITIVE

THE LAST DAYS

THE RISEN EMPIRE

SCOTT WESTERFELD

parasite

positive

www.atombooks.co.uk

ATOM

First published in the United States in 2005 by Razorbill,
Penguin Group (USA) Inc.
First published in Great Britain in 2007 by Atom

5 7 9 10 8 6 4

Interior design by Christopher Grassi

A CIP catalogue record for this book
is available from the British Library.

ISBN 978-1-905654-07-9

Typeset in Caxton and American Typewriter by M Rules
Printed and bound by CPI Group (UK) Ltd, Croydon, CR0 4YY

Papers used by Atom are from well-managed forests
and other responsible sources.

MIX
Paper from
responsible sources
FSC www.fsc.org   FSC® C104740

Atom
An imprint of
Little, Brown Book Group
Carmelite House
50 Victoria Embankment
London EC4Y 0DZ

An Hachette UK Company
www.hachette.co.uk

www.atombooks.co.uk

To the Australian science-fiction community
for their winning and welcoming ways

After a year of hunting, I finally caught up with Sarah.

It turned out she'd been hiding in New Jersey, which broke my heart. I mean, *Hoboken*? Sarah was always head-over-heels in love with Manhattan. For her, New York was like another Elvis, the King remade of bricks, steel, and granite. The rest of the world was a vast extension of her parents' basement, the last place she wanted to wind up.

No wonder she'd had to leave when the disease took hold of her mind. Peeps always run from the things they used to love.

Still, I shook my head when I found out where she was. The old Sarah wouldn't have been caught dead in Hoboken. And yet here I was, finishing my tenth cup of coffee in the crumbling parking lot of the old ferry terminal, armed only with my wits and a backpack full of Elvis memorabilia. In the black mirror of the coffee's surface, the gray sky trembled with the beating of my heart.

It was late afternoon. I'd spent the day in a nearby diner, working my way through the menu and waiting for the clouds to clear, praying that the bored and very cute waitress wouldn't start talking to me. If that happened, I'd have to leave and wander around the docks all day.

I was nervous – the usual tension of meeting an ex, with the added bonus of facing a maniacal cannibal – and the hours stretched out torturously. But finally a few shafts of sun had broken through, bright enough to trap Sarah inside the terminal. Peeps can't stand sunlight.

It had been raining a lot that week, and green weeds pushed up through the asphalt, cracking the old parking lot like so much dried mud. Feral cats watched me from every hiding place, no doubt drawn here by the spiking rat population. Predators and prey and ruin – it's amazing how quickly nature consumes human places after we turn our backs on them. Life is a hungry thing.

According to the Night Watch's crime blotters, this spot didn't show any of the usual signs of a predator. No transit workers gone missing, no homeless people turning psychotically violent. But every time New Jersey Pest Control did another round of poisoning, the hordes of rats just reappeared, despite the fact that there wasn't much garbage to eat in this deserted part of town. The only explanation was a resident peep. When the Night Watch had tested one of the rats, it had turned out to be of my bloodline, once removed.

That could only mean Sarah. Except for her and Morgan, every other girl I'd ever kissed was already locked up tight. (And Morgan, I was certain, was *not* hiding out in an old ferry terminal in Hoboken.)

Big yellow stickers plastered the terminal's padlocked doors, warning of rat poison, but it looked like the guys at pest control were starting to get spooked. They'd dropped off their little packets of death, slapped up a few warning stickers, and then gotten the heck out of there.

Good for them. They don't get paid enough to deal with peeps.

Of course, neither do I, despite the excellent health benefits. But I had a certain responsibility here. Sarah wasn't just the first of my bloodline – she was my first real girlfriend.

My *only* real girlfriend, if you must know.

We met the opening day of classes – freshman year, Philosophy 101 – and soon found ourselves in a big argument about free will and predetermination. The discussion spilled out of class, into a café, and all the way back to her room that night. Sarah was very into free will. I was very into Sarah.

The argument went on that whole semester. As a bio major, I figured 'free will' meant chemicals in your brain telling you what to do, the molecules bouncing around in a way that *felt* like choosing but was actually the dance of little gears – neurons and hormones bubbling up into decisions like clockwork. You don't use your body; it uses you.

Guess I won that one.

There were signs of Sarah everywhere. All the windows at eye level were smashed, every expanse of reflective metal smeared with dirt or something worse.

And of course there were rats. Lots of them. I could hear that even from outside.

I squeezed between the loosely padlocked doors, then stood waiting for my vision to adjust to the darkness. The sound of little feet skittered along the gloomy edges of the vast interior space. My entrance had the effect of a stone landing in a still pond: The rippling rats took a while to settle.

I listened for my ex-girlfriend but heard only wind whistling over broken glass and the myriad nostrils snuffling around me.

They stayed in the shadows, smelling the familiarity of me,

wondering if I was part of the family. Rats have evolved into an arrangement with the disease, you see. They don't suffer from infection.

Human beings aren't so lucky. Even people like me – who don't turn into ravening monsters, who don't have to run from everything they love – we suffer too. Exquisitely.

I dropped my backpack to the floor and pulled out a poster, unrolling it and taping it to the inside of the door.

I stepped back, and the King smiled down at me through the darkness, resplendent against black velvet. No way could Sarah get past those piercing green eyes and that radiant smile.

Feeling safer under his gaze, I moved farther into the darkness. Long benches lined the floor like church pews, and the faded smell of long-gone human crowds rose up. Passengers had once sat here to await the next ferry to Manhattan. There were a few beds of newspaper where homeless people had slept, but my nose informed me that they'd lain empty for weeks.

Since the predator had arrived.

The hordes of tiny footsteps followed me warily, still unsure of what I was.

I taped a black-velvet Elvis poster onto each exit from the terminal, the bright colors clashing with the dingy yellow of the rat-poison warnings. Then I postered the broken windows, plastering every means of escape with the King's face.

Against one wall, I found pieces of a shredded shirt. Stained with fresh-smelling blood, it had been flung aside like a discarded candy wrapper. I had to remind myself that this creature wasn't really Sarah, full of free will and tidbits of Elvis trivia. This was a cold-blooded killer.

Before I zipped the backpack closed, I pulled out an eight-inch

'68 Comeback Special action figure and put it in my pocket. I hoped my familiar face would protect me, but it never hurts to have a trusty anathema close at hand.

I heard something from above, where the old ferry administration offices jutted out from the back wall, overlooking the waiting room. Peeps prefer to nest in small, high places.

There was only one set of stairs, the steps sagging like a flat tire in the middle. As my weight pressed into the first one, it creaked unhappily.

The noise didn't matter – Sarah had to know already someone was here – but I went carefully, letting the staircase's sway settle between every step. The guys in Records had warned me that this place had been condemned for a decade.

I took advantage of the slow ascent to leave a few items from my backpack on the stairs. A sequined cape, a miniature blue Christmas tree, an album of *Elvis Sings Gospel*.

From the top of the stairs, a row of skulls looked down at me.

I'd seen lairs marked this way before, part territorialism – a warning to other predators to stay away – and partly the sort of thing that peeps just . . . liked. Not free will but those chemicals in the brain again, determining aesthetic responses, as predictable as a middle-aged guy buying a red sports car.

More tiny feet skittered when I kicked one of the skulls into the gloom. It rolled with a limping, asymmetrical *ka-thump*, *ka-thump* across the floor. As the echoes died away, I heard something human-size breathing. But she didn't show herself, didn't attack. I wondered if she recognized my smell.

'It's me,' I called softly, not expecting any response.

'Cal?'

I froze, not believing my ears. None of the other girls I'd ever dated had spoken at all when I'd tracked them down, much less said my name.

But I recognized Sarah's voice. Even raspy and desiccated, as dry and brittle as a lost contact lens, it was her. I heard her dry throat swallow.

'I'm here to help you,' I said.

There was no answer, no movement of rats' feet. The sounds of her breathing had stopped. Peeps can do that, subsist on pockets of oxygen stored in the parasite's cysts.

The balcony stretched before me, a row of doors leading to abandoned offices. I took a few steps and glanced into the first one. It was stripped of furniture, but I could see the outlines of tiny cubicles imprinted into the gray industrial carpet. Not a terrible place to work, though: Iron-framed windows overlooked the harbor, the views magnificent, even though the glass was broken and smeared.

Manhattan lay across the river, the downtown spires lighting up as the sun went down, painting the glass towers orange. Strange that Sarah would stay here, in sight of the island she'd loved. How could she stand it?

Maybe she was different.

Old clothes and a couple of crack vials littered the floor, along with more human bones. I wondered where she had been hunting and how the Watch had missed the kills. That's the thing about predators: They leave a huge statistical footprint on any ecosystem. Get more than a dozen of them in even the biggest city and the homicides show up like a house on fire. The disease has spent the last thousand years evolving to conceal itself, but it gets tougher and tougher for man-eaters to stay hidden. Human beings are prey with *cell phones*, after all.

I stepped back into the hall and closed my eyes, listening again. Hearing nothing.

When I opened them, Sarah stood before me.

I sucked in a breath and the most trivial of thoughts went

through me: *She's lost weight*. Her wiry body almost disappeared in the stolen rags she wore, like a child in borrowed, grown-up clothes. As always when running into an ex after a long time, there was the weirdness of seeing a once-familiar face transformed.

I could see why the legends call them beautiful: that bone structure right there on the surface, like heroin chic without the bad skin. And a peep's gaze is so intense. Adapted to the darkness, their irises and pupils are huge, the skin around the orbitals pulled back in a predatory face-lift, revealing more of the eyeballs. Like Botoxed movie stars, they always look surprised and almost never blink.

For a brief and horrible moment, I thought I was in love with her again. But it was just the insatiable parasite inside me.

'Sarah,' I breathed out.

She hissed. Peeps hate the sound of their own names, which cuts into the tangled channels of their brains just like an anathema. But she'd said, 'Cal . . .'

'Go away,' came the raspy voice.

I could see hunger in her eyes – peeps are always hungry – but she didn't want me. I was too familiar.

Rats began to swirl around my feet, thinking a kill was coming. I stamped one of my rat-proof cowboy boots down hard to send them scurrying. Sarah bared her teeth at the noise and my stomach clenched. I had to remind myself that she wouldn't eat me, *couldn't* eat me.

'I have to take you out of here,' I said, my fingers closing on the action figure in my pocket. They never went without a fight, but Sarah was my first real love. I thought maybe . . .

She struck like lightning, her open palm landing upside my head, a slap that felt like it had burst my eardrum.

I staggered back, the world ringing, and more blows

pummeled my stomach, driving the breath from me. And then I was lying on my back, Sarah's weight on my chest, her body as sinewy as a bag full of pissed-off snakes, her smell thick in my nostrils.

She pushed my head back, baring my throat, but then froze, something fighting behind her Botoxed eyes. Her love for me? Or just the anathema of my familiar face?

'Ray's Original, First Avenue and Eighth Street,' I said quickly, invoking her favorite pizza place. 'Vanilla vodka on the rocks. *Viva Las Vegas.*' That last one scored, so l added, 'His mother's middle name was Love.'

At this second Elvis reference, Sarah hissed like a snake, one hand curling into a claw. The fingernails, like a corpse's, keep growing as everything else is eaten away, and hers were as gnarled and black as dried beetle husks.

I stopped her with the password for our shared video store account, then rattled off her old cell-phone number and the names of the goldfish she'd left behind. Sarah flinched, battered by these old, familiar signifiers. Then she let out a howl, her mouth stretching wide to bare the awful teeth again. A dark claw raised up.

I pulled the action figure from my pocket and thrust it into her face.

It was the King, of course, in Comeback Special black, complete with leather wristband and four-inch guitar. This was my only keepsake from her former life – I'd stolen it from under her roommate's nose, dropping by a week after Sarah had disappeared, instinctively knowing she wasn't coming back. Wanting something of hers.

Sarah howled, closing her fist and bringing it down on my chest. The blow left me coughing, my eyes filling with tears. But her weight was suddenly gone.

I rolled over, gasping, trying to regain my feet. As my eyes cleared, I saw boiling fur in every direction, the rats in a panic at their mistress's distress.

She had started down the stairs, but now the anathema had taken hold of her mind. The Elvis memorabilia I'd placed on the steps did its job – Sarah twisted in midcourse at the sequined cape, like a horse glimpsing a rattlesnake, and crashed through the rickety banister.

I scrambled to the balcony's edge and looked down. She crouched on one of the pews, glaring up at me.

'Are you okay, Sarah?'

The sound of her own name got her moving, gliding across the waiting room, bare feet silent on the backs of the benches. But she stumbled to a halt as she came face-to-face with the black velvet King poster, a horrible wail filling the echoing terminal. It was one of those spine-tingling transformations, like when a forlorn cat suddenly makes the sound of a human child, Sarah uttering the cry of some other species.

Rats swept toward me from all sides – attacking, I thought for a moment. But they were simply freaking out, swirling without purpose around my boots, disappearing through holes and into office doorways.

As I ran down the staircase, the metal bolts that held it to the wall yanked at their berths in a screeching chorus. Sarah darted from exit to exit, mewling at the sight of the King's face. She froze and hissed at me again.

She knew I had her cornered and watched warily as I put the doll back in my pocket.

'Stay there. I won't hurt you.' I slowly climbed down the rest of the swaying stairs. It was about as steady as standing in a canoe.

The moment one of my feet touched the ground floor, Sarah

ran straight toward the far wall. She leaped high, her black claws grasping one of a web of steam pipes that fed a long radiator. Her long black fingernails made pinging sounds on the empty pipes as she climbed up and along the wall toward a high window I hadn't bothered to cover. She moved like a spider, fast and jerky.

There was no Elvis between her and freedom. I was going to lose her.

Swearing, I turned and dashed back up the swaying stairs. A series of pops came from behind me, bolts failing, and just as I reached the top, the whole staircase pulled away, freeing itself from the wall at last. But it didn't crash to the ground, just sagged exhaustedly, a few bolts still clinging to the upper floor like rusty fingernails.

Sarah reached the high window and put her fist through it, smeared glass shattering onto a jagged patch of gray sky. But as she pulled herself up into the window frame, a bright shaft of sun struck through the clouds, hitting her square in the face.

The rosy light filled the terminal, and Sarah screamed again, swinging from one hand, the other flailing. She tried to hoist herself through the broken window twice more, but the punishing sunlight forced her back. Finally she scurried away, fleeing along the pipes and leaping to the balcony, darting through the farthest doorway from me.

I was already running.

The last office was the darkest, but I could smell the rats, the main nest of her brood. When I reached the door they turned to face me in awful unison, red eyes illuminated by the dusty shaft of sunlight filtering in behind me. There was a bed in one corner, its rusty springs covered with rotting clothes. Most peeps didn't bother with beds. Had it been left here by squatters? Or had Sarah salvaged it from some rubbish heap?

She'd always been a fussy sleeper, bringing her own pillow to college from Tennessee. Did she still care what she slept on?

Sarah watched me from the bed, her eyes half closed. It was only because the sunlight had burned them, but it made her look more human.

I approached carefully, one hand on the action figure in my pocket. But I didn't pull it out. Maybe I could take her without any more struggle. She'd said my name, after all.

The motionless rats made me nervous. I took a plastic bag from my pocket and emptied it onto my boots. The brood parted, scenting Cornelius's dander. My ancient cat hadn't hunted in years, but the rats didn't know that. Suddenly, I smelled like a predator.

Sarah clung to the bed's spindly frame, which began to shudder. I paused to pull a Kevlar glove onto my left hand and dropped two knockout pills into its palm.

'Let me give you these. They'll make you better.'

Sarah squinted at me, still wary, but listening. She had always forgotten to take her pills, and it had been my job to remind her. Maybe this ritual would calm her, something remembered, but not fondly enough to be an anathema. I could hear her breathing, her heart still beating as fast as it had during the chase.

She could spring at me at any moment.

I took another slow step and sat down beside her. The bed's rusty springs made a questioning sound.

'Take these. They're good for you.'

Sarah stared at the small white pills cupped in my palm. I felt her relax for a moment, maybe recalling what it was like to be sick – just *normal* sick – and have a boyfriend look after you.

I'm not as fast as a full-blown peep, or as strong, but I am pretty quick. I cupped my hand over her mouth in a flash and heard the pills *snick* into her dehydrated throat. Her hands gripped my shoulders, but I pressed her head back with my whole weight, letting her teeth savage the thick glove. Sarah's black nails didn't go for my face, and I saw swallows pulsing along her pale neck.

The pills took her down in seconds. With a metabolism as fast as ours, drugs hit right away – I feel tipsy about a minute after alcohol touches my tongue, and I damn near need an IV to keep a coffee buzz going.

'Well done, Sarah.' I let her go and saw that her eyes were still open. 'You'll be okay now, I promise.'

I pulled the glove off. The outer water-resistant layer was shredded, but her teeth hadn't broken the Kevlar. (It *has* happened, though.)

My cell phone showed one lonely bar of reception, but the call went straight through. 'It was her. Pick us up.'

As the phone went dark, I wondered if I should have mentioned the crumbling stairs. Oh, well. They'd figure out how to get up.

'Cal?'

I started at the sound, but her slitted eyes didn't seem to pose a threat. 'What is it, Sarah?'

'Show me again.'

'Show you what?'

She tried to speak, but a pained look crossed her face.

'You mean . . .' His name would hurt her if I said it. 'The King?'

She nodded.

'You don't want that. It'll only burn you. Like the sun did.'

'But I miss him.' Her voice was fading, sleep taking her.

I swallowed, feeling something flat and heavy settle over me. 'I know you do.'

Sarah knew a lot about Elvis, but she enjoyed obscure facts the most. She loved it that his mother's middle name was Love. She searched the Web for MP3s of the B-sides of rare seventies singles. Her favorite movie was one that you've probably never heard of: *Stay Away, Joe*.

In it, Elvis is a half-Navajo bronco buster on a reservation. Sarah claimed it was the role he was born to play, because he really was part Native American. Yeah, right. His great-great-great-grandmother was Cherokee. And, like most of us, he had *sixteen* great-great-great-grandmothers. Not much genetic impact there. But Sarah didn't care. She said obscure influences were the most important.

That's a philosophy major for you.

In the movie, Elvis sells pieces of his car whenever he needs money. The doors go, then the roof, then the seats, one by one. By the end he's riding along on an empty frame – Elvis at the steering wheel, four tires and a sputtering engine on an open road.

As the disease had settled across her, Sarah had held onto Elvis the longest. After she'd thrown out all her books and clothes, erased every photograph from her hard drive, and broken all the mirrors in her dorm bathroom, the Elvis posters still clung to her walls, crumpled and scratched from bitter blows, but hanging on. As her mind transformed, Sarah shouted more than once that she couldn't stand the sight of me, but she never said a word against the King.

Finally, she fled, deciding to disappear into the night rather than tear down those slyly grinning faces she could no longer bear to look at.

As I waited for the transport squad, I watched her shivering on the bed and thought of Elvis clutching the steering wheel of his skeletal car.

Sarah had lost everything, shedding the pieces of her life one by one to placate the anathema, until she was left here in this dark place, clinging to a shuddering, rickety frame.

2. TREMATODES

The natural world is jaw-droppingly horrible. Appalling, nasty, vile.

Take trematodes, for example.

Trematodes are tiny fish that live in the stomach of a bird. (How did that happen? Horribly. Just keep reading.) They lay their eggs in the bird's stomach. One day, the bird takes a crap into a pond, and the eggs are on their way. They hatch and swim around the pond looking for a snail. These trematodes are microscopic, small enough to lay eggs in a snail's eye, as we used to say in Texas.

Well, okay. We never said that in Texas. But trematodes actually *do* it. For some reason, they always choose the left eye. When the babies hatch, they eat the snail's left eye and spread throughout its body. (Didn't I say this would be horrible?) But they don't kill the snail. Not right away.

First, the half-blind snail gets a gnawing feeling in the pit of its stomach and thinks it's hungry. It starts to eat but for some reason can never get enough food. You see, when the food gets to where the snail's stomach used to be, all that's left down there is trematodes, getting their meals delivered. The snail can't mate, or sleep, or enjoy life in any other snaily way. It has become a hungry robot dedicated to gathering food for its horrible little passengers.

After a while, the trematodes get bored with this and pull the plug on their poor host. They invade the snail's antennae, making them twitch. They turn the snail's left eye bright colors. A bird passing overhead sees this brightly colored, twitching snail and says, 'Yum . . .'

The snail gets eaten, and the trematodes are back up in a bird's stomach, ready to parachute into the next pond over.

Welcome to the wonderful world of parasites.

This is where I live.

One more thing, and then I promise no more horrific biology (for a few pages).

When I first read about trematodes, I always wondered why the bird would eat this twitching, oddly colored snail. Eventually, wouldn't the birds evolve to avoid any snail with a glowing left eye? This is a nasty, trematode-infected snail, after all. Why would you *eat* it?

Turns out the trematodes don't do anything unpleasant to their flying host. They're polite guests, living quietly in the bird's gut, not messing with its food or its left eye or anything. The bird hardly knows they're there, just craps them out into the next pond over, like a little parasite bomb.

It's almost like the bird and the trematodes have a deal between them. You give us a ride in your stomach, and we'll arrange some half-blind snails for you to eat.

Isn't cooperation a beautiful thing?

Unless, of course, you happen to be the snail . . .

Okay, let's clear up some myths about vampires.

First of all, you won't see me using the V-word much. In the Night Watch, we prefer the term *parasite-positives*, or *peeps*, for short.

The main thing to remember is that there's no magic involved. No flying. Humans don't have hollow bones or wings – the disease doesn't change that. No transforming into bats or rats either. It's impossible to turn into something much smaller than yourself – where would the extra mass go?

On the other hand, I can see how people in centuries past got confused. Hordes of rats, and sometimes bats, accompany peeps. They get infected from feasting on peep leftovers. Rodents make good 'reservoirs,' which means they're like storage containers for the disease. Rats give the parasite a place to hide in case the peep gets hunted down.

Infected rats are devoted to their peeps, tracking them by smell. The rat brood also serves as a handy food source for the peep when there aren't humans around to hunt. (Icky, I know. But that's nature for you.)

Back to the myths:

Parasite-positives *do* appear in mirrors. I mean, get real: How would the mirror know what was *behind* the peep?

But this legend also has a basis in fact. As the parasite

takes control, peeps begin to despise the sight of their own reflections. They smash all their mirrors. But if they're so beautiful, why do they hate their own faces?

Well, it's all about the anathema.

The most famous example of disease mind control is rabies. When a dog becomes rabid, it has an uncontrollable urge to bite anything that moves: squirrels, other dogs, you. This is how rabies reproduces; biting spreads the virus from host to host.

A long time ago, the parasite was probably like rabies. When people got infected, they had an overpowering urge to bite other humans. So they bit them. Success!

But eventually human beings got organized in ways that dogs and squirrels can't. We invented posses and lynch mobs, made up laws, and appointed law enforcers. As a result, the biting maniacs among us tend to have fairly short careers. The only peeps who survived were the ones who ran away and hid, sneaking back at night to feed their mania.

The parasite followed this survival strategy to the extreme. It evolved over the generations to transform the minds of its victims, finding a chemical switch among the pathways of the human brain. When that switch is thrown, we despise everything we once loved. Peeps cower when confronted with their old obsessions, despise their loved ones, and flee from any signifier of home.

Love is easy to switch to hatred, it turns out. The term for this is the *anathema effect*.

The anathema effect forced peeps from their medieval villages and out into the wild, where they were safe from lynch mobs. And it spread the disease geographically. Peeps moved to the next valley over, then the next country, pushed farther and farther by their hatred of everything familiar.

As cities grew, with more police and bigger lynch mobs, peeps had to adopt new strategies to stay hidden. They learned to love the night and see in the dark, until the sun itself became anathema to them.

But come on: They don't burst into flame in daylight. They just really, really hate it.

The anathema also created some familiar vampire legends. If you grew up in Europe in the Middle Ages, chances were you were a Christian. You went to church at least twice a week, prayed three times a day, and had a crucifix hanging in every room. You made the sign of the cross every time you ate food or wished for good luck. So it's not surprising that most peeps back then had major cruciphobia – they could actually be repelled by the sight of a cross, just like in the movies.

In the Middle Ages, the crucifix was the big anathema: Elvis and Manhattan and your boyfriend all rolled into one.

Things were so much simpler back then.

These days, we hunters have to do our homework before we go after a peep. What were their favorite foods? What music did they like? What movie stars did they have crushes on? Sure, we still find a few cases of cruciphobia, especially down in the Bible Belt, but you're much more likely to stop peeps with an iPod full of their favorite tunes. (With certain geeky peeps, I've heard, the Apple logo alone does the trick.)

That's why new peep hunters like me start with people they used to know, so we don't have to guess what their anathemas are. Hunting the people who once loved us is as easy as it gets. Our own faces work as a reminder of their former lives. *We* are the anathema.

So what am *I*? you may be asking.

I am parasite-positive, technically a peep, but I can still listen to Kill Fee and Deathmatch, watch a sunset, or put Tabasco on scrambled eggs without howling. Through some trick of evolution, I'm partly immune, the lucky winner of the peep genetic lottery. Peeps like me are rarer than hens' teeth: Only one in every hundred victims becomes stronger and faster, with incredible hearing and a great sense of smell, without being driven crazy by the anathema.

We're called *carriers*, because we have the disease without all the symptoms. Although there is this one extra symptom that we do have: The disease makes us horny. All the time.

The parasite doesn't want us carriers to go to waste, after all. We can still spread the disease to other humans. Like that of the maniacs, our saliva carries the parasite's spores. But we don't bite; we kiss, the longer and harder the better.

The parasite makes sure that I'm like the always-hungry snail, except hungry for sex. I'm constantly aroused, aware of every female in the room, every cell screaming for me to *go out and shag someone!*

None of which makes me wildly different from most other nineteen-year-old guys, I suppose. Except for one small fact: If I act on my urges, my unlucky lovers become monsters, like Sarah did. And this is not much fun to watch.

Dr. Rat showed up first, like she'd been waiting by the phone.

Her footsteps echoed through the ferry terminal, along with a rattling noise. I left Sarah's side and went out to the balcony. Dr. Rat had a dozen folding cages strapped to her back, like some giant insect with old-lady hair and unsteady metal wings, ready to trap some samples of Sarah's brood.

'Couldn't wait, could you?' I called.

'No,' she yelled up. 'It's a big one, isn't it?'

'Seems to be.' The brood was still behind me, quietly attending to its sleeping mistress.

She looked at the half-fallen staircase with annoyance. 'Did you do that?'

'Um, sort of.'

'So how am I supposed to get up there, Kid?'

I just shrugged. I'm not a big fan of the nickname 'Kid.' They all call me that at the Night Watch, just because I'm a peep hunter at nineteen, a job where the average age is about a hundred and seventy-five. All peep hunters are carriers. Only carriers are fast and strong enough to hunt down our crazy, violent cousins.

Dr. Rat's usually pretty cool, though. She doesn't mind her own nickname, mostly because she actually *likes* rats. And even though she's about sixty and wears enough hairspray to stick a bear to the ceiling, she plays good alternative metal and lets me rip her CDs – Kill Fee hasn't made a dime off me since I met Dr. Rat. And mercifully, she falls well off my sexual radar, so I can actually concentrate in the Night Watch classes she teaches (Rats 101, Peep Hunting 101, and Early Plagues and Pestilence).

Like most people who work at the Night Watch, she's not parasite-positive. She's just a working stiff who loves her job. You have to, working at the Night Watch. The pay's not great.

With one last look at the crumpled staircase, Dr. Rat began to set out her traps, then started laying out piles of poison.

'Isn't there enough of that stuff around already?' I asked.

'Not like this. Something new I'm trying. It's marked with Essence of Cal Thompson. A few swabs of your sweat on each pile and they'll eat hearty.'

'My what?' I said. 'Where'd you get my sweat?'

'From a pencil I borrowed from you in Rats 101, after that pop quiz last week. Did you know pop quizzes make you sweat, Cal?'

'Not *that* much!'

'Only takes a little – along with some peanut butter.'

I wiped my palms on my jacket, not sure how annoyed to be.

Rats are great smellers, gourmets of garbage. When they eat, they can detect one part of rat poison in a million. And they can smell their peeps from a mile away. Because I was Sarah's progenitor, my familiar smell would cover the taint of poison.

I supposed it was worth having my sweat stolen. We had to kill off Sarah's brood before it fell apart and scattered into the rest of Hoboken. A hungry brood that has lost its peep can be dangerous, and the parasite occasionally spreads from rats back into humans. The last thing New Jersey needed was another peep.

That's the interesting thing about Dr. Rat: She loves rats but also loves coming up with new and exciting ways to kill them. Like I said, love and hatred aren't that far apart.

The transport squad arrived ten minutes later. They didn't wait for sunset, just cut the locks off the biggest set of doors and backed their garbage truck right up to them, its reverse beep echoing through the terminal to wake the dead. Garbage trucks are perfect for the transport squad. They're like the digestive system of the modern world – no one ever thinks twice about them. They're built like tanks and yet are completely invisible to regular people going about their regular business. And if the guys who ride on them happen to be wearing thick protective suits and rubber gloves, well, nothing funny about that, is there? Garbage is dangerous stuff, after all.

Rather than chance the ruined staircase, the transport guys reached into their truck for rope ladders with grappling hooks. They climbed up, then lowered Sarah to the ground floor in a litter. They always carry mountain-rescue gear, it turns out.

I watched the whole operation while I did my paperwork, then asked the transport boss if I could come along in the truck with Sarah.

He shook his head and said, 'No rides, Kid. Anyway, the Shrink wants to see you.'

'Oh,' I said.

When the Shrink calls, you go.

By the time I got back into Manhattan, darkness had fallen.

In New York City, they grind up old glass, mix it into concrete, and make sidewalks out of it. Glassphalt looks pretty, especially if you've got peep eyesight. It sparkled underfoot as I walked, catching the orange glow of streetlights.

Most important, the glassphalt gave me something to look at besides the women passing by – trendy Villagers with chunky shoes and cool accessories, tourists looking around all wide-eyed and wanting to ask directions, NYU dance students in formfitting regalia. The worst thing about New York is that it's full of beautiful women, enough to make my head start spinning with unthinkable thoughts.

My senses were still at the pitch that hunting brings them to. I could feel the rumble of distant subway trains through my feet and hear the buzz of streetlight timers in their metal boxes. I caught the smells of perfume, body lotion, and scented shampoo.

And stared at the sparkling sidewalk.

I was more depressed than horny, though. I kept seeing Sarah on that bare and rickety bed, asking for one last glimpse of the King, however painful.

I'd always thought that once I found her, things would uncrumble a little. Life would never be completely normal again, but at least certain debts had been settled. With her in recovery, my chain of the infection had been broken.

But I still felt crappy.

The Shrink always warned me that carriers stay wracked with lifelong guilt. It's not an uplifting thing having turned lovers into monsters. We feel bad that we haven't turned into monsters ourselves – *survivor's guilt*, that's called. And we feel a bit stupid that we didn't notice our own symptoms earlier. I mean, I'd been sort of wondering why the Atkins diet was giving me night vision. But that hadn't seemed like something to *worry* about . . .

And there was the burning question: Why hadn't I been more concerned when my one real girlfriend, two girls I'd had a few dates with, and another I'd made out with on New Year's Eve had *all* gone crazy?

I'd just thought that was a New York thing.

Visiting the Shrink makes my ears pop.

She lives in the bowels of a Colonial-era town house, the original headquarters of the Night Watch, her office at the end of a long, narrow corridor. A soft but steady breeze pushes you toward her, like a phantom hand in the middle of your back. But it isn't magic; it's something called a *negative-pressure prophylaxis*, which is basically a big condom made of air. Throughout the house, a constant wind blows toward the Shrink from all directions. No stray microbes can escape from her out into the rest of the city, because all the air in the house moves *toward* her. After she's breathed it, this air gets microfiltered, chlorine-gassed, and roasted at about two hundred degrees Celsius before it pops out of the town house's always-smoking chimney. It's the same setup they have at bioweapons factories, and at the lab in Atlanta where scientists keep smallpox virus in a locked freezer.

The Shrink actually *has* smallpox, she once told me. She's a carrier, like us hunters, but she's been alive a lot longer, even longer than the Night Mayor. Old enough to have been around before inoculations were invented, back when measles and smallpox killed more people than war. The parasite makes her immune from all that stuff, of course, but she still wound up catching it, and she carries bits and pieces of various human scourges to this day. So they keep her in a bubble.

And yes, we peeps can live a really long time.

New York's city government goes back about three hundred and fifty years, a century and a half older than the United States of America. The Night Watch Authority may have split off from official City Hall a while back – like the peeps we hunt, we have to hide ourselves – but the Night Mayor was appointed for a life-long term in 1687. It just so happens he's still alive. That makes us the oldest authority in the New World, edging the Freemasons by forty-six years. Not too shabby.

The Night Mayor was around to personally watch the witch trials of the 1690s. He was here during the Revolutionary War, when the black rats who used to run the city got pushed out by the gray Norwegian ones who still do, and he was here for the attempted Illuminati takeover in 1794. We *know* this town.

The shelves behind the Shrink's desk were filled with her ancient doll collection, their crumbling heads sprouting hair made from horses' manes and hand-spun flax. They sat in the dim light wearing stiff, painted smiles. I could imagine the sticky scent left by centuries of stroking kiddie fingers. And the Shrink hadn't bought them as antiques; she'd lifted every one from the grasp of a sleeping child, back in the days when they were new.

Now *that's* a weird kink, but it beats any fetishes that would spread the disease, I suppose. Sometimes I wonder if the whole living-in-a-bubble thing is just a way to keep the Shrink's ancient and unfulfilled desires at bay. Summer days in Manhattan, when every woman in town is wearing a tank top or a sundress, I wish they'd lock me in a bubble somewhere.

'Hey, Kid,' she said, looking up from the papers on her desk.

I frowned but could hardly complain. After being around five centuries, you can pretty much call everybody 'Kid.'

I took a seat, careful to stay well behind the red line painted on the floor. If you step over it, the Shrink's minders take everything you're wearing and burn it, and you have to go home in these penalty clothes that are too small, like the jacket and tie they force you to wear at fancy restaurants when you show up underdressed. Everyone at the Watch remembers a carrier peep named Typhoid Mary, who wandered around too addled by the parasite to know that she was spreading typhus to everyone she slept with.

'Good evening, Doctor Prolix,' I said, careful not to raise my voice. It's always weird talking to other carriers. The red line kept me and the Shrink about twenty feet apart, but we both had peep hearing, so it was rude to shout. Social reflexes take a long time to catch up to superpowers.

I closed my eyes, adjusting to the weird sensation of a total absence of smell. This doesn't happen very often in New York City, and it *never* happens to me, except in the Shrink's super-clean office. As an almost-predator, I can smell the salt when someone's crying, the acid tang of used AA batteries, and the mold living between the pages of an old book.

The Shrink's reading light buzzed, set so low that its filament barely glowed, softening her features. As carriers get older, they begin to look more like full-blown peeps – wiry, wide-eyed, and gauntly beautiful. They don't have enough flesh to get wrinkles; the parasite burns calories like running a marathon. Even after my afternoon at the diner, I was a little hungry myself.

After a few moments, she took her hands from the papers, steepled her fingers, and peered at me. 'So, let me guess . . .'

This was how Dr. Prolix started every session, telling me what was in my own head. She wasn't much for the so-how-does-that-make-you-feel school of head-shrinking. I noticed that her voice had the same dry timbre as Sarah's, with a hint of dead, rustling leaves among her words.

'You have finally reached your goal,' she said. 'And yet your long-sought redemption isn't what you thought it would be.'

I had to sigh. The worst part of visiting the Shrink was being read like a book. But I decided not to make things *too* easy for her and just shrugged. 'I don't know. I had a long day drinking coffee and waiting for the clouds to clear. And then Sarah put up a wicked fight.'

'But the difficulty of a challenge usually makes its accomplishment more satisfying, not less.'

'Easy for you to say.' The bruises on my chest were still throbbing, and my ribs were knitting back together in an itchy way. 'But it wasn't really the fight. The messed-up thing was that Sarah recognized me. She said my name.'

Dr. Prolix's Botoxed eyes widened even farther. 'When you captured your other girlfriends, they didn't speak to you, did they?'

'No. Just screamed when they saw my face.'

She smiled gently. 'That means they loved you.'

'I doubt it. None of them knew me that well.' Other than Sarah, who I'd met before I turned contagious, every woman I'd ever started a relationship with had begun to change in a matter of weeks.

'But they must have felt something for you, or the anathema wouldn't have taken hold.' She smiled. 'You're a very attractive boy, Cal.'

I cleared my throat. A compliment from a five-hundred-year-old is like when your aunt says you're cute. Not helpful in any way.

'How's that going anyway?' she added.

'What? The enforced celibacy? Just great. Loving it.'

'Did you try the rubber band trick?'

I held up my wrist. The Shrink had suggested I wear a rubber band there and *ping* myself with it every time I had a sexual thought. Negative reinforcement, like swatting your dog with a rolled-up newspaper.

'Mmm. A bit raw, isn't it?' she said.

I glanced down at my wrist, which looked like I'd been wearing a razor-wire bracelet. 'Evolution versus a rubber band. Which would you bet on?'

She nodded sympathetically. 'Shall we turn back to Sarah?'

'Please. At least I know she really loved me; she almost killed me.' I stretched in the chair, my still-tender ribs creaking. 'Here's the funny thing, though. She was nested upstairs, with these big-ass windows looking out over the river. You could see Manhattan perfectly.'

'What's so strange about that, Cal?'

I glanced away from her gaze, but the blank eyes of the dolls weren't much better. Finally, I stared at the floor, where a tiny tumbleweed of dust was being sucked toward Dr. Prolix. Inescapably.

'Sarah was *in love* with Manhattan. The streets, the parks, everything about it. She owned all these New York photo books, knew the histories of buildings. How could she stand to look at the skyline?' I glanced up at Dr. Prolix. 'Could her anathema be, like, *broken* somehow?'

The Shrink's fingers steepled again as she shook her head. 'Not broken, exactly. The anathema can work in mysterious ways. My patients and the legends both report similar obsessions. I believe your generation calls it *stalking*.'

'Um, maybe. How do you mean?'

'The anathema creates a great hatred for beloved things. But that doesn't mean that the love itself is entirely extinguished.'

I frowned. 'But I thought that was the point. Getting you to reject your old life.'

'Yes, but the human heart is a strange vessel. Love and hatred can exist side by side.' Dr. Prolix leaned back in her chair. 'You're nineteen, Cal. Haven't you ever known someone rejected by a lover, who, consumed by rage and jealousy, never lets go? They look on from a distance, unseen but boiling inside. The emotion never seems to tire, this hatred mixed with intense obsession, even with a kind of twisted love.'

'Uh, yeah. That would pretty much be stalking.' I nodded. 'Kind of a fatal attraction thing?'

'Yes, *fatal* is an apt word. It happens among the undead as well.'

A little shiver went through me. Only the really old hunters use the word *undead*, but you have to admit it has a certain ring to it.

'There are legends,' she said, 'and modern case studies in my files. Some of the undead find a balancing point between the attraction of their old obsessions and the revulsion of the anathema. They live on this knife's edge, always pushed and pulled.'

'Hoboken,' I said softly. *Or my sex life, for that matter.*

We were silent for a while, and I remembered Sarah's face after the pills had taken effect. She'd gazed at me without terror. I wondered if Sarah had ever stalked me, watching from the darkness after disappearing from my life, wanting a last glimpse before her Manhattan anathema had driven her across the river.

I cleared my throat. 'Couldn't that mean that Sarah might be more human than most peeps? After I gave her the pills, she wanted to see her Elvis doll . . . that is, the anathema I'd brought. She *asked* to see it.'

Dr. Prolix raised an eyebrow. 'Cal, you aren't fantasizing that Sarah might recover completely, are you?'

'Um . . . no?'

'That you might one day get back together? That you could have a lover again? One your own age, whom you couldn't infect, because she already carries the disease?'

I swallowed and shook my head no, not wanting the lecture in Peeps 101 repeated to me: Full-blown peeps never come back.

You can whack the parasite into submission with drugs, but it's hard to wipe it out completely. Like a tapeworm, it starts off microscopic but grows much bigger, flooding your body with different parts of itself. It wraps around your spine, creates cysts in your brain, changes your whole being to suit its purposes. Even if you could remove it surgically, the eggs can hide in your bone marrow or your brain. The symptoms can be controlled, but skip one pill, miss one shot, or just have a really upsetting bad-hair day, and you go feral all over again. Sarah could never be let loose in a normal human community.

Worse, the mental changes the parasite makes are permanent. Once those anathema switches get thrown in a peep's brain, it's pretty hard to convince a peep that they really, really used to *love* chocolate. Or, say, this guy from Texas called Cal.

'But don't some peeps come back more than others?' I asked.

'The sad truth is, for most of those like Sarah, the struggle never ends. She may well stay this way for the rest of her life, on the edge between anathema and obsession. An uncomfortable fate.'

'Is there any way I can help?' My own words surprised me.

I'd never been to the recovery hospital. All I knew about it was that it was way out in the Montana wilds, a safe distance from any cities. Recovering peeps usually don't want their old boyfriends showing up, but maybe Sarah would be different.

'A familiar face may help her treatment, in time. But not until you deal with your own disquiet, Cal.'

I slumped in my chair. 'I don't even know what my disquiet is. Sarah freaked me out is all. I think I'm still . . .' I waved a hand in the air. 'I just don't feel . . . *done* yet.'

The Shrink nodded sagely. 'Perhaps that's because you aren't done, Cal. There is, after all, one more matter to be settled. Your progenitor.'

I sighed. I'd been over all this before, with Dr. Prolix and the older hunters, and in my own head about a hundred thousand times. It never did any good.

You may have been wondering: If Sarah was my first girlfriend, where did *I* catch the disease?

I wish I knew.

Okay, I obviously knew *how* it happened, and the exact date and pretty close to the exact time. You don't forget losing your virginity, after all.

But I didn't actually know *who* it was. I mean, I got her name and everything – Morgan. Well, her first name anyway.

The big problem was, I didn't remember *where*. Not a clue.

Well, one clue: 'Bahamalama-Dingdong.'

It was only two days after I first got to New York, fresh off the plane from Texas, ready to start my first year at college. I already wanted to study biology, even though I'd heard that was a tough major.

Little did I know.

At that point, I could hardly find my way around the city. I got the general concept of uptown and downtown, although they didn't really match north and south, I knew from my compass. (Don't laugh, they're useful.) I'm pretty sure that this all happened somewhere downtown, because the buildings weren't quite so tall and the streets were pretty busy that night. I remember lights rippling on water at some point, so I might have been close to the Hudson. Or maybe the East River.

And I remember the Bahamalama-Dingdong. Several, in fact. They're some kind of drink. My sense of smell wasn't superhuman back then, but I'm pretty sure they had rum in them. Whatever they had, there was *a lot* of it. And something sweet too. Maybe pineapple juice, which would make the Bahamalama-Dingdong a close cousin of the Bahama Mama.

Now, the Bahama Mama can be found on Google or in cocktail books. It's rum, pineapple juice, and a liqueur called Nassau Royale, and it is from the Bahamas. But the Bahamalama-Dingdong has much more shadowy origins. After I found out what I'd been infected with and realized who must have done it, I searched every bar I could find in the Village. But I never met a single bartender who knew how to make one. Or who'd even *heard* of them.

Like a certain Morgan Whatever, the Bahamalama-Dingdong had come out of the darkness, seduced me, then disappeared.

These searches didn't evoke a single memory flashback. No hazy images of pinball machines jumped out at me, no sudden glimpses of Morgan's long dark hair and pale skin. And, no – being a carrier doesn't make you pale-skinned or gothy-looking. Get real. Morgan was probably just some goth type who didn't know she was about to turn into a bloodthirsty maniac.

Unless, of course, she was someone like me: a carrier. But one who got off on changing lovers into peeps. Either way, I hadn't seen her since.

So this is all I can remember:

There I was, sitting in a bar in New York City and thinking, *Wow, I'm sitting in a bar in New York City*. This thought probably runs through the heads of a lot of newly arrived freshmen who manage to get served. I was drinking a Bahamalama-Dingdong because the bar I was sitting in was 'The Home of the Bahamalama-Dingdong.' It said so on a sign outside.

A pale-skinned woman with long dark hair sat beside me and said, 'What the hell is that thing?'

Maybe it was the frozen banana bobbing in my drink that provoked the question. I suddenly felt a bit silly. 'Well, it's this drink that lives here. Says so on the sign out front.'

'Is it good?'

It was good, but I only shrugged. 'Yeah. Kind of sweet, though.'

'Kind of girly-looking, don't you think?'

I did think. The drink had been a vague sort of embarrassment to me since it had arrived, frozen banana bobbing to the music. But the other guys in the bar had seemed not to notice. And they were all pretty tough-looking, what with their leather chaps and all.

I pushed the banana down into the drink, but it popped back up. It wasn't really trying to be obnoxious, but frozen bananas have a lower specific density than rum and pineapple juice, it turns out.

'I don't know about girly,' I said. 'Looks like a boy to me.'

She smiled at my accent. '*Yerr* not from around here, are *yew*?'

'Nope. I'm from Texas.' I took a sip.

'Texas? Well, hell!' She slapped me on the back. I'd already figured out in those two days that Texas is one of the 'brand-name' states. Being from Texas is much cooler than being from a merely recognizable state, like Connecticut or Florida, or a *huh?* state, like South Dakota. Texas gets you noticed.

'I'll have one of those,' she said to the bartender, pointing to my Bahamalama-Dingdong, which pointed back. Then she said her name was Morgan.

Morgan drank hers, I drank mine. We both drank a few more. My recall of subsequent events gets steadily worse. But I do remember that she had a cat, a flat-screen TV, black satin sheets, and a knack for saying what she thought – and that's pretty much all I remember, except for waking up the next morning, getting kicked out of an unfamiliar apartment because she had to go somewhere and was looking all embarrassed, and heading home with a hangover that made navigation difficult. By the time I got back to my dorm room, I had no idea where I'd started out.

All I had to show for the event was a newfound confidence with women, slowly manifesting superpowers, and an appetite for rare meat.

'We've been over all that,' I said to Dr. Prolix. 'I still can't help you.'

'This is not about helping me,' she said firmly. 'You won't come to terms with your disease until you find your progenitor.'

'Yeah, well, I've tried. But like you've said before, she must have moved away or died or something.' That had always been the big mystery. If Morgan was still around, we'd be seeing her handiwork everywhere – peeps popping up all over the city, a bloodbath every time she picked up some foolish young Texan in a bar. Or at least a few corpses every now and then. 'I mean, it's been over a year, and we don't have a single clue.'

'*Didn't* have a clue,' she said, and rang a small, high-pitched bell on her desk. Somewhere out of sight but within earshot, a minder tapped away at a computer keyboard. A moment later, the printer on my side of the red line began to hum, its cartridge jerking to life below the plastic cover.

'This was recently brought to my attention, Cal. Now that you've dealt with Sarah, I thought you might want to see it.'

I stood and went to the printer and lifted with trembling fingers the warm piece of paper that slid into its tray. It was a scanned handbill, like they pass out on the street sometimes:

Dick's Bar Is Back in Business!
– Seven Days a Week –
The Health Department Couldn't Keep Us Down!
The One and Only Home of the Bahamalama-Dingdong

Dr. Prolix watched me read it, steepling her fingers again.
'Feeling thirsty?' she asked.

Flip a coin.

Tails? Relax.

Heads? You've got parasites in your brain.

That's right. Half of us carry the *Toxoplasma gondii* parasite. But don't reach for the power drill just yet.

Toxoplasma is microscopic. Human immune systems usually kick its ass, so if you've got it, you'll probably never even know. In fact, toxoplasma doesn't even *want* to be in your head. Trapped inside your thick skull, under assault by your immune defenses, it can't lay eggs, which is a big evolutionary Game Over.

Toxoplasma would much rather live in your cat's digestive system, eating cat food and laying eggs. Then, when kitty takes a crap, these eggs wind up on the ground, waiting for other scurrying creatures. Like, say, rats.

A quick word about rats: They're basically parasite subway trains, carrying them from place to place. In my job, we call this being a *vector*. Rats go everywhere in the world, and they breed like crazy. Catching a ride on the Rat Express is a major way that diseases have evolved to spread themselves.

When toxoplasma gets into a rat, the parasite

starts to make changes to its host's brain. If a normal rat bumps into something that smells like a cat, it freaks out and runs away. But toxoplasma-infected rats actually *like* the smell of cats. Kitty pee makes them curious. They'll explore for hours trying to find the source.

Which is a cat. Which eats them.

And that makes toxoplasma happy, because toxoplasma really, really wants to live in the stomach of a cat.

Parasite geeks have a phrase for what cats are to toxoplasma: the 'final host.'

A final host is the place where a parasite can live happily ever after, getting free food, having lots of babies. Most parasites live in more than one kind of animal, but they're all trying to reach their final host, the ultimate vector . . . parasite heaven.

Toxoplasma uses mind control to get to its heaven. It makes the rat *want* to go looking for cats and get eaten. Spooky, huh?

But nothing like that would work on us humans, right?

Well, maybe. No one's really sure what toxoplasma does to human beings. But when researchers collected a bunch of people with and without toxoplasma, gave them personality tests, observed their habits, and interviewed their friends, this is what they learned:

Men infected with toxoplasma don't shave every day, don't wear ties too much, and don't like following social rules. Women infected with toxoplasma like to spend money on clothes, and they tend to have lots of friends.

The rest of us think they're more attractive than non-infected women. In general, the researchers found that infected people are more interesting to be around.

On the other hand, people *without* toxoplasma in their brains *like* following the rules. If you lend them money, they're more likely to pay you back. They show up for work on time. The men get into fewer fights. The women have fewer boyfriends.

Could this be toxoplasma mind control?

But that's just *too* weird, isn't it? There has to be another explanation.

Maybe some people *always* hated getting to work on time, and they like having felines around because cats wouldn't go to work on time either, if they had any work to go to. These people adopted cats and *then* got toxoplasma.

Maybe the other half of humanity, the ones who enjoy following the rules, usually get dogs. Fetch. Sit. Stay. So, their brains stay toxoplasma-free.

Maybe these are two kinds of people who were *already* different.

Or maybe not.

That's the thing about parasites: It's hard to tell if they're the chicken or the egg. Maybe we're all really robots, walking around doing the bidding of our parasites. Just like those hungry, twitching snails . . .

Do you really love your cat? Or is the toxoplasma in your head telling you to take care of kitty, its final host, so that one day it too will reach parasite heaven?

Dick's Bar hadn't changed all that much, but I had.

It wasn't just my superpowers. I was older, wiser, and had lived in New York for just over a year now. I had grown-up eyes.

It turned out that Dick's Bar didn't get a lot of female patronage. Not much at all. Just a lot of guys playing pool in their leather chaps, drinking beer and swigging the occasional Jell-O shot, listening to a mix of country and classic disco. A typical West Village bar.

It was a relief, really. I could hang out here without having to stare into my drink, trying to avoid contact with any hot girls. Even better, any woman who was a regular would stick out like a banana in a highball glass. Surely *someone* would remember a tall, pale-skinned creature wearing a long black dress and picking up wayward Texans.

'Drink?' the bartender asked.

I nodded. A little stimulus for my fugitive memories wouldn't hurt.

'A Bahamalama-Dingdong, please.

The bartender raised an eyebrow, then turned to ring a bell over the bar. A few guys playing pool in the back chuckled, and something dislodged itself from the cloudy sky of memories inside my head.

Ding! said my brain, as I recalled that whenever anyone ordered a Bahamalama-Dingdong, they rang a special bell. Hence the 'dingdong' part of the name.

Well, partly. I watched the bartender take a banana from the freezer. He put it in a tall highball glass and poured rum over it, then mystery juice from a plastic container marked *B/D*, and finally a careful layer of red liqueur across the top. I detected a scent like cough medicine rising up.

'Nassau Royale?' I asked.

The bartender nodded. 'Yeah. Do I remember you?'

'You mean, from before the Health Department shut you down?' I asked.

'Yeah,' he said. 'You don't look so familiar, though.'

I nodded. 'I've only been here once, actually. But I had a friend who used to come all the time. Named Morgan?'

'Morgan?'

'Yeah. Tall, dark hair, pale skin. Black dresses. Kind of gothy?'

Pause. 'A woman?'

'Yeah.'

He shook his head. 'Not ringing a bell. You sure you got the right place?'

I looked down at the Bahamalama-Dingdong, the Nassau Royale-stained banana looking back at me like a bloodshot eye, and took a sip. Tropical fruit sweetness poured over my tongue, textured by strips of rind shedding from the frozen banana. That night of more than a year before began to flood back into my mind, carried on pineapples and the burnt taste of dark rum.

'I'm positive,' I said.

There wasn't much to do but get drunk.

The bartender asked around, but no one remembered Morgan or even vaguely recalled a gothlike woman who had hung out here in the old days. Maybe, like me, she'd randomly wandered in off the street that night.

On the other hand, if her inner parasite had been pulling her strings, making her desperately horny, then why had she chosen a gay bar, the place she was least likely to get lucky? (Had she been as clueless as my younger self? Hmm.)

I let the drinks take hold, ringing more bells, bringing back stray fragments of memory from that night. There definitely had been a river involved; I recalled reflected lights rippling in boat wakes. All the Bahamalama-Dingdongs that Morgan and I had drunk had put a little stumble into our step. I'd been worried she'd go over the rail and I'd have to leap into the cold water to save her, even though I wasn't fit to walk a dog.

We had strolled out to the end of a long pier and stood looking at the river. The Hudson or the East River, though?

Then I remembered: At some point I'd checked my compass and announced that we were facing northwest, which made her laugh. Definitely the Hudson, then. We'd been looking at New Jersey.

What had happened next?

I tried to press the hazy memories forward in time, but my mind was stuck on that image of New Jersey reflected in the river – Hoboken already teasing me from across the water. No matter how hard I concentrated, I couldn't recall a single step of the route we'd taken back to Morgan's apartment.

A guy came up next to me, back here in the present.

It took a few moments to pull myself out of my Bahamalama-Dingdong reverie, but I could tell from his scent that he'd just come back into the bar from catching a smoke outside. His leather vest was cow-smell new, and he wore an intrigued expression. Maybe he'd heard I'd been asking about Morgan.

'Hey,' I said.

'Hey. What's your name?'

'Cal.' I reached to shake his hand.

'I'm Dave. So . . . what are you into, Cal?' he asked.

I paused for a second before answering.

I couldn't tell him what I was *really* into: finding the woman who had turned me into a superhuman freak, taking the next step in destroying my bloodline – dealing with my progenitor, then hunting down any more peeps she had created, and then delving further into the endless, knotted tree of the parasite's spread. So I cast my mind back to the homework I'd been reading in the diner that morning as I'd waited for the clouds to clear.

'Hookworms,' I said.

'Hookworms?' He took the seat next to me. 'Never heard of that.'

I sipped from my third Bahamalama-Dingdong.

'Well, they burrow in through your feet, using this enzyme that breaks down skin tissue, then travel along the bloodstream till they get into your lungs. They mess up your breathing, so you cough them up. But you know how you always swallow a little bit of phlegm?'

One of his eyebrows raised, but he admitted he did.

'Well, a few hookworm eggs get swallowed along with the phlegm and travel down into your intestines, where they grow to be about half an inch long.' I held up my fingers a hookworm's length apart. 'And they develop this circle of teeth in their mouths, like a coil of barbed wire. They start chomping into your intestinal wall and sucking your blood.' I realized I was going into drunken detail here and paused to check if he was still interested.

'Really?' His voice sounded a bit dry.

I nodded. 'Wouldn't lie to you, Dave. But here's the cool thing. They produce this special anticlotting factor, kind of like blood antifreeze, so the wound doesn't scab over. You become a sort of

42

temporary hemophiliac, just in that one spot. Your intestines won't stop bleeding until the hookworm gets its fill!'

'Hookworms, huh?' he asked.

'That's what they're called.'

Dave nodded gravely, standing back up. He grasped my shoulder firmly, a serious expression on his face. His thoughtful features seemed to reflect for a moment the hard road I had in front of me.

'Good luck with that,' he said.

I figured seven Bahamalama-Dingdongs would do the job.

That was probably more than I'd drunk my first time at Dick's, but these days I was older and more superhuman. I did a professional job of getting off my stool, and my feet got into a pretty good rhythm after shuffling a bit at first. My metabolism may be peeped up, but there's only so much rum even my body can process before it starts to sputter. All in all, I'd managed a pretty fair reconstruction of my first really wicked buzz in New York City.

I headed off to retrace my stumbling path from a year before.

The bartender watched me go with an impressed-looking nod, and Dave waved from behind the pool table. As the evening had progressed, he'd sent some of his friends over to ask about hookworms, and they'd all listened attentively. I'd thrown in some stuff about blood flukes, too. So it hadn't been like drinking alone.

Outside Dick's Bar, the streetlights wore coronas of orange, and the glassphalt shimmered like sugar crystals on top of lemon meringue pie. My breath curled out steamy, but the warmth from inside Dick's still saturated my jacket, its fingers nestled around me like a cluster of liver worms.

Okay, bad image. But I *was* a little drunk.

My feet carried me toward the river automatically, but I wasn't remembering the route to Morgan's yet. It was just gravity doing its job.

Skateboarding around the city, I'd noticed the Hump, how the ground rises in the center of Manhattan and falls away toward the rivers, like the slippery back of a giant whale emerging from the harbor. A *really* giant whale: The slope is barely perceptible – you only feel it on a board or a bike, or if your stride is lubricated by seven or so Bahamalama-Dingdongs.

My feet had wheels, and I rolled toward the water effortlessly.

Soon I glimpsed the river at the end of the street, sparkling as it had that night. A walkway stretched along the water. By instinct, I turned north. It was a little tricky staying between the pedestrian lines, though. A few bikers and skaters whirred around me, leaving annoyed comments in their wake. I commented right back at them, my words a little slurred. Outside the warm company of Dick's Bar, my Bahamalama-Dingdongs had made me antisocial.

But my mood lifted when I saw the pier.

It stretched out into the water, as long as a football field. Mismatched beats from various boom boxes echoed across the water from it, and bright lights beamed down from high posts.

Was that the same pier Morgan and I had stood on that night?

There was one way to find out. I shambled to the end of the pier, trying to ignore kissing couples and a group of very cute roller-dancing girls, and pulled my trusty compass out. The needle steadied itself to magnetic north.

I was facing northwest, the exact reading I'd taken a year before.

I breathed in deeply, tasting ocean salt, green algae, and motor oil in the air, all familiar from that night. This had to be the place.

But what now?

I gazed out onto the river. On either side of me, the timbers of abandoned piers rose up from the water like rotting black teeth. More pieces of my memory were falling into place, like a blurry picture downloading in waves, gradually becoming clearer.

Then I saw the dark hulk of a building across the Hudson, its three giant maws open to the river. The Hoboken Ferry Terminal. Without knowing it, I'd had a glimpse of my future that night a year before.

My peep-strength eyes caught a flicker of lights in its second-story windows. Dr. Rat was still up there, probably with a dozen or so of her colleagues from Research and Development, studying the nesting habits of Sarah's brood. Weighing and measuring poisoned alpha rats and punks. Maybe looking for a rare 'rat king' – a bunch of rats with tangled-up tails who travel in a pack all tied together, like dogs being walked by a professional dog walker, ten leashes in hand.

With Sarah gone, her brood would be disintegrating over the next few days, scattering into nearby alleys and sewers like runoff from an autumn storm. I wondered if the rats would miss her. Did they get something more than leftovers from their peeps? A sense of belonging?

The thought of all those orphaned creatures depressed me, and I turned back toward Manhattan.

My heart drunkenly skipped a beat.

Before me, just across the highway, a razor-thin high-rise stood.

Buildings get their personality from their windows, just like people express themselves with their eyes. This building had a schizophrenic look. Its lower floors were cluttered with tiny balconies, but along the top floor stretched floor-to-ceiling windows, wide open with surprise. I remembered Morgan pointing the building out to me, giggling and squeezing my hand . . .

'That's where I live!' she'd said, thus marking the exact moment when I had been absolutely *positive* I was going to get laid.

How the hell does anyone forget a moment like that? I wondered.

Shaking my head in amazement, I stumbled back up the pier.

The first trick was getting in.

Funny. I hadn't remotely remembered that Morgan lived in a luxury building: river views and duplex penthouses, a lobby encased in marble and brass, the uniformed doorman watching six TV monitors.

Give a boy the loss of his virginity and much else is forgotten.

I watched from across the street, hiding behind a cluster of newspaper boxes, waiting for just the right bunch of residents to follow through the door – my age or so, a little bit drunk, and enough of them for me to follow along unnoticed.

Of course, if I was really lucky I'd see Morgan herself. But what was I going to say to her? *Hey, do you know you're carrying vampirism? What's up with that?*

The minutes passed slowly, the night growing steadily colder. The wind roaring off the river stopped being invigorating and veered over into cruel. My Bahamalama-Dingdong buzz began to wear off, and soon my system started demanding more blood sugar. It occurred to me that the only solid food I'd had for dinner was seven frozen bananas, not enough for my voracious parasites.

Bad host. Hungry parasites can provoke crazy behavior.

Worst of all, I felt like *I* was being the stalker now, stuck between anathema and obsession.

Just after midnight, I spotted my ticket inside.

They were three girls and two guys, college-aged, dressed for a night out. They shouted jokes at one another, their voices still pitched for whatever loud bar they had spent the evening in.

I left my cover and started across the street, timing my move to reach the outer door just as they did.

They hardly noticed me, still arguing about what kind of pizza to order. 'Lots of cheese. Hangover helper,' one guy was saying. The others laughed and voted their way to a split ticket of two large – one mushroom and one pepperoni, both with extra cheese. Sounded pretty good to me, after all those drinks. As we approached the door, I tried to look interested in the conversation while hanging at the back of the pack.

Through the glass, the doorman looked up with a smile of weary and indulgent recognition, and the inner door buzzed as one of the women reached for its handle. Warm air rushed over us, and I was inside.

As we crossed the lobby toward the elevators together, the woman who'd opened the door glanced back at me. A questioning look troubled her expression. I returned her gaze blankly. With four friends around her, she shouldn't be so nervous about a stranger, but sometimes normal humans get a weird feeling from us predator types.

Of course, I was getting a weird feeling about her too.

She wore a leather jacket over a short plaid dress that left her knees bare to the cold. Her hair lay across her forehead in a jet-black fringe that had grown out too long, ending just above her dark brown eyes. It took me a moment to realize that in the days before I lusted after *all* women *all* the time, this girl would have been my type.

She kept watching me as her friends prattled on, her expression more thoughtful than suspicious. When she ran her tongue between her lips in a distracted way, a little shudder went through me, and I tore my eyes away.

Bad carrier, I scolded myself, snapping a mental rubber band against my wrist.

The elevator dinged and opened, and the six of us crowded inside. I tucked myself into the corner. The pizza consensus had become unglued, and everyone besides the girl in the leather jacket was arguing again, the reflected sound from the shiny steel walls sharpening their voices.

Then a smell reached me – jasmine shampoo. I glanced up and saw the girl pushing her fingers through her hair. Somehow, the fragrance cut through the cigarette smoke clinging to their clothes, the alcohol on their breath; it carried her human scent to my nose – the smell of her skin, the natural oils on her fingers.

I shuddered again.

She pressed seven, glanced at me. 'What floor?'

I stared at the controls. The array of buttons covered one through fifteen (without the thirteen), in three columns. I tried to imagine Morgan's hand reaching out and pressing one of them, but my mind was in turmoil over the smell of jasmine.

The Bahamalama-Dingdong memory injection had finally let me down.

'Any particular floor?' she said slowly.

'Um, I uh . . .' I managed, my voice dry. 'Do you know Morgan?'

She froze, one finger still hovering near the buttons, and the rest of them fell into a sudden silence. They all stared at me.

The elevator *meep*ed away a couple of floors.

'Morgan on the seventh floor?' she said.

'Yeah . . . I think so,' I answered. How many Morgans could there be in one building?

'Hey, isn't that the – ?' one of the boys asked, but the other three shushed him.

'She moved out last winter,' leather-jacket girl said, her voice controlled and flat.

'Oh, wow. It's been a while, I guess.' I lit up a big fake smile. 'You don't know where she lives now, do you?'

She shook her head slowly. 'Not a clue.'

The elevator slid open on the seventh floor. The doors stirred the air, and I caught something under the cigarettes and alcohol on their breath, an animal smell that cut through even the jasmine. For a moment, I smelled fear.

Morgan's name had scared them.

The other four piled out efficiently, still in silence, but leather-jacket girl held her ground, one fingertip squashed white against the OPEN DOOR button. She was staring at me like I was someone she half recognized, thinking hard. Maybe she was trying to figure out why I set her prey hackles on fire.

I wanted to drop my eyes to the floor, sending a classic signal from Mammal Behavior 101: *I don't want to fight you*. Humans can be touchy when they feel threatened by us, and I didn't want her telling the doorman I had snuck in behind them.

But I held her gaze, my eyes captured.

'Guess I'll just go, then.' I settled back against the elevator wall.

'Yeah, sure.' She took one step back out of the elevator, still staring.

The doors began to slide closed, but at the last second her hand shot through. There was a binging sound as her leather-clad forearm was squeezed; then the doors jumped back.

'Got a minute, dude?' she asked. 'Maybe there's something you can explain for me.'

*

Apartment 701 was full of déjà vu.

The long, narrow living room had a half kitchen at one end. At the other, glass doors looked out onto a tiny balcony, the river, and the ghostly lights of New Jersey. Two more doors led to a bathroom and a small bedroom.

A classic upscale Manhattan one-bedroom apartment, but the devil was in the details: the stainless steel fridge, sliding dimmers instead of regular light switches, fancy brass handles on the doors – everything was sending waves of recognition through me.

'Did she live here?' I asked.

'Morgan? Hell, no,' the girl said, slipping off her leather jacket and tossing it onto a chair. The other four kept their coats on, I noticed. Their expressions reminded me of people at a party right after the cops turn the lights on, their buzz thoroughly killed. 'She lived down the hall.'

I nodded. All the apartments in the building must have looked pretty much the same. 'So you know her?'

She shook her head.

'Lace moved in after,' one of the boys volunteered. The rest of them gave him a *Shut up!* look.

'After what?' I said.

She didn't answer.

'Come on, Lace,' the boy said. 'You're going to show him the thing, aren't you? That's why you asked him in, right?'

'Roger, why don't you call for the pizza?' Lace said sharply.

He retreated to the kitchen muttering. I heard the manic beeps of speed-dialing, then Roger specifying extra cheese in a wounded tone.

The rest of us had filtered into the living room. Lace's three other friends took seats, still keeping their coats on.

'How well do you know Morgan?' Lace asked. She and I

remained standing, as if faced off against each other, but out of the confines of the elevator, her smell was more diffuse, and I found it easier not to stare so maniacally.

To distract myself I cataloged the furniture: urban rescue, musty couches and other cast-offs, a coffee table held up by a pair of wooden produce boxes. The tattered decor didn't go with the sanded floorboards or the million-dollar views.

'Don't know her that well, really,' I said. She frowned, so I added, 'But we're related. Cousins.'

Kind of a fib, I know. But our *parasites* are related, after all. That has to count for something.

Lace nodded slowly. 'You're related, but you don't know where she lives?'

'She's hard to find sometimes.' I shrugged, like it was no big deal. 'My name's Cal, by the way.'

'Lace, short for Lacey. Look, Cal, I never met this girl. She disappeared before I got here.'

'Disappeared?'

'Moved out.'

'Oh. How long ago was that?'

'I got in here at the beginning of March. She'd already been gone a month, as far as anyone knows. She was the weird one, according to the other people in the building.'

'*The* weird one?'

'The weirdest on the seventh floor,' she said. 'They were all kind of strange, people tell me.'

'The whole floor was strange?'

Lace just shrugged.

I raised an eyebrow. New Yorkers don't usually bond with their neighbors, not enough to gossip about former tenants – unless, of course, there are some *really* good stories to tell. I wondered what Lace had heard.

But my instincts told me to back off for the moment. The five of them were still twitchy, and there was something Lace didn't want to say in front of the others. I could smell her indecision, tinged with a weird sort of embarrassment. She wanted something from me.

I opened my hands, like I had nothing to hide. 'In the elevator, you said you had a question?'

Lace bit her lip, having a long, slow think. Then she sighed and sat down in the center of the couch. The other two girls scrunched into its corners to make room for her.

'Yeah, maybe there's something you can tell me, dude.' She swallowed and lowered her voice. 'Why am I only paying a thousand bucks a month for this place?'

When the shocked silence finally broke, the others were appalled.

'You told me sixteen hundred when I stayed here!' Roger screamed through the kitchen doorway.

Lace rolled her eyes at him. 'That was just so you'd pay your long-distance bill. It's not like *you* were paying any rent!'

'A thousand? That's *all*?' said one of the girls, sitting bolt upright on the couch. 'But you've got a *doorman*!'

Hell hath no fury like New Yorkers in someone else's cheap apartment. And what with the elevator, the doorman in his marble lobby, and those sunset views across the river, I reckoned the place should be about three thousand a month at least. Or maybe four? So far out of my league I wouldn't even know.

'I take it this isn't a rent-control thing?' I said.

Lace shook her head. 'They just built this place last year. I'm only the second tenant in my apartment, like everyone else on the seventh floor. We all moved in around the same time.'

'You mean all the first tenants moved out *together*?' I asked.

'From all four apartments on the seventh floor. Yeah.'

'A thousand bucks?' Roger said. 'Wow. That makes me feel a *lot* better about the thing.'

'Shut *up* about the thing!' Lace said. She looked at me, rolled her eyes again. 'It never made any sense. I spent all last winter sleeping on my sister's couch in Brooklyn, trying to find a place to stay closer to school. But everything in Manhattan was too expensive, and I was *way* over roommates.'

'Hey, thanks a lot,' Roger said.

Lace ignored him. 'But then my sister's super says he's got a line on this building they're trying to fill up fast. A whole floor of people totally skipped out on their rent, and they want new tenants right away. So it's cheap. Way cheap.' Her voice trailed off.

'You sound unhappy,' I said. 'Why's that?'

'We only signed up to finish the previous tenants' leases,' she said. 'There's only a couple of months left. Everyone on seven's talking about how they're going to raise the rent, push us out one by one.'

I shrugged. 'So how can I help you?'

'You know more than you're saying, dude,' she said flatly.

The certainty in her eyes silenced me – I didn't deny it, and Lace nodded slowly, positive now I wasn't some long-lost cousin.

'Something happened here,' Lace said. 'Something the land-lords wanted to cover up. I *need* to know what it was.'

'Why?'

'Because I need leverage.' She leaned forward on the couch, fingers gripping the cushions with white-knuckled strength. 'I'm *not* going back to my sister's couch!'

Like I said: hell hath no fury.

I held up my hands in surrender. To get anything more out of her, I was going to have to give her some of the truth, but I needed time to get my story straight.

'Okay. I'll tell you what I know,' I said. 'But first . . . show me the thing.'

She smiled. 'I was going to anyway.'

'The thing is *so* cool,' Roger said.

They'd done this before.

Without being told, the other two women turned off the lamps at either end of the couch. Roger flicked off the kitchen light and came through, sitting cross-legged in front of the white expanse of wall, almost like it was a TV screen.

It was dark now, the room glowing with dim orange from distant Jersey streetlights, accented by a bluish strip of night-light from under the bathroom door.

The other guy got out of his chair, scraping it out of our way, turning around to get his own view of the blank white wall.

'Is this a slide show?' I asked.

'Yeah, sure,' Roger said, giggling and hugging his knees. 'Fire up the projector, Lace.'

She grunted, rooting around under the coffee table and pulling out a fat candle and a pack of matches. She crossed the room carefully in the darkness and knelt beside the blank wall, setting the candle against the baseboard.

'Farther away,' Roger said.

'Shut *up*,' Lace countered. 'I've done this more than you have.'

The match flared in her hand, and she put it to the candle's wick. Just before the scent of sandalwood overpowered my nostrils, I detected the human smell of nervous anticipation.

The wall flickered like an empty movie screen, little peaks of stucco casting elongated shadows, like miniature mountains at sunset. The mottled texture of the wall became exaggerated, and my peep vision sharpened in the gloom, recording every imperfection. I could see the hurried, uneven paths that the rollers had followed up and down when the wall had been painted.

'What am I looking at?' I asked. 'A bad paint job?'

'I told you,' Roger said. 'Move it *out* a little.'

Lace growled but slid the candle farther from the wall.

The words appeared . . .

They glowed faintly through the shadows, their edges indistinct. A slightly darker layer of paint showed through the top coat, as often happens when landlords don't bother with primer.

Like when they're in a big rush.

The wall said:

so pRetty i hAd to Eat hiM

I crossed to the wall. The darker layer was less noticeable up close. I ran my fingertips across the letters. The cheap water-based paint felt as dry as a piece of chalk.

With one fingernail, I incised a curved mark in the paint, about the size of a fully grown hookworm. The dark color showed through a little more clearly there.

I brought my fingertip to my nose and sniffed.

'Dude, that's weird,' Roger said.

'Smell is the most sensitive of our senses, Roger,' I said. But I didn't mention the substance humans are most sensitive to: ethyl mercaptan, the odorant that gives rotten meat its particular tang. Your nose can detect one four-billionth of a gram of it in a single breath of air.

My nose is about ten times better.

I also didn't mention to Roger that my one little sniff had made me certain of something – the words had been painted in blood.

It turned out to be more than blood, though. As I incised the wall again with my steel-hard fingernails, breathing in the substances preserved under the hasty coat of paint, I caught a whole range of tissues from the human body. The iron tang of blood was joined by the mealy smell of ground bone, the saltiness of muscle, the flat scent of liver, and the ethyl mercaptan effluence of skin tissues.

I believe the layman's term is *gristle*.

There were other, sharper smells mixed in – chemical agents used to clean away the message. By the time they'd found it, though, the blood must have already soaked deep into the plaster, where it still clung tenaciously. They had painted it over, but the letters remained.

I mean, really: *water-based* paint? What is it with New York landlords?

'What the hell are you doing?' Lace said softly.

I turned and saw that they were all sitting there wide-eyed. I tend to forget how normal humans are made uncomfortable by the sniffing thing.

'Well . . .' I started, searching for a good excuse among the dregs of rum in my system. What was I going to say?

The buzzer sounded.

'Pizza's here!' Roger cried, jumping up and running to the door.

'Sounds good to me,' I said.

For some reason, I was starving.

6. SLIMEBALLS

Ants have this religion, and it's caused by slime-balls.

It all starts with a tiny creature called *Dicro-coelium dendriticum* – though even parasite geeks don't bother saying that out loud. We just call them 'lancet flukes.'

Like a lot of parasites, these flukes start out in a stomach. Stomachs are the most popular organs of final hosts, you may have noticed. Well, duh – there's *food* in them. In this case, we're talking about the stomach of a cow.

When the infected cow makes a cow pie, as we say in Texas, a passel of lancet fluke eggs winds up in the pasture. A snail comes along and eats some of the cow pie, because that's what snails do. Now the snail is infected. The fluke eggs hatch inside the unlucky snail's belly and then start to drill their way out through its skin.

Fortunately for the snail, it has a way to protect itself: slime.

The sliminess of the snail's skin lubricates the flukes as they drill their way out, and the snail survives their exit. By the time the flukes escape, they're entirely encased in a slimeball, unable to move. They'll never mess with any snails again, that's for sure.

But the flukes don't mind this turn of events. It turns out they *wanted* to be covered in slime. The whole trip through the snail was just evolution's way of getting the flukes all slimy. Because they're headed to their next host: an ant.

Here's something you didn't want to know: Ants love slimeballs.

Slimeballs make a delicious meal, even when they have a few hundred flukes inside. So sooner or later, some unlucky ant comes along, eats the slimeball, and winds up with a bellyful of parasites.

Inside the ant, the lancet flukes quickly organize themselves. They get ready for some parasite mind control.

'Do ants even have minds?' you may ask. Hard to say. But they do have tiny clusters of nerves, about midway in complexity between human brains and TV remote controls. A few dozen flukes take up a position at each of these nerve clusters and begin to change the ant's behavior.

The flukey ant gets religion. Sort of.

During the day, it acts normal. It wanders around on the ground, gathering food (possibly more slimeballs) and hanging out with the other ants. It still smells healthy to them, so they don't try to drive it off as they would a sick ant.

But when night falls, the ant does something flukey.

It leaves the other ants behind and climbs up a tall blade of grass, getting as high as it can off the ground. Up there under the stars, it waits all night alone.

What does it think it's doing? I always wonder.

Ants may not think anything ever. But if they do, maybe they have visions of strange creatures coming along to carry them to another world, like *X-Files* geeks in the Roswell desert waiting for a spaceship to whisk them away. Or perhaps *Dicrocoelium dendriticum* really is a religion, and the ant thinks some great revelation will strike if it just spends enough nights up at the top of a blade of grass. Like a swami meditating on a mountain, or a monk fasting in a tiny cell.

I'd like to think that in its final moments the ant is happy, or at least relieved, when a cow's mouth comes chomping down on its little blade of grass.

I know the flukes are happy. They're back in a cow's stomach, after all.

Parasite heaven.

I didn't really sleep that night. I never do.

Sure, I take my clothes off, get into bed, and close my eyes. But the whole unconsciousness thing doesn't quite happen. My mind keeps humming, like in those hours when you're coming down with something – not quite sick yet, but a bit light-headed, a fever threatening, illness buzzing at the edge of your awareness like a mosquito in the dark.

The Shrink says it's the sound of my immune system fighting the parasite. There's a war in my body every minute, a thousand T- and B-cells battering the horned head of the beast, prying at its hooks along my muscles and spine, finding and destroying its spores hidden inside transmuted red blood cells. On top of which there's the parasite fighting back, reprogramming my own tissues to feed it, tangling up my immune defenses with false alarms and bogus enemies.

This guerrilla war is always going on, but only when I'm lying in silence can I actually *hear* it.

You'd think this constant battle would tear me apart, or leave me exhausted come daylight, but the parasite is too well made for that. It doesn't want me dead. I'm a carrier, after all – I have to stay alive to ensure its spread. Like every parasite, the thing inside me has evolved to find a precarious balance called *optimum virulence*. It takes as much as it can get away with, sucking out the nutrients it needs to create more offspring. But no parasite wants to starve the host *too* quickly, not while it's getting a free ride. So, as long as it gets fed, it backs off. I may eat like a four-hundred-pound guy, but I never get fat. The parasite uses the nutrients to churn out its spores in my blood and saliva and semen, with enough left over to give me predatory strength and hyped-up senses.

Optimum virulence is why most deaths from parasites are long and lingering – in the case of a carrier like me, the time it takes to die happens to be longer than a normal human life span. That's the way the older peep hunters talk about it: not so much immortality as a centuries-long downward spiral. Maybe that's why they use the word *undead*.

So I lie awake every night, listening to the gnawing, calorie-burning struggle inside me, and getting up for the occasional midnight snack.

That particular long night, I found myself thinking about Lace, remembering her smell, along with another flood of details I hadn't even known I'd spotted. Her right hand sometimes made a fist when she talked, her eyebrows moved a lot beneath their concealing fringe, and – unlike girls back in Texas – her voice didn't rise in pitch at the end of a sentence, unless it really was a question, and sometimes not even then.

We'd agreed to meet in my favorite diner at noon the next day, after her morning class. Neither of us wanted to discuss things in front of her friends, and something about the aftertaste of pepperoni doesn't go with talk of gristle on the wall.

Normally, I don't like to torture myself, hanging around with cute girls my age, but this was job-related, after all. Besides, maybe a *little* bit of torture is okay. I didn't want to wind up like the Shrink, after all, collecting old dolls or something even weirder.

And I figured it would be nice to hang out with someone from outside the Night Watch once in a while, someone who thought I was a normal guy.

So I stayed awake all night, thinking of lies to tell her.

I got up early and reported to the Night Watch first.

The Watch's offices are pretty much like any other city government building, except older, danker, and even deeper underground. There are the usual metal detectors, petty bureaucrats behind glass, and ancient wooden file drawers stuffed with four centuries' worth of paperwork. Except for the odd fanatic like Dr. Rat, no one looks remotely happy to be at work there, or even slightly motivated.

It's a wonder the whole city isn't infected.

I went to Records first. In terms of square footage, Records is the biggest department of the Watch. They've got back doors into regular city data, and also their own paper trails going back to the days when Manhattan was called New Amsterdam. Records can find out who owns what anywhere in the city, who owned it before that, and before that . . . back to the Dutch farmers who stole it from the Manhattan Indians.

And they're not just into real estate – Records has a database of every suspicious death or disappearance since 1648 and can produce a clipping of pretty much every newspaper story involving infectious diseases, lunatic attackers, or rat population explosions published since the printing press reached the New World.

Records has two mottos. One is:

The Secrets of the City Are Ours

The other:

NO, WE DO NOT HAVE PENS!

Bring your own. You'll need them. You see, like every other

department in the city, Records runs on Almighty Forms. There are forms that tell the Night Mayor's office what we hunters are doing – starting an investigation, ending one, or reaching various points along the way. There are forms that make things happen, from installing rat traps to getting lab work done. There are forms with which to requisition peep-hunting equipment, from tiger cages to Tasers. (The form for commandeering a genuine NYC garbage truck may be thirty-four pages long, but one day I *will* think of some reason to fill it out, I swear to you.) There are even forms that activate other forms or switch them off, that cause other forms to mutate, thus bringing newly formed forms into the world. Put together, all these forms are the vast spiral of information that defines us, guides our growth, and makes sure our future looks like our past – they are the DNA of the Night Watch.

Fortunately, what I wanted that morning wasn't quite DNA-complicated. First, I requisitioned some standard equipment, the sort of peep-hunting toys that you can pull off the rack. Then I asked for some information about Lace's building: who owned it, who had originally rented all the seventh-floor apartments, and if anything noticeably weird had ever happened there. Getting answers to these simple questions wasn't easy, of course. Nothing ever is, down in the bowels of a bureaucracy. But after only three hours, my paperwork passed muster with the ancient form-dragon behind the bulletproof glass, was rolled into a pneumatic-tube missile, and was launched on its journey into the Underworld with a *swish*.

They'd call me when it came back, so I headed off to meet Lace at my favorite diner. On the way, I realized that this was my first date in six months – even if it was only a 'date' in the lame sense of being an arrangement to meet someone. Still, the concept made me nervous, all my underused muscles of dating anxiety springing into action. I started checking out my reflection in shop windows and wondering if Lace would like the Kill Fee T-shirt I was wearing. Why hadn't I put on something less threadbare? And what was with my hair these days? Apparently, Dr. Rat, the Shrink, and my other Night Watch pals didn't feel compelled to tell me it was sticking out at the sides.

After two minutes in front of a bank window, trying to stick it behind my ears, I despaired of fixing it. Then I despaired of my life in general.

What was the point of a good haircut when nothing could come of it anyway?

Lace sat down across from me, wearing the same leather jacket as the night before, this time over a wool dress. Under a beret that was the same dark brown as her eyes, her hair still smelled like jasmine-scented shampoo. She looked like she'd had about as much sleep as I had.

Seeing Lace in the daylight, both of us sober, I realized for the first time that she might be a few years older than me. Her leather jacket was brown – with buttons, not black and zippered like mine – and the rest of her outfit looked like something you would wear to an office job. My Kill Fee T-shirt felt suddenly dorky, and I hunched my shoulders together so my jacket would fall across the screaming demon on my chest.

'What up?' she said, feeling my scrutiny, and I dropped my eyes back to the table.

'Uh, nothing. How was your class?' I asked, spattering some more Tabasco over my scrambled eggs and bacon. Before she'd arrived, I'd already consumed a pepper steak to calm my nerves.

'All right, I guess. Some guest lecturer yakking about ethics.'

'Ethics?'

'Journalistic ethics.'

'Oh.' I stirred my black coffee for no particular reason. 'Journalists have ethics?'

Lace cast her eyes around for a waiter or waitress, one finger pointing at my coffee. She nodded as the connection was made, then turned back to me. 'They're supposed to. You know, don't reveal your sources. Don't destroy people's lives just to get a story. Don't pay people for interviews.'

'You're studying journalism?'

'Journalism and the law, actually.'

I nodded, wondering if that was an undergraduate major. Somehow, it didn't sound like one. I revised Lace's age up to the lower to mid-twenties and felt myself relax a little. Suddenly, this was even less a date than it had been a moment before.

'Cool,' I said.

She looked at me like I might be retarded.

I tried to smile back at her, realizing that my small-talk muscles were incredibly rusty, the result of socializing only with people in a secret organization who pretty much only socialized with one another. Of course, if I could just steer the conversation to rinderpest infection rates in Africa, I knew I'd blow her away.

Rebecky – at sixty-seven and three hundred pounds, my favorite waitress in the world to flirt with – appeared and handed Lace a cup of coffee and a menu.

'How're you doing there, Cal?' she asked.

'Just fine, thanks.'

'You sure? You haven't been eating much lately.' She gave me a sly wink.

'On a diet,' I said, patting my stomach.

Her standard response: 'Wish that diet worked on me.'

Rebecky chuckled as she walked away. She's amazed by my appetite, but her repertoire of where-does-Cal-put-it-all jokes had shrunk to the bare minimum over the last months. As a guy with something to hide, there's one thing I've learned: People only worry about the uncanny for about a week; that's the end of their attention span. After that, suspicions turn into shtick.

Lace looked up from her menu. 'Speaking of funny diets, Cal, what the hell happened in my building last winter?'

I leaned back and sipped coffee. Evidently, Lace wasn't up for small talk either. 'You in a hurry or something?'

'My lease is up in two months, dude. And last night you promised you wouldn't jerk me around.'

'I'm not jerking you around. You should try the pepper steak.'

'Vegetarian.'

'Oh,' I said, my parasite rumbling at the concept.

Lace flagged down Rebecky and ordered potato salad, while I crammed some bacon into my mouth. Potato salad is an Atkins nightmare, and more important, the parasite hates it. Peeps prefer protein, red in tooth and claw.

'So tell me what you know,' she said.

'Okay.' I cleared my throat. 'First of all, I'm not really Morgan's cousin.'

'Duh.'

I frowned. This revelation hadn't provided the same *oomph* that it had on my mental flowchart of the conversation. 'But I am looking for her.'

'Again: *duh*, dude. So you're like a private detective or something? Or stalker ex-boyfriend?'

'No. I work for the city.'

'Cal, you are *so* not a cop.'

I wasn't quite sure how she'd come to this assessment, but I couldn't argue. 'No, I'm not. I work for the Department of Health and Mental Hygiene, Sexually Transmitted Disease Control.'

'Sexually transmitted?' She raised an eyebrow. 'Wait. Are you *sure* you're not a stalker?'

I reached for my wallet and flopped it open, revealing one of the items I'd picked up from the Night Watch that morning. We've got a big machine that spits out laminated ID cards and badges, credentials for dozens of city agencies, both real and imaginary. This silver-plated badge was very impressive, with the words *Health Field Officer* curving along the bottom. In the ID case next to it, my photo stared grimly out at her.

She stared at it for a moment, then said, 'You know you're wearing the same shirt today as in that picture?'

I froze for a second, realizing that, yep, I hadn't changed since that morning. In a brilliant save, I glanced down at my Kill Fee T-shirt and said, 'What? You don't like it?'

'Not particularly. So what's that job all about? Do you, like, hunt people down and arrest them for spreading the clap?'

I cleared my throat, pushing my empty plate away. 'Okay, here's how it works. About a year ago, I was given a disease. Um, let me put that another way – I was *assigned* a specific carrier of a certain disease. I tracked down all his sexual partners and encouraged them to get tested, then I tracked down their sexual partners, and so on.' I shrugged. 'I just keep going where the chain of infection leads me, informing people along the way. Sometimes I don't get enough specific information about someone, so I have to poke around a little, like I was last night. For one thing, I don't even know Morgan's last name.' I raised my eyebrows hopefully.

Lace shrugged. 'Me neither. So let me get this straight: You tell people they've got STDs? That's your *job*, dude?'

'No, their doctors do that. All I'm allowed to do is tell them they're at risk. Then I try to get them to cooperate and give me a list of people *they've* slept with. Someone's got to do it.'

'I guess. Wow, though.'

'So far I've spent a whole year tracking down the offspring –

or rather, the infections from that one carrier.' I smiled at my cover story's cleverness. Nifty how I worked the truth in there, huh?

'Wow,' Lace repeated softly, her eyes still wide.

Now that I thought about it, the job I'd chosen for myself did sound pretty cool. A little bit of undercover work, some social consciousness, an air of illicit mystery and human tragedy. One of those careers where you'd have to face life's harsh realities *and* be a good listener. By now, she had to figure I was older than nineteen – more like her age, and probably wise beyond my years.

Her potato salad arrived, and after a fortifying bite of carbs, she said, 'So what's your disease?'

'My disease? I didn't say I had a disease.'

'The one you're *tracking*, dude.'

'Oh. Right. I'm not at liberty to say. Confidentiality. We have ethics too.'

'Sure you do.' Her eyes narrowed. 'And that's why you didn't want to talk in front of my friends last night?'

I nodded. My cover story was sliding into place perfectly.

She put down her fork. 'But it's one of those sexually transmitted diseases that makes people *paint stuff on the walls in blood*?'

I swallowed, wondering if perhaps my cover story might have a few loose ends.

'Well, some STDs can cause dementia,' I said. 'Late-stage syphilis, for example, makes you go crazy. It eats your brain. Not that syphilis is what we're talking about here, necessarily.'

'Wait a second, Cal. You think all the people on the seventh floor of my building were shagging one another? And going all demented from it?' She made a face at her potato salad. 'Do you guys get a lot of that kind of thing?'

'Um, it happens. Some STDs can cause . . . promiscuity. Sort of.' I felt my cover story entering the late stages of its life span and suppressed an urge to mention rabies (which was a little too close to the truth, what with the frothing and the biting). 'Right now, I can't be sure what happened up there. But my job is to find out where all those people went, especially if they're infected.'

'And why the landlord is covering it up.'

'Yeah, because this is all about your rent.'

She raised her hands. 'Hey, I didn't know you were all into saving the world, okay? I just thought you were a stalker ex-boyfriend or a weird psycho cousin or something. But I'm glad you're the good guys, and I want to help. It's not just my rent situation, you know. I have to *live* with that thing on the wall.'

I put down my coffee cup with authoritative force. 'Okay. I'm glad you're helping. I thank you, and your city thanks you.'

In fact, I was just glad the cover story had made it through the worst of Lace's suspicions. I'd never really worked undercover before; lies aren't my thing. She frowned, eating a few more bites of potato salad, and I wondered if Lace's help was worth involving her. So far, she'd been a little too smart for comfort. But smart wasn't all bad. It wouldn't hurt to have a pair of sharp eyes on the seventh floor.

And frankly, I was enjoying her company, especially the way she didn't hide her thoughts and opinions. That wasn't a luxury I could indulge in myself, of course, but it was good to hear Lace voicing every suspicion that went through her head. Saved me from being paranoid about what she was thinking.

On top of which, I was feeling very in control, hanging out with a desirable woman without having a sexual fantasy every few seconds. Maybe every few *minutes* or so, but still, you have to crawl before you can walk.

'Dude, why are you scratching your wrist like that?'

'I am? Oh, crap.'

'What the hell, Cal? It's all red.'

'Um, it's just . . .' I ransacked my internal database of skin parasites, then announced, 'Pigeon mites!'

'Pigeon whats?'

'You know. When pigeons sit on your window and shake their feathers? Sometimes these little mites fall off and nest in your pillows. They bite your skin and cause . . .' I waved my oft-pinged wrist.

'Eww. One more reason not to like pigeons.' She glared out the window at a few of them scavenging on the sidewalk. 'So what do we do now?'

'How about this? You take me back to your building and show me which apartment used to be Morgan's.'

'And then what?'

'Leave that to me.'

As we passed the doorman I made sure to catch his eye and smile. If I came in with Lace a few more times, maybe the staff would start to recognize me.

On the seventh floor, she led me to the far end of the hall, gesturing at a door marked 704. There were just four apartments on this floor, all the one-bedrooms you could squeeze into the sliver-thin building.

'That's where she lived, according to the two guys upstairs. Loud and freaky in bed, they tell me.'

I coughed into a fist, again damning my fugitive memories. 'You know who lives here now?'

'Guy called Max. He works days.'

I knocked hard. No answer.

Lace sighed. 'I told you he wouldn't be home.'

'Glad to hear it.' I pulled out another of the items requisitioned that morning and knelt by the door: The lock was a standard piece-of-crap deadbolt, five tumblers. Into its keyhole I sprayed some graphite, which is the same gray stuff that gets on your fingers if you fiddle with the end of a pencil, and does the same thing to locks that Bahamalama-Dingdongs do to repressed memories – lubricates them. Two of the tumblers rolled over as my pick slid in. Easy-peasy.

'Dude,' Lace whispered, 'shouldn't you get a warrant or something?'

I was ready for this one. 'Doesn't matter. You only need a warrant if you want the evidence to stand up in court. But I'm not taking anyone to court.' Another tumbler rolled over. 'This isn't a criminal investigation.'

'But you can't just break into people's apartments!'

'I'm not breaking. Just looking.'

'Still!'

'Look, Lace, maybe this isn't strictly legal. But if people in my job didn't cut a few corners every now and then, everyone in this city would be infected, okay?'

She paused for a moment, but the ring of truth had filled my words. I've seen simulations of what would happen if the parasite were to spread unchecked, and believe me, it's not pretty. Zombie Apocalypse, we call it.

Finally, she scowled. 'You better not steal anything.'

'I won't.' The last two tumblers went, and I opened the door. 'You can stay out here if you want. Knock hard if Max comes out of that elevator.'

'Forget it,' she said. 'I'm going to make sure you don't do anything weird. Besides, he's had my blender for four months.'

She pushed in past me, heading for the kitchen. I sighed, putting my lock-pick away and closing the door behind us.

The apartment was a carbon copy of Lace's, but with better furniture. The shape of the living room refired my recognition pistons. Finally, I had found the place where the parasite had entered me, making me a carrier and changing my life forever.

It was much tidier than Lace's apartment, which might be a problem. After seven months of living there, an obsessive cleaner would have swept away a lot of evidence.

I crossed to the sliding glass doors and shut the curtains to make it darker, trying to ignore the clatter of pots and pans from the kitchen.

'You know,' I called, *you're* the one who's going to have to explain to Max how you got your blender back.'

'I'll tell him I astral-projected. Butt-head.'

'Huh?'

'Him, not you. He had my blender all summer. Margarita season.'

'Oh.' I shook my head – infection, cannibalism, blender appropriation. The Curse of 704 was alive and well.

I pulled out another little toy I'd picked up that morning – an ultraviolet wand – and flicked it on. The demon's eyes on my Kill Fee shirt began to give off an otherworldly glow. I swept the wand across the same wall that, back in Lace's apartment, had held the words written in gristle.

'Dude! Flashback!' Lace said, crossing the living room. She smiled, and her teeth flickered as white as a radioactive beach at noon.

'Flashback?'

'Yeah, your teeth are glowing, like at a dance club.'

I shrugged. 'Don't go to clubs much since I . . . got this job.'

'No, I guess you wouldn't,' she said. 'All that sexual transmission just waiting to happen.'

'Huh? Hey, I don't have anything against – '

She smiled. 'Just kidding, dude. Relax.'

'Ah.' I cleared my throat.

Nothing glowed on the wall in the ultraviolet. I held the wand closer, casting weird shadows across the stucco mountainscape. No pattern of a hurried paint roller appeared. I cut into a few spots at random with my fingernail, but nothing bright shone through.

The other walls were just as clean.

'So does that thing make blood show up?' she asked.

'Blood and other bodily fluids.'

'Bodily fluids? You are so *CSI*.' She said this like it was a cool thing, and I gave her a smile.

'Let's try the bedroom,' she said.

'Good idea.'

We went through the door, and my déjà vu ramped up to another level. This was where I had lost my virginity and become a monster, all in one night.

Like the living room, the bedroom was impeccably clean. Lace sat on the bed while I scanned the walls with UV.

'This goo you're looking for, it isn't still . . . active, is it?'

'Active? Oh, you mean infectious.' I shook my head. 'One thing about parasites – they're great at living inside other organisms, but once they hit the outside world, they're not so tough.'

'Parasites?'

'Oh, pretend you didn't hear that. Anyway, after seven months, you're totally safe from catching it.' I cleared my throat. 'As am I.'

'So, what's with the glow stick?'

'I'm trying to see if the same thing happened here as in your apartment.'

'The wall-writing dementia festival, you mean? Does that really happen a lot?'

'Not really.'

'Didn't think so. Lived in New York all my life, and I never saw anything like that on the news.'

I shot her a look, the word *news* making me wonder if her journalistic instincts were kicking in. Which would be a bad thing.

'What disease is this again?' she asked.

'Not telling.'

'*Please!*'

I waved the wand at her, and several luminous streaks appeared on the blanket underneath her.

'What's *that*?'

I grinned. 'Bodily fluids.'

'Dude!' She leaped to her feet.

'That's nothing compared to the skin mites.'

Lace was rubbing her hands together. 'Which are what?'

'Microscopic insects that hang out in beds, feeding on dead skin cells.'

'I'll be washing out my blender,' she said, and left me alone.

I chuckled to myself and turned the wand on the other walls, the floors, inside the closet. Other than Max's blanket and a pair of underwear under the bed, the UV didn't get a rise out of anything. Picking at the stucco didn't help; nothing had been painted over in this apartment.

Max was a lot neater than most single men, I'd say that for the guy. Or maybe Morgan knew not to eat where she slept.

Suddenly, my ears caught a jingling sound. Keys in a lock.

'Crap,' I said. Max was home early.

'Uh, Cal?' Lace's voice called softly, her vocal cords tight.

'Shh!' I flicked off the wand, shoved it into my pocket, and ran into the living room. Lace was standing there, clutching her wet blender.

'Put that down!' I hissed, dragging her toward the glass doors that led to the balcony.

I heard the lock's bolt shoot closed. A lucky break – I had left the apartment unlocked behind us, so whoever was coming in had just *re*locked the door, thinking they were *un*locking it.

Muffled Spanish swearing filtered through, a female voice, and I realized that Max's apartment was spotless because he had a cleaner.

I yanked the sliding glass door open and pushed Lace out into the cold. When it was shut behind us, I watched the thick curtains swing lazily to a halt, hiding us from the living room. Pressing one ear to the icy glass, palming the other to mute the roar of traffic, I listened. My heartbeat was ramped up with excitement, adrenaline making the parasite start to churn, my muscles tightening. Through the glass came the sound of a graphite-lubricated deadbolt shooting free, and the door creaked open.

'*Mio!*' an annoyed voice muttered. Fingers fumbling for a light switch. The apartment was too dark to work in – she would probably be opening the curtains in a few moments.

I turned to Lace, whose eyes were wide, her pupils huge from the excitement. On the tiny balcony, we were only a foot apart, and I could smell her perfectly – the jasmine hair, a salt smell of nerves. We were too close for comfort. I pulled my eyes away from her and pointed at the next balcony over. 'Who lives there?'

'Um, this girl called Freddie,' Lace whispered.

'She at home?'

Lace shrugged.

'Well, let's hope not.' I jumped up onto the rail and across.

'Jesus, dude!' Lace squeaked.

I turned back to look down through the two-and-a-half-foot gap, realizing I should at least *pretend* to show fear, if only for

Lace's sake. The parasite doesn't want its peeps too cautious; it wants us picking fights, complete with the biting and the scratching and other disease-spreading activities. We carriers don't mind a little danger.

Lace, though, was fully human, and her eyes widened farther as she stared down.

'Come on,' I whispered soothingly. 'It's just a couple of feet.'

She glared at me. 'A couple of feet *across*. Seven stories down!'

I sighed and jumped back up, steadied myself with one foot on each rail, and leaned back against the building. 'Okay, I'll swing you across. I promise I won't drop you.'

'No way, dude!' she said, her panic breaking through the whisper.

I wondered if the cleaner had heard us and was already calling the cops. My Health and Mental badge looked real, and if a policeman called the phone number on the ID, there would be a Night Watch employee sitting at the other end. But Lace had been right about the whole illegal entry thing, and if someone went looking to complain to my boss in person, they would find only a bricked-up doorway in a forgotten basement of City Hall. The Night Watch had cut most of its official ties two hundred years ago; only a few bureaucrats remained who knew the secret histories.

I leaned down and grabbed Lace's wrist. 'Sorry, but . . .'

'What are you – ?' She squealed as I lifted her up and over, setting her down on the next balcony.

When I jumped down beside her, Lace's face was white.

'You . . . I could have . . .' she sputtered. Her mouth was open, and she was breathing hard. On the tiny balcony, my senses started to tangle up with one another, smell and sight and taste, the parasite pushing its advantage. Excitement radiated from

Lace; I knew it was only fear making her pupils expand, her heart pound, but my body responded in its own blind way, construing it all as signs of arousal. My hands were itching to take hold of her shoulders and taste her lips.

'Excuse me,' I squeaked, pushing her away from the balcony door.

I knelt and pulled out lock-picking equipment, desperate to get off that balcony and inside, anything to be a few feet farther away from Lace. My fingers fumbled, and I banged my head against the glass on purpose, clearing my brain long enough to squirt the keyhole with graphite.

Seconds later, the door slid open.

I stumbled inside Freddie's apartment, away from Lace's smell, sucking in the odors of industrial carpet, recently assembled Ikea furniture, and a musty couch. Anything but jasmine.

When I managed to get back under control, I put my ear to the wall. The welcome roar of a vacuum cleaner rumbled back and forth next door. Taking another deep breath, I collapsed onto the couch. I hadn't kissed Lace and the cops weren't on their way – two near disasters averted.

Without catching Lace's eye, I looked around. Another clone of Morgan's apartment, the walls innocently white. 'Might as well check in here too.'

Lace didn't say a word, staring at me from where she stood just inside the balcony door. Her expression was still intense, and when I switched on the UV light, the whites of her eyes glowed fiercely. She was rubbing her wrist where I'd grabbed it to lift her across.

She said calmly, 'How did you do that?'

'Do what?'

'Pick me up. Swing me like a cat.'

I attempted a cavalier smile. 'Is that how cats are swung?'

She snarled, revealing a flash of ultraviolet teeth. 'Tell me.'

I realized she was still angry and tried to channel Dr. Rat's lecture voice. 'Well, the human body is capable of great strength, you know. Mothers whose babies are in danger have been known to lift cars. And people high on PCP can snap steel handcuffs or even pull their own teeth out with pliers.'

This was a point often made in Hunting 101: Peeps aren't stronger than normal people in any healthy sense – the parasite just turns them into psychos, setting their muscles at emergency strength, like a car with its gas pedal stuck down. (Which would sort of make carrier peeps controlled psychos, I suppose, though nobody at the Night Watch ever put it like that.)

'So which category do you fall into?' Lace said. 'Concerned mother or insane drug addict?'

'Um . . . more like concerned mother, I guess?'

Lace advanced on me, stuck one stiff forefinger into the center of my chest, her smell overwhelming me as she shouted, 'Well, let's get something straight, Cal. I am *not . . . your . . . baby!*'

She spun on her heel and stomped to the apartment door, unlocking it and yanking it open. She turned back, pulling something from her pocket. For a second, I thought she was going to throw it at me in a wild rage.

But her voice was even. 'I found this in Max's kitchen trash. Guess Morgan never bothered to get her mail forwarded.'

She flicked it at me after all, the envelope spinning like a ninja's star.

I plucked it from the air and turned it over. It was addressed to Morgan. Just a random piece of junk mail, but now I had a last name.

'Morgan Ryder. Hey, thanks for – '

The door slammed shut. Lace was gone.

I stared after her for a while, the echo of her exit ringing in my exquisite hearing. I could still smell the jasmine fragrance in the air, the scent of her anger, and traces of her skin oil and sweat on my fingers. Her departure had been so sudden, it took a moment to accept it.

It was better this way, of course. I'd been lucky so far. Those moments on the balcony had been too intense and unexpected. It was one thing sitting across a table from Lace in a crowded restaurant, but I couldn't be alone with her, not in small spaces. I liked her too much, and after six months of celibacy, the parasite was stronger than I was.

And once she thought about my cover story a little more, she'd probably figure I was some kind of thief or con man or just plain freaky. So maybe she'd steer clear of me from now on.

I let out a long, sad sigh, then continued sweeping for bodily fluids.

A long time ago human beings were hairy all over, like monkeys. Nowadays, however, we wear clothes to keep us warm.

How did this switch happen? Did we lose the fur and then decide to invent clothes? Or did we invent clothing and then lose the body hair that we no longer needed?

The answer isn't in any history books, because writing hadn't been invented yet when it happened. But fortunately, our little friends the parasites remember. They carry the answer in their genes.

Lice are bloodsuckers that live on people's heads. So small that you can barely see them, they hide in your hair. Once they've infested one person, they spread like a rumor, carrying trench fever, typhus, and relapsing fever. Like most bloodsuckers, lice are unpopular. That's why the word *lousy* is generally not a compliment.

You can't fault lousy loyalty, though. Human lice have been with us for five million years, since our ancestors split off from chimpanzees. That's a long run together. (The tapeworm, for comparison, has only been inside us for about eight thousand years, a total parasite-come-lately.) At the same time we were evolving away from monkeys, our parasites were evolving from monkey parasites — coming along for the ride.

But I bet that *our* lice wish they hadn't bothered. You see, while the chimps stayed hairy, we humans lost most of our body hair. So now human lice have only our hairy heads to hide in. On top of that, they're always getting poisoned by shampoo and conditioner, which is why lice have become rare in wealthy countries.

But lice aren't utterly doomed. When people started wearing clothing, some lice evolved to take advantage of the new situation. They developed claws that are adapted for clinging to fabric instead of hair. So these days, there are two species of human lice: hair-loving head lice and clothes-loving body lice.

Evolution marches on. Maybe one day we'll have space suit lice.

So what does this have to do with the invention of clothing?

Not long ago, scientists compared the DNA of three kinds of lice: head lice, body lice, and the old original chimp lice. As time passes, DNA changes at a fixed rate, so scientists can tell roughly how long ago any two species split up from each other. Comparing lice DNA soon settled the question of what came first — the clothes or the nakedness.

Here's how it happened:

Human lice and monkey lice split off from each other about 1.8 million years ago. That's when ancient humans lost their body hair and the lice we inherited from the chimps had to adapt, evolving to stick to our heads.

But head lice and body lice didn't split until seventy-two thousand years ago, an eternity later (especially in lice years). That's when human beings invented clothes, and body lice evolved to reclaim some of their lost real estate. They got brand-new claws and spread down into our brand new clothing.

So that's the answer: Clothes got invented *after* we lost our body hair. And not right away; our primate ancestors ran around naked and hairless for well over a million years.

That part of human evolution is written in lousy history, in the genes of the things that suck our blood.

Just as I finished Freddie's apartment (finding no glimmer of bodily fluids), my phone buzzed. One of the Shrink's minders was on the other end, saying that she wanted to see me again. My stack of forms had returned from Records, chock-full of enough intrigue to bounce all the way up to the Shrink. That was always a sign of progress.

Still, I sometimes wished she would just talk to me on the phone and not insist on quite so much face time. But she's so old-school that telephones just aren't her thing. In fact, *electricity* isn't her thing.

I wonder if I'll ever get that ancient.

I took the subway down to Wall Street, then walked across. The Shrink's house is on a crooked alley paved with cobblestones, barely one car wide. It's one of those New Amsterdam originals that the Dutch laid down four centuries ago, running on the diagonal, flouting the grid in the same grumpy way that the Shrink ignores telephones. Those early streets possess their own logic; they were built atop the age-old hunting trails of the Manhattan Indians. Of course, the Indians were only following even more ancient paths created by deer.

And who were the deer copying? I wondered. Maybe my route had first been cut through the primeval forest by a line of hungry ants.

One thing about carrying the parasite – it makes you

feel connected to the past. As a peep, I'm a blood brother to every other parasite-positive throughout the ages. There's an unbroken chain of biting, scratching, unprotected sex, rat reservoirs, and various other forms of fluid-sharing between me and that original slavering maniac, the poor human who was first infected with the disease.

So where did he or she get it from? you may ask. From elsewhere in the animal kingdom. Most parasites leap to humanity from other species. Of course, it was a long time ago, so the original parasite-positive wasn't exactly what we'd call human. More likely the first peep was some early Cro-Magnon who was bitten by a dire wolf or giant sloth or saber-toothed weasel.

I kicked a bag of garbage next to the Shrink's stoop and heard the skittering of tiny claws inside it. A few little faces peeked out to glare at me; then one rat jumped free and scampered a few yards down the alley, disappearing down a hole among the cobblestones.

There are more of those holes than you'd think.

When I first came to the city, I saw only street level, or sometimes caught glimpses of the netherworld through exhaust grates or down empty subway tracks. But in the Night Watch we see the city in layers. We *feel* the sewers and the hollow sidewalks carrying electrical cables and steam pipes, and below that the older spaces: the basements of fallen buildings, the giant buried caskets of abandoned breweries, the ancient septic tanks, the forgotten graveyards. And, struggling to get free underneath, the old streambeds and natural springs – all those pockets where rats, and much bigger things, can thrive.

Dr. Rat says that the only creatures that ever come out onto the surface are the weak ones, the punks who aren't competitive enough to feed themselves down where it's safe. The really big things, the rat kings and the other alpha beasties, live and die without ever troubling the daylight world. Think about that for a second: There are creatures down there who've never seen a human being.

The laden sky rumbled overhead, and I smelled rain.

History. Nature. Weather. My head was pounding, full of those big, abstract words that have their own cable channels.

But it was the sound of those tiny scratching feet inside the garbage bag that followed me into the Shrink's house and down the corridor to her session room, pushed along by an invisible wind.

'Most impressive, Cal.' She leafed through papers on her desk. 'All it took was a few drinks to get you back to Morgan's house.'

'Yeah. But it was an apartment, Dr. Prolix. Not many houses in Manhattan these days, you might have noticed.'

The guy from Records in the other visitor's chair raised his eyebrows at my tone, but the Shrink only folded her hands and smiled. 'Still glum? But you're making such progress.'

I chewed my lip. The Shrink didn't need to know what I was bummed about. Not that it mattered anymore, the whole stupid way I'd had Lace help me. Even if she'd gone on believing me, hanging out with her would have just gotten more and more torturous.

Worse than that, it had been *dangerous*. Lace hadn't showed a bit of interest – not *that* kind of interest anyway – and I'd still come close to kissing her.

Never again. Lesson learned. Move on. I was back in lone-hunter mode now.

'Yeah, gallons of progress,' I said. 'You saw what I found on the wall?'

'I read your 1158-S from this morning, yes.'

'Well, I went back there today but didn't find anything more on the creepy graffiti front. Or much else. Morgan moved out at least seven months ago. Not exactly an oven-fresh trail.'

'Cal, eight months is the blink of an eye for Records. To find out where Morgan has gone, perhaps we should look at where she came from.'

'What do you mean?'

'The history of that property has proven interesting.' She turned to the Records guy and waved her pale hand.

'When the landlords in question filed their initial rent-control forms,' he began, 'there were four residents on the seventh floor.' His voice quivered slightly, and once or twice as he read, his eyes darted up to the creepy dolls, confirming that he wasn't comfortable in the Shrink's office. Not a hunter, just an average working stiff with a city job. His chair was backed as far away from the red line as it could go. No typhoid germs for him. 'We ran the names of these individuals through the city databases and hit a missing persons report from March this year.'

'Only one?' I asked. 'I figured they'd all be missing.'

He shook his head. 'More than one missing person from the same address, and we would have already filed an MP-2068 with you guys. But there was only one hit. NYPD has no leads, and at this point it's pretty much a dead investigation.'

Given what I'd seen in Lace's apartment, that wording was appropriate. 'So let me guess: The guy who lived in 701 is gone.' *So pretty I just had to eat him.*

The man from Records nodded. 'That's right, 701. Jesus Delanzo, age twenty-seven. Photographer.' He looked up at me, and when I didn't say anything, he continued, 'Apartment 702 was occupied by Angela Dreyfus, age thirty-four. Broker.'

'Where does she live now?'

He frowned. 'We don't exactly have an address for her. Just a post office box in Brooklyn, and a cell phone that doesn't answer.'

'Rather anonymous, don't you think?' the Shrink said.

'And her friends and family don't think it's weird she lives in a post office box?' I asked.

'We don't know,' the Records guy said. 'If they're worried, they haven't filed with the NYPD.'

I frowned, but the Records guy kept going. 'A couple lived in the other apartment – 703. Patricia and Joseph Moore, both age twenty-eight. And guess what: Their mail forwards to the same post office box as Angela Dreyfus's, and they have the same phone number.' He leaned back, crossed his legs, and smiled, rather pleased to have put such a juicy coincidence on my plate.

But his last words hadn't even gotten through to me yet. Something else was really wrong.

'That's only three apartments. What about 704?'

He raised an eyebrow, looked down at his printouts, and shrugged. 'Unoccupied.'

'Unoccupied?' I turned to the Shrink. 'But that's where Morgan lived. Her junk mail is still showing up there.'

The Records guy nodded. 'The post office doesn't forward junk mail.'

'But why don't you have a record of her?'

He leafed through his folder as he shook his head. 'Because the landlord never filed an occupancy form for that apartment. Maybe they were letting her live there for free.'

'For *free*? Fat chance,' I said. 'That's a three-grand-a-month apartment.'

'Actually, more like thirty-five hundred,' the Records guy corrected.

'Ouch,' I said.

'The rent is not the most unsettling thing about that building,

Cal,' the Shrink said. 'There was something else Records didn't notice until you prompted them to look.'

The guy glanced sheepishly down at his papers. 'It's not anything we usually flag for investigation. But it is . . . odd.' He shuffled papers and unrolled a large set of blueprints across his knees. 'The building plans show an oversize foundation, much deeper and more elaborate than one would expect.'

'A foundation?' I said. 'You mean, the part that's *underground*?'

He nodded. 'They didn't have the air rights to put up a tall building, because it would block views of the river. So they decided to make some extra space below. There are several sub-basements descending into the granite bedrock, spreading out wider than the building overhead. Room for a two-floor health club, supposedly.'

'Health club in the basement.' I shrugged. 'Not surprising in a ritzy place like that.'

The Shrink drew herself up. 'Unfortunately, this health club is not in a particularly healthy location. They excavated too close to the PATH tunnel, an area where the island is very . . . porous. That tunnel was only finished in 1908. Not everything stirred up by the intrusion has settled yet.'

'Not settled yet?' I said. 'After a hundred years?'

The Shrink steepled her fingers. 'The big things down there awaken slowly, Kid. And they settle slowly, too.'

I swallowed. Every old city in the world has a Night Watch of some kind, and they all get nervous when the citizens start digging. The asphalt is there for a very good reason – to put something solid between you and the things that live underneath.

'It's possible that this excavation has opened the lower environs,' the Shrink said, 'allowing something old to bubble up.'

'You think they uncovered a reservoir?'

Neither of them said anything.

Remember what I said about rats carrying the disease? How broods store the parasite in their blood when their peeps die? Those broods can last a long time after the peeps are gone, spreading the disease down generations of rats. Old cities carry the parasite in their bones, the way chicken pox can live in your spinal column for decades, ready to pop out as horrible blisters in old age.

'The health club, huh?' I said, shaking my head. 'That's what people get for working out.'

'It may be more than a reservoir, Cal. There may be larger things than rats and peeps to worry about.' The Shrink paused. 'And then . . . there are the owners.'

'The owners?' I asked.

The man from Records glanced at the Shrink, and the Shrink looked at me.

'A first family,' she said.

'Oh, crap,' I answered. One thing about the carriers of the Night Watch: They have a special affection for the families after whom the oldest streets are named. Back in the 1600s, New Amsterdam was a small town, only a few thousand people, and everyone was someone's cousin or uncle or indentured servant. Certain loyalties go back a long way, and in blood.

'Who are they? Boerums? Stuys?'

The Shrink's eyes slitted as she spoke, one hand gesturing vaguely toward the half-forgotten world outside her town house. 'If I remember correctly, Joseph once lived on this very street. And Aaron built his first home on Golden Hill, where Gold Street and Fulton now meet. Medcef Ryder's farm was up north a ways – he grew wheat in a field off Verdant Lane, although that field is called Times Square these days. And they had more farmland in Brooklyn. They were good boys, the Ryders, and the Night Mayor has kept up with their descendants, I believe.'

I found my voice. 'Ryder, you said?'

'With a *y*,' the Records guy offered softly.

I swallowed. 'My progenitor's name is Morgan Ryder.'

'Then we have a problem,' said the Shrink.

The guy from Records, whose name was Chip, took me down to his cubicle. We were going over the history of the Hoboken PATH tunnel, which was a lot more exciting than you'd think.

'The first incident was in 1880, killed twenty workers,' Chip said. 'Then another in 1882 killed a few more than that. They were supposedly explosions, and the company had the body parts to prove it.'

'Handy,' I said.

'And leggy,' he chuckled. Out from under the soulless eyes of the Shrink's doll collection, Chip was a certified laugh riot. 'That brought the project to a halt for a couple of decades. Those incidents were in Jersey, but on this side of the river we never bought the cover story.'

'Why not?'

'There are ancient tunnels that travel through the bedrock, all around these parts. And around the PATH train, the tunnels are . . . newer.' His fingers drifted along the tunnel blueprints on his desk. 'Check it out, Cal: If you add up the weight of all the plants and animals that live under the ground, it's actually *more* than everything that lives above. About a billion organisms in every pinch of soil.'

'Yeah, none of which is big enough to *eat twenty people*.'

He lowered his voice. 'But that's what happens after you're buried, Kid. Things in the ground eat you.'

Great, now *Records* was calling me Kid. 'Okay, Chip,' I said. 'But worms don't eat people who are still alive.'

'But there's a food chain down there,' he said. *'Something* has to be at the top.'

'You guys don't have a clue, do you?'

Chip shook his head. 'We have clues. Those tunnels? They're a lot like the trails of an earthworm through the dirt.'

I frowned and dropped my eyes back to the blueprints for Lace's building. The fine-lined drawings – precisely scaled and covered in tiny symbols – showed only the shapes that human machines had carved from the soil. No hint at the environment surrounding our descent into the earth. 'So you think there are giant *worms* down there? I thought you guys in Records were a little more . . . factual.'

'Yeah, well, we read a lot of weird stuff.' He pointed his pen at the edge of the level labeled Health Club, Lower. 'This is what somebody should have noticed – and then filed a great big ST-57.' The pen tapped. 'The excavation goes too deep for comfort; it's only a few yards above part of the exhaust system for the PATH tunnel. Any variation from these plans, and they're connected.'

'Connected to what?'

'You ever seen those big exhaust towers by the river? The fans are about eighty feet across, sucking air all day. Bad.'

'Air is bad?'

'They're *pumping oxygen* down there!' Chip shook his head, tossed the pen disgustedly down onto the plans. 'That's like pouring fertilizer on your weeds. Lack of oxygen is the growth-limiting factor in a subterranean biome!'

'Ah, so things are growing. But those "explosions" in Jersey were a hundred and twenty years ago, after all. We're just talking *rats* these days, right?'

'Probably,' Chip said.

'Probably. Wonderful.' Standing there in the gloom, I realized that Chip and I were underground right now, tons of bricks and mortar piled up over our heads. The squeaking ceiling fan labored to bring oxygen down to us; without the flickering fluorescents it would be too dark even for my peep eyes to see. Down here was hostile territory – a place for corpses and worms, and the bigger things that ate the worms, and the *bigger* things that ate them . . .

'But our guys at the PATH say that there are a few places under the exhaust towers that their workers have abandoned,' Chip added. 'They aren't officially condemned, but nobody goes down there anymore.'

'Great. And how close is that to Morgan's building?'

'Not far. A couple hundred yards?'

My nose wrinkled, as if a bad smell had wafted into the cubicle. Why couldn't I have just lost my virginity the normal way? No vampiric infections, no subterranean menaces. 'Okay, so what's the best way for me to get down there?'

'Through the front door.' Chip ran a finger across the building plans, pointing out a set of symbols. 'They've got major security all over the joint; cameras everywhere, especially in the lower levels.'

'Crap.'

'I thought you had an inside line. That girl you mentioned in your 1158-S, the one who lives there now? Tell her you want to check out the basement.'

'She had an attitude problem. I'd rather break in. I'm good with locks.'

Chip raised an eyebrow.

'Or a Sanitation badge,' I flailed. 'Maybe a Health Inspector of Health Clubs?'

'What happened between you and her?'

'Nothing!'

'You can tell me, Kid.'

I groaned, but Chip fixed me with his big brown eyes. 'Look, it's just that she . . . We had this . . .' My voice fell. 'There was a Superhuman Revelation Incident, sort of.'

'There was?' Chip frowned. 'Have you filed an SRI-27/45?'

'No, I *haven't* filed an SRI-27/45. It's not like she saw me climbing up a wall or anything. All I did was sort of . . . lift her up, and only for a second.'

'And?'

'And swing her from one balcony to another. Otherwise we were going to get caught breaking and entering. *Just* entering, I mean – nothing was broken.' I decided not to get into the Grand Theft Blender issue. 'Look, Chip, all I need are some traps and a Pest Control badge. Catch a few rats, let the Doctor test their blood, see if we've got a running reservoir. First things first. No big deal.'

Chip nodded slowly, then looked down and continued detailing the lower depths of the Hoboken PATH tunnel, letting his expression say it all.

'Pretty late, isn't it?'

'Tell me about it,' I grunted at the doorman, willing him not to look too closely at my face. He was the same guy from that afternoon, but now I was dressed in a standard city-issue hazmat suit, a wool cap pulled down to my eyebrows. My oven-fresh Sanitation badge was flopped open in his face. In more ways than one, I was presenting a different picture than I had nine hours before.

'Yeah, I'm on till midnight myself,' he said, his eyes dropping from my face as he pulled out a desk drawer. He hadn't recognized me. The clothes *do* make the man, as far as most people are concerned.

He yanked out a clattering ring of keys, and we headed to the elevator.

'Did you guys get a complaint from one of our tenants? I never heard nothing about rats here.'

'No, just some problems nearby. Population explosion by the river.'

'Yeah, the river. Always smells damp down in the basement. Kind of fishy.' The elevator door opened. He leaned one shoulder against it, blocking its attempts to close while he counted through the keys until he found one marked with a green plastic ring. He slipped it into a keyhole marked B2 at the bottom of the controls and gave it a half turn.

'You ever heard of a tenant getting bitten here?' I asked. 'Maybe a year ago or so?'

He looked up at me. 'Didn't work here then. No one did. They hired all new staff early this year. The old guys were running some kind of payroll scam, I hear.'

'Ah. I see.' I made a mental note to run all those doormen's and janitors' names through Records.

He pressed the B2 button, keeping one hand on the door's rubber bumpers. 'Not that hardly that many people use it down there. Only a few diehards. Like I said, smells funny. By the way, when you come back up, don't forget to mention you're leaving to whoever's on the door. It's supposed to be locked up down there this time of night.'

'No problem.' I lifted my duffel bag in weary half salute.

He smiled and let the door close. The elevator took me down.

It did smell funny.

There were about fifty kinds of mold growing down there, and

I could smell the rot of wooden beams behind the walls, dried human sweat on the padded weight benches, assorted shoes decaying behind the slats of locker doors.

But behind the health club smells, something else was brewing. I couldn't quite figure out what. Smells are not as easy to place as sights and sounds. They're like suppressed memories: You sometimes have to let them bubble up on their own.

I let the elevator close its door and glide away, not switching on any lights. I didn't want the doorman watching me on the security cameras. I was hoping he would forget I was down here and go off his shift without mentioning me to the next guy.

Once my eyes adjusted, the red glow of the thermostats and exercise machine controls were enough to see by. For a few minutes, though, I just stood there, listening for the sounds of tiny feet.

It didn't seem a likely spot for a rat invasion; there wasn't any source of food down here, not even a candy machine. In any case, street-level garbage eaters weren't the only issue here. I was looking for big alpha rats – and, if Chip was right, unnamed other things – bubbling up from below. Things that had never heard of M&M's.

All I could hear was the refrigerator in the juice machine, the hiss of steam heat, and a distant steady rumble. I knelt and pressed one palm flat against the floor, feeling the vibration spreading into my flesh along with the chill of the cement. The rumble was cycling slowly – maybe it was those eighty-foot fan blades that gave Chip nightmares.

But I didn't hear any rats, or any of Chip's monsters, for that matter. I moved among the dark shapes of machines, the red eyes of their controls winking at me. The smell of chlorine rose from a covered Jacuzzi. That other scent, the one I couldn't identify, seemed to grow stronger as I moved toward the back wall.

Then I felt a draft, the slightest hint of cold. I swept my eyes across the baseboard behind the radiator, searching for a rat-hole letting in the autumn chill of the earth. Rats don't need much space to crawl through; they can break down their own skeletons and squeeze through holes the size of quarters. (We peeps can supposedly do that too, but it hurts like hell, I've heard.)

There weren't any openings along the floor. The fittings around the steam pipes were tight. I didn't spot any doors to slip under, no loose tiles in the ceiling. No way for anything to bubble up from the depths.

But in the farthest corner of the gym, the paneled walls themselves radiated cold.

I gave the wall a thump.

It was hollow.

Hearing the empty sound, I realized something about the darkened health club – it didn't have any stairs down. The second level promised in the blueprints didn't exist. Or it was hidden.

My duffel bag clanked against the concrete floor. From a pocket, I pulled the plans that Chip had printed for me, checking my compass. According to the blueprints, the subbasement stairs were only a few yards away, on the other side of the wall.

The wood paneling didn't give at all when I pushed; there was something solid behind it. Of course, my duffel bag was full of drills, hacksaws, bolt cutters, and a crowbar, or I could have just put my fist through the wall. But I still had to come back in my Sanitation costume to reclaim any rats my traps caught, and the staff doesn't like it when you break their building.

I moved along the wall, pressing and thumping. The echoes were muffled, which meant that lots of crisscrossed beams supported the paneling. The stairs were solidly sealed off as well, with no easy way in. Had they just abandoned a whole sub-basement down there?

The wood paneling ended at a row of lockers – too heavy to move, even with my peep muscles. I tapped the floor with my feet, wondering what was hidden beneath. From the ceiling, the red eyes of security cameras glowed mockingly in the darkness.

Then I realized something: All of the cameras were pointed more or less at *me*. Were they tracking me?

I moved a few yards, back into the cold corner, but the cameras didn't follow. They all stayed pointed at the same target – the row of lockers. Whoever had set the security system up didn't care what happened in the rest of the health club, as long as they could watch that one spot.

I walked along the lockers, running my fingers against them, smelling the dirty socks and chlorinated swimsuits inside. The metal grew colder as I went.

In the center, one locker was icy to my touch, and through its ventilation slats that half-familiar scent – the one I couldn't quite identify – floated on a draft of chilled air. I looked up at the cameras; they were all pointed directly at me now.

The padlock was an off-the-shelf Master Lock, though with four tumblers instead of the usual three, more expensive than the others. I knelt, cradling it like a cell phone to my head. As the numbers spun left, then right, I heard the tiny steel teeth connecting, the tumblers aligning . . . until it sprang open, as loud as a gunshot in my ear.

Sliding the lock off the hasp, I opened the door.

There was nothing inside – nothing*ness*, in fact. No hanging clothes, no hooks or shelves, just a black void that consumed the dim light of the gym. A chill wind came from the darkness, bearing that same half-familiar smell, sharpened now.

I reached into the locker. My hand went back into the darkness and cold, disappearing into nothingness.

Let me get this straight about my night vision: When I'm at home, the only light I keep on is the red LED of my cell phone charger; I can read fine print by starlight; I have to tape over the glowing clock face of my DVD player, because otherwise it's too bright to sleep in my bedroom.

But I couldn't see *jack* inside this locker.

There is something called *cave darkness*, which is ten times darker than sitting in a closet with towels stuffed under the door, covering your eyes with your hands – basically darker than anything you've ever experienced except down in a cave. Your hands disappear in front of your face, you can't tell whether your eyes are open or not, random red lights seem to flicker in your peripheral vision as your brain freaks out from the total absence of light.

'Great,' I said.

Hoisting my duffel bag, I slipped through into the void.

The standard Night Watch flashlight has three settings. One is a low-light mode designed not to burn out peep night vision. The second setting is a normal flashlight, useful for normal people. The third is a ten-thousand-lumen eyeball-blaster intended to blow away peeps, scare away rat hordes, and generally indicate panic. Held a few inches from your skin, it will actually give you a suntan.

Switching on the tiny light, I found myself in a narrow hallway, squeezed between the foundation's cement wall and the back side of the maniacally reinforced wood paneling. The floor was covered with little globs of something gooey. I knelt and sniffed and realized what I'd been smelling all along – peanut butter, mixed with the chalky funk of rat poison. Someone had laid out about a hundred jars of weaponized extra-crunchy back here. The bottom of the false wall was smeared with it to prevent the wood paneling from being gnawed through.

I stepped carefully among the gooey smears, and the hallway led me back to the corner where the missing stairs should have been. An industrial-strength metal door stood there, reinforced with yards of chain and generous wads of steel wool stuffed into the crack beneath it.

Steel wool is one thing rats can't chew through. Someone was working conscientiously on the rat issue. Hopefully that meant Chip was crazy on the giant monster issue, and all there was down here was some peep's long-lost brood.

The chains wound back and forth between the door's push-bar handle and a steel ring cemented into the wall, secured with big, fat padlocks that took keys instead of combinations. To save time, I pulled bolt cutters from my bag and snipped the chains. As taut as rubber bands, they snapped loose and clattered to the floor.

Funny, I thought, *chains don't keep out rats*.

Ignoring that uncomfortable fact, I gave the door a good hard push; it scraped inward a few inches. Through the gap, the promised stairs led downward into smellier smells and colder air and darker darkness. Sounds filtered up: little feet scurrying, the snufflings of tiny noses, the nibblings of razor-sharp teeth. An all-night rat fiesta – but what were they *eating* down there?

Not chocolate, was my guess.

I pulled on thick rubber gloves.

The gap was just big enough to squeeze through. As I descended, I kept one thumb on the flashlight's eyeball-blaster switch, ready to blaze away if there was a peep down here. I couldn't hear anything bigger than a rat, but, as I've said, parasite-positives can hold their breath for a long time.

The rats must have heard me cutting the chains, but they didn't sound nervous. Did they get a lot of visitors?

At the bottom of the stairs, my night vision began to adjust to the profound darkness, and the basement eased into focus. At first I thought the floor was slanted, then I saw that a long swimming pool dominated the room, sloping away from me. The paired arcs of chrome ladders glowed on either side, and a diving board thrust out from the edge of the deep end.

The pool contained something much worse than water, though.

Along its bottom skittered a mass of rats, a boiling surface of pale fur, slithering tails, and tiny rippling muscles. They scrambled along the pool's edges, gathered in feeding frenzies around piles of something I couldn't see. All of them had the wormy look of deep-underground rats, slowly losing their gray camouflage – and ultimately even their eyesight – as they spent generation after generation out of the sun.

A fair number of ratty skeletons were lined up on one side of the basement, bare ribs as thin as toothpicks – as if someone had put out glue traps in a neat row.

There were a lot of smells (as you might imagine) but one stood out among the others, raising my hackles. It was the scent-mark of a predator. In Hunting 101, we had been taught to call it by its active molecule: 4-mercapto-4methylpentan-2-1. But most folks just call it 'cat pee.'

What the hell was a *cat* doing down here? Sure, there are feral felines in New York. But they live on the surface, in abandoned buildings and vacant lots, within paw's reach of humanity. They stay out of the Underworld, and rats stay away from them. When it comes to rats, cats are on *our* side.

If one had stumbled down here, it would be lean pickings by now.

I forced that last image from my mind and reached into the duffel bag for an infrared camera. Its little screen winked to life, turning the horde of rats into a blobby green snowstorm. I set the camera on the pool's edge, pointing down into the maelstrom. Dr. Rat and her Research and Development pals could watch this stuff for hours.

Then I realized something: I didn't smell chlorine.

With my nose, even a swimming pool that's been drained for years retains that tangy chemical scent. The pool had never been filled, which meant that the rat invasion had happened *before* they'd finished construction down here. I looked at the pool: The black line at water height had been half started, then abandoned.

I remembered Dr. Rat's standard checklist: My first job was to figure out if this brood had access to the surface. I began a slow walk around the edge of the basement, flashlight still set low, moving carefully, looking for any holes in the walls.

The rats hardly noticed me. If this was the brood that had infected Morgan, they would find my scent comforting – our parasites were closely related, after all. On the other hand, true Underworld rats might behave this way with anyone. Never having seen a human being before, their little pink eyes wouldn't know what to make of me.

The walls looked solid, not even hairline cracks in the cement. Of course, this building was just over a year old – the foundation should have been rat-proof for another decade or so.

I peered over the edge. In the deep end, right where the drain should have been, was a boiling mass of rats. Pale bodies struggled against one another, some disappearing into the mass, others thrashing their way up and out. The brood did have a way out of this basement, I realized, but it didn't go up to the surface . . .

It went down.

I swallowed. The Night Watch would want to know exactly how big this opening was. Merely rat-size? Or were bigger things afoot?

I walked slowly back around to the shallow end of the pool and picked up the infrared camera. With it in one hand and the flashlight in the other, I put one tentative foot into the pool.

The sole of my boot didn't make a sound. A layer of something soft was strewn across against the bottom of the pool, fluttering beneath the claws of darting rats. It was too dark to see what.

Something ran across my boot, and I shuddered.

'Okay, guys, let's observe some personal space here,' I said, then took another step.

Something answered my words, something that wasn't a rat. A long, high-pitched moan echoed through the room, like the sound of a mewling infant . . .

At the very end of the diving board, two reflective eyes opened, and another annoyed growl rumbled out.

A *cat* was looking at me, its sleepy eyes floating against invisibly black fur. A host of big, gnarly alpha rats sat around it on the diving board, like kingly attendants to an emperor, when they should have been running for their lives.

The eyes blinked once, strangely red in the flashlight's glow. The cat looked like a normal cat of normal-cat size, but this was *not* a normal place for any cat to be.

But cats didn't carry the parasite. If they did, we'd *all* be peeps by now. They live with us, after all.

My eyes fell from the feline's unblinking gaze, and I saw what the rats were eating: pigeons. Their feathers were the soft layer lining the pool. The cat was hunting for its brood, just like a peep would. And I heard a sound below the ratty squeaks – the cat purring softly, as if trying to calm me down.

It was family to me.

Suddenly, the floor began trembling, a vibration that traveled up through my cowboy boots and into my muscle-clenched stomach. My vision began to shudder, as if an electric toothbrush had been jammed into my brain. A new smell rose up from the swimming pool drain, something I couldn't recognize – ancient and foul, it made me think of rotten corpses. It made me want to run screaming.

And through it all, the cat's low purr of satisfaction filled the room.

I squeezed my eyes shut and switched the flashlight to full power.

I could only hear (and feel) what happened next: a thousand rats panicking, pouring out of the pool to race for the dark corners of the room, flowing past my legs in a furry torrent. Hundreds more scrambled to escape down the drain and into the darkness below, their claws scraping the broken concrete as they fought to flee the horrifying light. Bloated rat king bodies flopped from the diving board and landed on the struggling mass, squealing like squeaky toys dropped from a height.

I fumbled a pair of sunglasses out of a pocket, got them on, and opened one eye a slit: The cat was unperturbed, still curled at the end of the diving board, eyes shut against the light, looking like an ordinary cat lying happily in the sun. It yawned.

The trembling of the floor had begun to fade, and the traffic jam of escaping rats was starting to break up. The drain hole looked to be more than *a yard* across; the deep end of the pool had cracked open, crumbling into some larger cavity below. The rats were still roiling, disappearing into it like crap down a flushing toilet.

Squinting up at the cat again, I saw that it had risen to its feet.

It was stretching lazily, yawning, its tongue curling pink and obscene.

'You just stay there, kitty,' I called above the din, and took another step toward the drain. How deep *was* the hole? Cat-size? Peep-size? *Monster*-size?

I only needed one glimpse and I was out of there.

Between my blazing flashlight and the squeaks and scrambling feet echoing off the sides of the pool, I was almost blind and practically deafened. But the weird smell of death was fading, and just as the last rats were finally clearing out, I caught the slightest whiff of something new in the air. Something close . . .

A sharp hiss sounded behind me, someone sucking in air. As I spun around, the flashlight slipped from my sweaty fingers . . .

It cracked on the swimming pool floor, and everything went very dark.

I was completely blind, but before the flashlight had died I'd glimpsed a human form at the edge of the pool. Following the bright image burned into my retinas, I ran the few steps up the slope and leaped from the pool, raising the camera like a club.

As I swung, I caught her smell again, freezing just in time.

Jasmine shampoo, mixed with human fear and peanut butter . . . and I knew who it was.

'Cal?' Lace said.

Howler monkeys live in the jungles of Central America. They have a special resonating bone that amplifies their cries — hence the name 'howler monkey.' Even though they're only two feet tall, you can hear a howler monkey scream from three miles away.

Especially if they've got screwworms.

Meet the screwfly, which lives in the same jungles as howler monkeys. Screwflies look pretty much like normal houseflies, except bigger. They aren't parasites themselves, but their babies are.

When it comes time to have baby flies, screwflies look for a wounded mammal to lay their eggs in. They're not picky about what kind of mammal, and they don't need a very large wound. Even a scratch the size of a flea bite is plenty big.

When the eggs hatch, the larvae — also known by such charming names as 'maggots' or 'screwworms' — are hungry. As they grow, they begin to devour the flesh around them.

Most maggots are very fussy and only eat dead flesh, so they're not a problem for their host. They can actually help to clean the wounds that they hatch into. In a pinch, doctors still use maggots to sterilize the wounds of soldiers.

But screwworms – screwfly maggots – are another matter. They are born ravenous, and they consume *everything* they can get their teeth into. As they devour the animal's healthy flesh, the wound gets bigger, luring more screwflies to come and lay their eggs. Those eggs hatch, and the wound gets even bigger . . .

Eww. Yuck. Repeat.

At the end of this cycle is a painful death for many a howler monkey.

But screwflies also bring a message of peace.

Like all primates, howler monkeys want mates, food, and territory – all the stuff that makes being a howler monkey fun. So they compete with one another for these resources – in other words, they get into fights.

But no matter how angry they get, howler monkeys *never* use their teeth or claws. Even if one of the monkeys is much bigger, all it ever does is slap the other one around and (of course) howl a lot.

You see, it's just not worth it to get into a real fight. Because even if the smaller monkey gets its monkey ass totally kicked, all it has to do is get in *one tiny scratch*, and the fight becomes a lose-lose proposition. One little scratch, after all, is all a screwfly needs to lay its eggs inside you.

Many scientists believe that the howler monkeys developed their awesome howling ability *because* of screwworms. Any monkeys who resolved their conflicts by scratching and biting (and getting bitten and scratched in return) were eaten from within by screw-worms. Game over for all the scratchy and bitey howler monkey genes.

Eventually, all that was left in the jungle were non-scratchy monkeys. Survival of the fittest, which in this case were the non-scratchiest.

But there were still mates and bananas to be fought over, so the non-scratchy monkeys evolved a non-scratchy way to compete: howling. Survival of the loudest. And that's how we got howler monkeys.

See? Parasites aren't all bad. They take primates who otherwise might be killing one another and leave them merely yelling.

'What are you *doing* down here?' I yelled.

'What are *you* doing down here?' Lace yelled back, grabbing two blind fistfuls of my hazmat suit in the darkness. 'Where the hell are we anyway? Were those *rats*?'

'Yes, those were rats!'

She started hopping. 'Crap! I thought so. Why did it go all dark?'

'I kind of dropped my flashlight.'

'Dude! Let's get *out* of here!'

We did. I could see only leftover streaks etched into my retinas by the flashlight, but Lace's eyes weren't as sensitive as mine. She pulled me stumbling back up the stairs, and as we squished through the poisoned-peanut-butter hallway, my vision began to return – light was pouring in from the health club through the open locker door.

Lace squeezed out, and I followed, slamming the locker shut behind me. Fluorescents buzzed overhead, and the basement looked shockingly normal.

'What *was* that down there?' Lace cried.

'Wait a second.' I pulled her away from the security cameras and over to a row of weight benches. Sitting down, I tried to blink away the spots on my vision. Lace stayed standing, eyes wide, nervously shifting from one foot to the other.

'What the hell?' was all she could say.

I stared at her, half blind and still astonished by her sudden appearance. Then I remembered the doorman setting the elevator's controls, leaving them unlocked so that I could return to the ground floor.

I hadn't paid close enough attention. It was all my fault. I'd blown the first rule of every Night Watch investigation: Secure the site. But I was *positive* I'd closed the locker door behind me . . .

'How did you get down here?' I sputtered. 'I thought the health club was closed at night!'

'Dude, you think I came down here to *exercise*?' She was still shifting from foot to foot. 'I was headed out and Manny said, "You know that guy you came in with this afternoon? He's here spraying for rats." And I'm like, "*What?*" And he's like, "Yeah, did you know he was an exterminator? He's down in the health club right now, looking to kill some rats!"' Lace spread her open palms wide. 'But *you* told me you were looking for Morgan. So what the hell?'

I didn't answer, just sighed.

'And when I came down here,' she continued in a breathless rush, 'the lights weren't even on. I thought Manny had lost his mind or something. But when the elevator closed behind me, it was totally dark.' She pointed. 'Except suddenly that locker was doing this . . . *glowing* thing.'

I groaned. On its killer setting, my Night Watch flashlight had been visible from up here.

Still hyperventilating, Lace continued. 'And there was a hidden hallway, and the floor was covered with weird goo, and there were stairs at the end, with this insane squeaky pandemonium coming up from below. I called your name, but all I heard was rats!'

'And that made you *want* to go down the stairs?' I asked.

'No!' Lace cried. 'But by then I figured you *were* down here, somewhere, maybe in trouble.'

My eyes widened. 'You came down to help me?'

'Dude, things didn't look so good down there.'

I couldn't argue with that. No one else could have messed this up quite as totally as I had. Things were bad enough, with a great big rat reservoir bubbling up from the Underworld, along with a weird peeplike cat and something big enough to make the earth shudder. And right smack in the middle of it all, I'd managed to insert Lace – a Major Revelation Incident.

I was screwed. But I found myself staring at Lace with admiration.

'All those rats . . .' A note of exhaustion crept into her voice as hysteria subsided. 'Do you think they'll follow us?'

'No.' I pointed at her shoe. 'That stuff will stop them.'

'What the . . .?' She stood on one foot, staring at the bottom of her other shoe. 'What the hell is this crap anyway?'

'Watch out! It's poisonous!'

She sniffed the air. 'It smells like peanut butter.'

'It's *poisonous* peanut butter!'

She let out a sigh. 'Whatever – I wasn't going to eat it. Note to Cal: I do not eat stuff off my shoe.'

'Right. But it's dangerous!'

'Yeah, no kidding. This whole place should be condemned. There were, like, *thousands* of rats in that pool.

I swallowed, nodding slowly. 'Yeah. At least.'

'So what's the deal? What are you doing here, Cal? You're not an exterminator. Don't tell me that you investigate STDs *and* spray for rats.'

'Um, not usually.'

'So does this building have *the plague* or something?'

Rats and plague did go together. Would Lace believe that one? My mind began to race.

'No, dude,' Lace said firmly, rising to her feet and putting a finger in my face. 'Don't sit there making shit up. Tell me the truth.'

'Uh . . . I can't.'

'You're trying to *hide* this? That's nuts!'

I stood and put my hands on her shoulders. 'Listen, I can't say anything. Except that it's very important that you don't tell anyone about what's down there.'

'Why the hell would I keep quiet? There's a swimming pool full of rats in my basement!'

'You just have to trust me.'

'Trust you? Screw that!' She set her jaw, and her voice rose. 'There's a disease that makes people write on the walls in blood spreading through my building, and I'm supposed to keep it a secret?'

'Um, yes?'

'Well, listen to this, then, Cal. You think this should be a secret? Wait till I tell Manny what I saw down there, and Max and Freddie and everyone else in the building, and the *New York Times* and the *Post* and *Daily News*, for that matter. It won't be very secret then, will it?'

I tried to pull off a shrug. 'No. Then it'll just be a building in New York City with rats in the basement.'

'Not with that thing on my wall.'

I swallowed and had to admit she had something there. With Morgan's gristle graffiti added into the mix, the NYPD would have a reason to reopen apartment 701's missing persons case, which might lead them in all sorts of uncomfortable directions. The Night Watch was usually pretty good at making investigations go away, but this one would be tricky.

Which meant I was supposed to call the Shrink right now and tell her what had happened. But the problem with that was, I already knew what she'd tell me to do. Lace would have to disappear forever. All because she'd tried to help me.

I stood there in silence, paralyzed.

'I just want the truth,' Lace said softly. She sat down heavily on a weight bench, as if her nervous energy had run out.

'It's really complicated, Lace.'

'Yeah, well, it's pretty simple for me – I *live* here, Cal. Something really hideous is going on under our feet, and something insane happened right in my living room. It's starting to *freak me out.*'

On those last words, her voice broke.

She could smell it now. With all she'd seen, Lace could *feel* the capital-*N* Nature bubbling up from below – not the fuzzy Nature at the petting zoo, or even the deadly but noble kind on the Nature Channel. This was the appalling, nasty, real-world version, snails' eyes getting eaten by trematodes; hookworms living inside a billion human beings, sucking at their guts; parasites controlling your mind and body and turning you into their personal breeding ground.

I sat down next to her. 'Listen, I understand you're scared. But knowing the truth won't make it any better. The truth sucks.'

'Maybe. But it's still the truth. All you've done is lie since you met me, Cal.'

I blinked. She didn't. 'Yeah,' I said. 'But – '

'But what?'

At that moment, I knew what I really wanted. After six months of the natural world getting steadily more horrible, of my own body turning against me, I was just as scared as Lace. I needed someone to share that fear with, someone to cling to.

And I wanted it to be her.

'Maybe I can explain some of it.' I breathed out slowly, a shudder going through me. 'But you'd have to promise not to tell anyone else. This isn't some journalism class project, okay? This is deadly serious. It has to stay secret.'

Lace thought for a few seconds. 'Okay.' She raised a finger in warning. 'As long as you don't lie to me. Ever.'

I swallowed. She'd agreed way too fast. How could I believe her? She was studying to be a *reporter*, after all. Of course, my only other choice was the phone call that would make her disappear.

I stared into her face, trying to divine the truth of her promise, which probably wasn't the best idea. Her brown eyes were still wide with shock, her breathing still hard. My whole awareness focused itself upon her, a tangle of hyped-up senses drinking her in.

My guess is the parasite inside me made the choice. Partly anyway.

'Okay. Deal.' I put out my hand. As Lace shook it, a strange thing happened: Instead of shame, I felt relief. After keeping this secret from the whole world for half a year, I was finally telling someone. It was like kicking my boots off at the end of a really long day.

Lace didn't let go of my hand, her grip strengthening as she said, 'But you can't lie to me.'

'I won't.' My mind was clearing, beginning to work logically for the first time since the earth had started to tremble, and I realized what I had to do next. 'But before I tell you, I have to sort out a couple of things.'

Lace narrowed her eyes. 'Like what?'

'I need to secure the basement: Chain up that big door behind the wall and lock that locker.' I could leave my duffel bag downstairs, I realized. The rats wouldn't steal it, and I'd need the equipment right where it was the next time I went down. But there was one last thing I had to get before we left. 'Um, do you have a flashlight? Or a lighter on you?'

'Yeah, I've got a lighter. But Cal, tell me you're not going down those stairs again.'

'Just for a second.'

'What the hell *for*?'

I looked into her brown eyes, wide with rekindled fear, but if Lace wanted to know the truth, it was time she found out how nasty it could be.

'Well, since we're already down here and everything, I really should catch a rat.'

'Okay, I'm tracking a disease. That part of my story was true.'

'No kidding. I mean, rats? Madness? Bodily fluids? What else could it be?'

'Oh, right. Nothing, I guess.'

We were up in Lace's apartment. She was drinking chamomile tea and staring out at the river; I was cleaning poisonous peanut butter out of my boot treads, hoping the task would distract me from the fact that Lace was wearing a bathrobe. A rat called Possible New Strain was sitting under a spaghetti strainer held down with a pile of journalism textbooks, saying rude things in rat-speak.

I'd caught PNS at the top of the stairs, snatching him up in a rubber-gloved hand as he sniffed one of Lace's peanutty foot-prints.

Lace cleared her throat. 'So, is this a terrorist attack or some-thing? Or a genetic engineering thing that went wrong?'

'No. It's just a disease. The regular kind, but secret.'

'Okay.' She didn't sound convinced. 'So how do I avoid get-ting it?'

'Well, you can be exposed through unprotected sex, or if someone bites you and draws blood.'

'*Bites* you?'

'Yeah. It's like rabies. It makes its hosts want to bite other animals.'

'As in "So pretty I had to eat him"?'

'Exactly. Cannibalism is also a symptom.'

'That's a *symptom*?' She shuddered and took a sip. 'So what's with all the rats?'

'At Health and Mental they call rats "germ elevators," because they bring germs that are down in the sewers up to where people live, like this high-rise. A rat bite is probably how Morgan, or someone else up here, got infected in the first place.'

I saw another shudder pass through the shoulders of her bathrobe. Lace had taken a shower while I'd called Manny and told him to lock up the health club. Her face looked pink from a hard scrubbing, and her wet hair was still giving off curls of steam. I turned my attention back to my boots.

At the mention of rat bites, she lifted her feet up from the floor and tucked them under her on the chair. 'So, sex and rats. Anything else I should worry about?'

'Well, we think there used to be a strain that infected wolves, based on certain historical . . . evidence.' I decided not to mention the bigger things that Chip was worried about, or whatever had made the basement tremble, and I cleared my throat. 'But as far as we know, wolves are too small a population to support the parasite these days. So, you're in luck there.'

'Oh, good. Because I was really worried about wolves.' She turned to me. 'So, it's a parasite? Like a tick or something?'

'Yeah. It's not like a flu or the common cold. It's an animal.'

'What the hell *kind* of animal?'

'Sort of like a tapeworm. It starts off as a tiny spore, but it grows big, taking over your whole body. It changes your muscles, your senses, and most of all, your brain. You become a crazed killer, an animal.'

'Wow, that is really freaky and disgusting, Cal,' she said, cinching her bathrobe tighter.

Tell me about it, I thought, but didn't say anything. I might have promised not to lie to her, but my personal medical history was not her business.

'So,' Lace said, 'does this disease have a name?'

I swallowed, thinking about the various things it had been called over the centuries – vampirism, lycanthropy, zombification, demonic possession. But none of those old words was going to make this any easier for Lace to deal with.

'Technically, the parasite is known as *Echinococcus cannibillus*. But seeing as how that takes too long to say, we usually just call it "the parasite." People with the disease are "parasite-positives," but we mostly say "peeps," for short.'

'Peeps. Cute.' She looked at me, frowning. 'So who's this *we* you're talking about anyway? You're not really with the city, are you? You're some sort of Homeland Security guy or something.'

'No, I do work for the city, like I said. The federal government doesn't know about this.'

'What? You mean there's some insane disease spreading and the government doesn't even know about it? That's crazy!'

I sighed, beginning to wonder if this had been a really bad idea. Lace didn't even understand the basics yet – all I'd managed to do was freak her out. The Shrink employed a whole department of psych specialists to break the news to new carriers like me; they had a library full of musty but impressive books and a spanking new lab full of blinking lights and creepy specimens. All I was doing was haphazardly answering questions, strictly amateur hour.

I pulled a chair over and sat down in front of her. 'I'm not explaining this right, Lace. This isn't an acute situation. It's chronic.'

'Meaning what?'

'That this disease is ancient. It's been part of human biology and culture for a long time. It almost destroyed Europe in the fourteenth century.'

'Hang on. You said this wasn't the plague.'

'It isn't, but bubonic plague was a side effect. In the 1300s, the parasite began to spread from humans to rats, which had just arrived from Asia. But it didn't reach optimum virulence with rodents for a few decades, so it mostly just killed them. As the rats died, the fleas that carried plague jumped over to human hosts.'

'Okay. Excuse me, but *what*?'

'Oh, right. Sorry, got ahead of myself,' I said, knocking my head with my fists. The last six months had been one big crash course in parasitology for me; I'd almost forgotten that most people didn't spend days thinking about final hosts, immune responses, or optimum virulence.

I took a deep breath. 'Okay, let me start over. The parasite goes way back, to before civilization even. The people I work for, the Night Watch, also go way back. We existed before the United States did. It's our job to protect the city from the disease.'

'By doing what? Sticking rats in spaghetti strainers?'

Release me! squeaked PNS.

'No. By finding people with the parasite and treating them. And by destroying their broods – um, I mean, killing any rats who carry the disease.'

She shook her head. 'It doesn't make sense, Cal. Why keep it a secret? Aren't you Health Department guys supposed to *educate* people about diseases? Not lie to them?'

I chewed my lip. 'There's no point in making it public, Lace. The disease is very rare; there's only a serious outbreak every few decades. Nobody *tries* to get bitten by a rat, after all.'

'Hmm. I guess not. But still, this secrecy thing seems like a bad idea.'

'Well, the Night Watch up in Boston once tried what you're talking about – a program of education to keep the citizens on the lookout for possible symptoms. They wound up with nonstop accusations of witchcraft, a handful of seventeen-year-olds claiming they'd had sex with the devil, and a lot of innocent bystanders getting barbecued. It took about a hundred years for things to settle down again.'

Lace raised an eyebrow. 'Yeah, we did that play in high school. But wasn't that a long time ago? Before science and stuff?'

I looked her in the eye. 'Most people don't know jack about science. They don't believe in evolution because it makes them *uncomfortable*. Or they think AIDS is a curse sent down from God. How do you think those people would deal with the parasite?'

'Yeah, well, people are stupid. But you wouldn't keep AIDS a secret, would you?'

'No, but the parasite is different. It's special.'

'How?'

I paused. This was the tricky part. In my own debriefing, the Night Watch psychs had presented all the science stuff for hours before talking about the legends, and it had been a solid week before they'd uttered the V-word.

'Well, some fears go farther back than science, deeper than rational thought. You can find peep legends in almost every culture on the globe; certain of the parasite's symptoms lend themselves to scary stories. If we ever get a major outbreak of this, there will be hell to pay.'

'Certain symptoms? Like what?'

'Think about it, Lace. Peeps are light-fearing, disease-carrying cannibals who revel in blood.'

As the words left my mouth, I realized I'd said too much too quickly.

She snorted. 'Cal, are we talking about *vampires*?'

As I struggled to find the right words, her amused expression faded.

'Cal, you are *not* talking about vampires.' She leaned closer. 'Tell me. You're not supposed to lie to me!'

I sighed. 'Yeah, peeps are vampires. Or zombies in Haiti, or *tengu* in Japan, or *nian* in China. But like I said, we prefer the term *parasite-positive*.'

'Oh. Vampires,' Lace said softly, looking away. She shook her head, and I thought for a moment that the slender thread of her trust had broken. But then I realized that her gaze was directed at the wall where the words written in blood many months before showed through.

Lace's shoulders slumped in defeat, and she drew the robe tightly around her. 'I still don't see why you have to lie about it.'

I sighed again. 'Okay, imagine if people heard that vampires were real. What would they do?'

'I don't know. Freak out?'

'Some would. And some wouldn't believe it, and some would go see for themselves,' I said. 'We figure at least a thousand amateurs would head down into the bowels of New York to look for adventure and mystery, and they would become human germ elevators. Your building is just one acute case. There are dozens of rat reservoirs full of the parasite down there, enough to infect everyone who takes the time to look for them.'

I stood up and started to move around the room, recalling all the motivational classes in Peep Hunting 101.

'The disease sits under us like a burned-down campfire, Lace, and all it needs is for a few idiots to start stirring the embers. Peeps were deadly enough to terrorize people back in tiny, far-flung villages. Imagine massive outbreaks in a modern-day city, with millions of people piled on top of one another, close enough to sink their teeth into any passing stranger!'

Lace raised her hands in surrender. 'Dude, I already promised. I'm not going to tell anyone, unless you lie to me.'

I took a deep breath, then sat down. Maybe this was going better than I'd thought. 'I'll be handling this personally. All you have to do is sit tight.'

'Sit tight? Yeah, right! I bet Morgan was sitting tight when she got bitten. There's probably some little rat tunnel that leads all the way up here from the basement!' Her eyes swept the apartment, searching for tiny cracks in the walls, holes that could let the pestilence inside. Already the old fears were stirring inside her.

'Well, maybe a year ago there was,' I said soothingly. 'But now there's steel wool stuffed under that chained-up door, and a ton of peanut butter behind the false wall. The disease is probably contained for the moment.'

'Probably? So you're asking me to trust my life to steel wool and *peanut butter*?'

'*Poisoned* peanut butter.'

'Cal, I don't care if it's *nuclear* peanut butter.' She stood up and stomped into her bedroom. I heard the scrape of vinyl across the floor, the sound of zippers, and the clatter of clothes hangers.

I went to her doorway and saw that she was packing a bag.

'You're splitting?'

'No shit, Sherlock.'

'Oh,' I said. The sight of her packing had sent a twinge through me. I'd just shared my biggest secret in the world with

Lace, and she was leaving. 'Well, that's probably a good idea. It won't take long to clear things up downstairs, now that we know what's going on.' I cleared my throat. 'You should tell me where you're going, though, so I can keep in touch. Tell you when it's safe.'

'No problem there. I'm coming to your place.'

'Um . . . you're doing *what*?'

She stopped with a half-folded shirt in her hands and stared at me. 'Like I told you last night: I'm *not* going back to my sister's couch. Her boyfriend's there all the time now, and he's a total dick. And my parents moved out to Connecticut last year.'

'But you *can't* stay with me!'

'Why not?'

'Why would you *want* to? You don't even know me! What if I . . . turn out to be a psychopath or something?'

She returned to folding the shirt. 'You? Every time I think you're talking crazy, I remember what I saw down in the basement, or what's in there.' She nodded toward the living room, where the thing on the wall lurked. 'And nuts or not, you've got the inside line on a *huge* story. Did you really expect me to go off and read textbooks tonight or something? Why do you think I went into journalism anyway?'

My voice went up an octave. 'A *story*? What about keeping this a secret? You promised. Aren't you supposed to have journalistic ethics or something?'

'Sure.' She smiled. 'But if you break your promise and lie to me, I can break mine. So maybe I'll get lucky.'

I opened my mouth and a strangled noise came out. How was I supposed to explain that I *was* a psycho, that a raging parasite inside me desperately wanted to spread itself by any means possible? That just standing here in the same room with her was already torture?

'Besides,' she continued, 'you don't want me staying any-where else if you want to keep this a secret.'

'I don't?'

She finished folding the shirt. 'No, you don't. I talk in my sleep like crazy.'

By the time we left her apartment, it was the dead of night.

I stabbed the button for the health club repeatedly as we rode down. It didn't light up.

'Dude, don't do that.'

'Just making sure Manny locked the elevator.'

Lace shifted her suitcase from one hand to another. 'Yeah, but it'll be open again tomorrow, won't it?'

Not for long.' I could requisition a fake court order in the morning, enough to shut down the lower levels for a week or so. And as soon as possible, I was going down there with Dr. Rat and a full extermination team, carrying enough poison to exterminate this particular slice of the Underworld halfway to the earth's core.

The doormen had changed shifts, and the new guy looked up at us through thick glasses as we crossed the lobby, reflections of the little TVs on his console flickering in them. It gave me an idea.

'Talk to him for a second,' I whispered.

'About what?'

'Anything.'

'Like what's in your bag?'

I will be avenged! came PNS's muffled squeak. He was trapped between the spaghetti strainer and a dinner plate, duct-taped together and wrapped in a towel for silence, the whole thing shoved inside the Barneys shopping bag in my hand. I fig-ured his little rat lungs had another minute of oxygen left before I'd have to take the towel off.

'No. Just distract the guy. Quick.'

I steered Lace over to the doorman's desk, elbowing her until she launched into a rant about her water taking too long to heat up. As the doorman tried to placate her, I eased around to where I could see his security monitors.

The little screens showed the insides of elevators, hallways, the sidewalk outside the building's entrance, but nothing from the floor below. That was why no one had noticed our comings and goings – the cameras downstairs didn't work anymore.

Or did they? I remembered their red lights glowing in the dark. This building was owned by an old family, after all. They hadn't simply walled up the rat invasion; they'd left a secret passage through the locker and turned the cameras to face it. Someone was interested in what was going on downstairs. There could be videotape of us somewhere, waiting to be watched . . .

'Come on,' I said, pulling Lace away in mid-sentence.

The air outside was cold and damp. I paused to unwrap a corner of PNS's cage to let him breathe. He squeaked vengeance and rebellion, and Lace glanced at the bag and took a step back.

'You owe me a plate and a strainer, dude,' she said.

'You owe me an earth-shattering secret history.'

'I'd rather have a spaghetti strainer.'

'Fine, take mine when you leave.' I pointed east, up Leroy Street. 'We can catch the B on Fourth.'

'What? Take the subway? Go *underground* all the way to Brooklyn?' Lace shuddered. 'No way. We're cabbing it.'

'But that's like twenty bucks!'

'Split two ways, it's only ten. Duh. Come on, we can grab one on Christopher.'

She started off, and I walked a little behind her, realizing that my lifestyle was already changing, and my guest hadn't even set foot in my apartment yet. I'd considered giving Lace my keys and taking PNS downtown for immediate testing, but the thought of her tromping through my personal space alone had killed that idea – there were books lying around that detailed the few Night Watch secrets I hadn't already spilled. I'd promised to tell her the truth about the disease, not teach a college course on it.

As we walked up Leroy, I glanced at the loading docks of the big industrial buildings, wondering if any of the brood had found a way up to street level. A couple of rats sat atop a glistening pile of plastic garbage bags, but they had the furry look of surface-dwellers, not the pale greasiness of the brood in the basement.

Then I saw another shape, something lean and sleek moving in the shadows. It had the stride of a predator – a cat.

I couldn't spot any markings, only a dark silhouette and the shine of fur. The cat in the basement had also been solid black, but so were about a million other cats in the world.

Suddenly the animal froze, looking straight at me. Its eyes caught a streetlight, the reflective cells behind them igniting with a flash. My stride slowed to a halt.

'What is it?' Lace asked from a few yards ahead. At the sound of her voice, the cat blinked once, then disappeared into the darkness.

'Cal? What's wrong?'

'Um, I just remembered something I didn't tell you, another vector for the disease.'

'Just what I was hoping for. Another thing to worry about.'

'Well, it's not very likely, but you should be careful of any cats you see in this neighborhood.'

'Cats?' Her gaze followed mine into the shadows. 'They can get it too?'

'Maybe. Not sure yet.'

'All right.' She pulled her coat tighter again. 'You know,

Cal . . . the guys upstairs from Morgan said that she had a cat. A loud one.'

A shudder traveled through me, another memory from that fateful night. There *had* been a cat in Morgan's apartment, greeting us as we came in the door, watching as I dressed to leave the next morning. But had it been the one down in the basement?

Or the one watching us right now?

'That reminds me, Lace,' I said. 'Are you allergic to cats?'

'No.'

'Good. You'll like Cornelius.'

'You have a cat? Even though they spread *the disease*?'

'Not this one. Rats are afraid of him. Now let's get out of here.'

Cornelius was waiting for us, yowling from the moment my keys jingled in the lock, demanding food and attention. Once the door was open, he slipped out into the hall and did a quick figure eight through my legs, then darted back inside. We followed.

'Hey, baby,' I said, picking Cornelius up and cradling him.

Save me from the beast! squeaked PNS from his Barneys bag.

Cornelius's claws unsheathed as he climbed painfully up my coat and down my back, leaping to the floor to paw the bag and yowl.

'Um, Cal?' Lace said. 'I'm seeing a possible vector-thingy here.'

'Huh? Oh.' I whisked the bag away from Cornelius and across the room to the closet. Kicking aside a pile of dirty laundry, I deposited PNS's entire containment system on the floor inside and shut the closet door tight.

'So that's enough?' Lace asked. 'A closet?'

'Like I said, the parasite has to be spread by biting,' I explained. 'It's not like the flu; it doesn't travel through the air.'

'*Ynneeeeow!*' complained Cornelius, and sounds of ratty panic answered from inside the closet.

'But we're going to be listening to that all night?'

' No. Watch this.' I picked up a can of cat food and ransacked the silverware drawer for a can opener. 'Nummy-time!'

As the opener's teeth incised the can, a million years of predatory evolution was sandblasted from Cornelius's brain by the smell of Crunchy Tuna. He padded back over to the kitchen and sat on his haunches, staring raptly up at me.

'See? Cornelius has priorities,' I said, spooning the tuna into a bowl.

'"Nummy-time"?' Lace asked.

I swallowed, realizing that I wasn't used to filtering my cat-to-owner gibberish. Lace was the first guest ever to set foot in this apartment. Between peep hunting and parasitology textbooks, I hadn't had much time for socializing. Especially not with women.

The whole thing made me nervous, like I was being invaded. But I kept reminding myself that I wouldn't lose control like I almost had on the balcony. That had been a moment of fear and excitement in a *very* small space.

I was considering, however, putting another rubber band around my wrist.

'It's just a thing Cornelius and I do,' I said, placing his bowl on the floor.

Lace didn't respond. She was touring the apartment, all one room of it, stretching from the kitchen to the futon squished into one corner. It was the same size as most, but I was suddenly self-conscious. Scoring an apartment in a fancy building had probably dampened Lace's enthusiasm for slumming.

She was inspecting my CD tower.

'Ashlee Simpson?'

'Oh, wait, *no*. That was an old girlfriend's obsession.' Actually, more of an anathema, lately. When I'd tracked Marla – the unfortunate girl I'd made out with at a New Year's Eve party – to an abandoned 6-train station below Eighteenth Street, I'd brought a boom box full of Ashlee for self-defense. 'I'm more into Kill Fee.'

'Kill Fee? Aren't they, like, heavy metal?'

'Excuse me, *alternative* metal.'

She rolled her eyes. 'Whatever. But you realize that having a girlfriend who's into Ashlee Simpson isn't much better than liking it yourself.'

'*Ex*-girlfriend,' I said, moving around the room and putting away my books from the Night Watch library. 'And she wasn't really . . . It was a short-term thing.'

'But you stocked up on tunes she liked? Very smooth.'

I groaned. 'Listen, you can stay here, but you don't *have* to snoop.'

Lace glanced at a T-shirt on the floor. 'Yeah, well, at least I didn't bring my ultraviolet wand.'

'Hey, that was for work. I don't usually seek out bodily fluids.' I crossed to the futon and pulled it out straight. 'Speaking of which, I'll put clean sheets on this. You can have it.'

'Listen, I don't want to kick you out of your bed.' She looked at my run-down couch. 'I'll be okay there. It's not like I'm sleeping that close to the floor again *ever*, especially not with an infected rat about ten feet away.'

I glanced at the closet, but apparently PNS had no comment.

'No, I can take the couch.'

She shook her head. 'You're too tall. You'll wake up crumpled.'

She sat down, her houndstooth-check coat still wrapped around her. 'And I'm too tired to care; I'm even too tired to worry about your pigeon mites. So keep your bed, okay?'

'Um, sure.' At least the couch and the futon were a decent distance apart. Lace's jasmine smell was already filling the apartment, making my palms sweat.

She lay down, coat and all. 'Just wake me up before ten.'

'Aren't you going to brush your teeth?'

'I forgot to pack a toothbrush. Got an extra one?'

'No. Sorry.'

'Man, I forgot pretty much everything. That happens when things scare me.'

'Sorry.'

'Not your fault, dude.'

She closed her eyes, and I went into the bathroom, trying to be silent, every sound I made rattling my super-hearing. I hid my toothbrush, just in case Lace got desperate in the morning. It's not a good idea to share a toothbrush with a positive, seeing as your gums bleed a tiny amount every time the brush scrapes across them. Not a very likely vector, but it could happen.

When I emerged, Cornelius had finished eating and was eyeing the closet. I knelt to stroke him for a while, building up a good purr. He wasn't strong enough to open the closet door – but I didn't want him and PNS yelling at each other all night. As always, I saved the fur that shed from his coat in a plastic Ziploc bag.

I went to bed in my clothes. Lace hadn't stirred since closing her eyes. She looked pretty crumpled herself, huddled there, and I felt guilty for having the almost-real bed, and for having blown up her world.

It took a long time for silence to come. At first, I was too aware of Cornelius purring at my feet and the panicky short breaths of PNS as he shivered in his metal prison. I could smell cat food and Cornelius dander and even the scent of infected rat with its weird hint of family. I could also smell Lace's jasmine shampoo and the oils in her hair. From her breathing, I knew she wasn't asleep yet.

Finally, she stirred and pulled her coat off.

'Cal?' she said softly. 'Thanks for letting me stay here.'

'That's okay. Sorry for messing up your life.'

She made the slightest movement – something like a shrug.

'Maybe you saved it. I knew that damn apartment was too good to be true. But I didn't think it would try to kill me.'

'It won't.'

'No, thanks to you.' She sighed. 'I mean, I always figured one day I'd be a fearless reporter and everything, but *your* job? Going down into that basement knowing what might be down there? Looking for those peep thingies instead of running away? You must be really brave, dude. Or really stupid.'

I felt a flush of pride, even though she didn't know the pathetic truth. I hadn't really chosen my job; I'd been infected by it.

'Hey, you followed me down there,' I said. 'That was pretty brave.'

'Yeah, but that was before I knew about the cannibals, you know?'

'Mmm,' was all I said.

'Anyway, I don't think I would've slept at all tonight, if I'd been alone. Thanks.'

We fell silent, and the glow inside me from Lace's words stayed for a long time. Her smell was intense, all around me, and I seemed to be expanding as I breathed it in. I really did want to get up and kiss her good night, but I don't think it was the parasite that wanted her. Not entirely.

And somehow, that made it easier to lie there, unmoving.

After a while, Lace's breathing slowed. My ears grew accustomed to the stirrings of cat and mouse. The rattle of steam heating and the rush of passing traffic gradually faded away. Finally, all that was left was the unfamiliar sound of someone breathing close to me. It was something I hadn't heard since the Night Watch had informed me that any lovers in my future were guaranteed to go crazy.

It kept spinning around in my head that Lace trusted me, a guy she'd only met the day before. Maybe it was something *more* than trust. Before the parasite, I'd wondered every few minutes if one girl or another liked me, but it had been a long six months since I'd entertained the question seriously. The fact that the answer was worthless didn't stop my brain from turning it over and over again. It was pure torture, but in a funny way it was better than nothing. Better than being alone.

I listened for hours as Lace drifted deeper into sleep, rose up slowly, almost breaching the surface of consciousness to utter a few words of some imagined conversation, then descended again into dreamlessness.

Even those sounds faded as I reached my own half-waking slumber, trapped alone inside my head with the rumble of the beast, the hum of the never-ending war raging inside me, the keen of optimum virulence . . . until something strange and wonderful happened. I fell asleep.

Meet wolbachia, the parasite that wants to rule the world.

Wolbachia is tiny, smaller than a single cell, but its powers are enormous. It can change its hosts genetically, tamper with their unborn children, and create whole new species of carriers ... whatever it takes to fill the world with wolbachia.

No one knows how many creatures on earth are infected. At least twenty thousand insect species carry it, and so do a lot of worms and lice. That's *trillions* of carriers as far as we know. And every new place scientists look, they find more.

So, do *you* have to worry about wolbachia? We'll get back to that later.

Here's the strangest thing about wolbachia: No living creature has ever been infected with it. That's right, you don't *catch* wolbachia; you are *born* with it.

Huh?

You see, wolbachia is like one of those scrawny supervillains with a big brain. Wolbachia is a wimp: It can never leave its host's body, not even in a drop of blood. At some point in its evolutionary history, wolbachia gave up the whole jumping-between-creatures thing and adopted a strategy of staying in safe territory – it spends its whole life inside one host.

So how does it spread? Very cunningly. Rather than risk the outside world, wolbachia infects new carriers *before they're born.* That's right: Every infected creature gets the disease from its own mother.

But what happens when wolbachia is born into a male host? Males can't have children, so they're a dead end for the infection, right?

This is the evil genius part.

In many insect species, wolbachia scrambles its male hosts' genes with a secret code. Only other wolbachia (living inside a female) know how to decode the genes and make them work right. So when an infected insect tries to mate with a healthy one, the kids are born with horrible mutations, and they all die.

Over hundreds of generations of breeding only with one another, the infected insects slowly evolve into a new species. This species is one hundred percent infected with wolbachia and dependent on its own parasite to have children. (Insert evil laugh here.)

And this isn't wolbachia's only species-altering trick.

In some kinds of wasps, wolbachia has an even more power-crazed solution to the male problem. It simply changes all its host's unborn children into females. No boys ever get born. Then wolbachia gives these females a special power: They can have kids without mating. And of course, all of *those* kids are born female too. In other words, males become completely irrelevant. Because of wolbachia, some species of wasp have become entirely female. All the boys are dead.

In fact, some scientists believe that wolbachia's tricks

may be responsible for creating a big chunk of the insect and worm species on our planet. Some of those species, like parasitic wasps, go on to infect *other* creatures. (That's right, even *parasites* have parasites. Isn't nature wonderful?) In this way, wolbachia is slowly remaking the world in its own image, without ever leaving the safety of home.

So what about you? You're not an insect or a worm. Why worry about wolbachia?

Meet the filarial worm, a parasite that infects biting flies. It happens to be one of wolbachia's big success stories. *All* of these worms are infected. If you 'cure' a filarial worm with antibiotics, it can't have kids anymore. It's dependent on its own parasites – one of many species genetically engineered to be wolbachia carriers.

So what happens when a fly infected with filarial worms bites you? The worms crawl into your skin and lay eggs there. The eggs hatch, and the babies swim around in your bloodstream, some of them winding up in your eyeballs. Fortunately, the baby worms don't hurt your eyes. Unfortunately, the wolbachia they carry sets off a red alert in your immune system. Your own immune system attacks your eyeballs, and you go blind.

Why does wolbachia do this? What is its evolutionary strategy in blinding human beings?

No one knows. One thing is for sure, though:

Wolbachia wants to rule the world.

'Dude, get up.'

My brain came awake slowly, appalled at the interruption of its first real sleep in ages. Then I smelled Lace's jasmine hair, heard Cornelius's claws scratching the closet door, felt the rat's infection in the air . . . and all of yesterday's memories crashed into place.

There was a deadly reservoir bubbling to the surface near the Hudson River. The parasite had jumped to a new vector species. I had betrayed the Night Watch, risking civilization as I knew it. And the most important thing? For the first time in six months I had spent the night with a girl, if only in the most narrow, technical sense.

Suddenly, I was awake, and feeling pretty decent.

'Come on, dude,' Lace said, stabbing my shoulder with the toe of her shoe. 'I've got class, but I want to show you something.'

'Okay.' I pulled myself from the bed, eyes gummy, my slept-in clothes clinging to me. Lace had already showered and changed, and a wondrous smell filled the apartment, even more wondrous than hers. 'Is that coffee?'

She handed me a cup, smiling. 'You got it, Sherlock. Man, you sleep like a dead dog.'

'Huh. Guess I needed it.' I gulped the coffee, strong and welcome, while crossing to the fridge and pulling out a package of emergency franks. My parasite was screaming for meat, having missed out on its usual midnight snacks. I ripped the plastic open and shoved a cylinder of cold flesh in my mouth.

'Whoa,' Lace said. 'Breakfast of crackheads.'

'Hungry.' It came out muffled through the half-chewed meat.

'Whatever wakes you up.' Lace sat at the tiny table that separated the kitchen from my living room and pointed to a piece of paper on it.

Cornelius was screaming for food, winding around my feet. On autopilot, I opened a can.

'So I got this out of your coat pocket,' Lace said. 'And I noticed something weird.'

'Wait. You did what?' I looked over her shoulder – spread across the table were the building plans Chip had printed for me. 'You went through my pockets?'

'It was sticking out, dude. Besides, you and I have no secrets now.' She shuddered. '*Except* that food; close your mouth while chewing.'

I did, managing a necessary swallow.

'This is the basement of my building, right?' Lace continued. 'No, don't open your mouth. I know it is.' She stabbed at one corner of the printout. 'And this is the rat pool below the health club. Did you get these plans from city records?'

'Mmm-hmm.'

'Very interesting. Because they don't match reality. They don't show a swimming pool at all.'

I swallowed. 'You know how to read blueprints?'

'I know how to do research – and how to read.' Her fingers traced a grid of little squares that filled one corner of the page. Next to it, the words *Storage Units* were neatly written. 'See? No pool.'

I studied the plans silently for a moment – remembering what Chip had said the day before. The pool was a few yards deep, just deep enough to reach the Underworld. Because someone had added a swimming pool, Morgan had been infected. Then me and Sarah and Marla . . .

'A simple little change,' I said softly. 'How ironic.'

'Dude, screw irony. I just wanted you to see how clever we journalism students are.'

'You mean how snoopy you are.'

Lace just grinned, then ran her eyes across my crumpled clothes and up-sticking hair. 'Dude, you are bed-raggled.'

'I'm what?'

'Bed-raggled. You know, you're all raggled from being in bed.'

The gears in my head moved slowly. 'Um, isn't it *bedraggled*?'

'Yeah, no kidding. But my version makes more sense, you know?' Lace checked the time on her phone. 'Anyway, I've got to run.' She swept up her bag from the table and headed for the door. Opening it, she turned back to face me.

'Oh, I don't have any keys to this place.'

'Right. Well, I might get back pretty late tonight – I'm already behind schedule today.' I cleared my throat, pointing at the fruit crate by the door. 'There's an extra set in that coffee can.'

Lace stuck her fingers into the can, rummaging through laundry quarters until she pulled out a ring of keys.

'Okay. Thanks. And, um, see you tonight, I guess.'

I smiled. 'See you tonight.'

She didn't move for a moment, then shuddered. 'Wow, all the discomfort of a one-night stand, with none of the sex. Later, dude.'

The door slammed shut as I stood there, wondering what

exactly she'd meant by that. That she was uncomfortable with me? That she hated being here?

That she'd *wanted* to have sex the night before?

Then I realized something else: I had trusted the biggest secret in the world to this woman, and I didn't even know her last name.

'There's actually a *form* for that?'

'Well, not for cats specifically.' Dr. Rat tapped a few keys on her computer. 'But yeah, here it is. ZTM-47/74: Zootropic Transmission to New Species.' She pressed a button, and her printer whirred to life.

I blinked. I had imagined a citywide Watch alert, an extermination team scrambling and heading for the West Side, maybe even a meeting with the Night Mayor. Not a one-page form.

'That's it?' I asked.

'Look, it says, "Process immediately" at the top. That's not nothing.'

'But . . .'

'What are you so worried about, Kid? You secured the site, didn't you?'

'Um, of course. But does this happen a lot? A whole new *species* getting infected?'

'Don't you remember Plagues and Pestilence?' Dr. Rat said, disappointment on her face. 'That whole week we spent on the 1300s?'

'Yes. But I don't consider once in the last seven hundred years to be *a lot.*'

'Don't forget werewolves, and those bats in Mexico last century.' She leaned back in her chair, staring up into the mysteries of the squeaking row of rat cages.

Dr. Rat's lair sort of freaks me out, what with all the rattling cages of rodents, the brand-new textbooks and musty bestiaries, and the shiny tools lined up to one side of the dissection table. (There's just something about dissection tables.)

'You know,' Dr. Rat said, 'there might even be some history of a cat-friendly strain. The Spanish Inquisition thought that felines were the devil's familiars and barbecued a whole bunch of them. Their theory was that cats stole your breath at night.'

'I can see where they got that one,' I said, remembering how often I'd woken up with all fourteen pounds of Cornelius sitting on my chest.

'But it's paranoid to focus on a handful of transmissions, Cal,' Dr. Rat said. 'You've got to keep your eye on the big picture. Evolution is always cranking out mutations, and parasites are constantly trying out new hosts – some kind of worm takes a crack at your intestines pretty much every time you eat a rare steak.'

'Oh, nice. Thanks for that image.'

'But most of them *fail*, Kid. Evolution is mostly about mutations that *don't* work, sort of like the music business.' She pointed at her boom box, which was cranking Deathmatch at that very moment. 'For every Deathmatch or Kill Fee, there are a hundred useless bands you never heard of that go nowhere. Same with life's rich pageant. That's why Darwin called mutations "hopeful monsters." It's a crapshoot; most fail in the first generation.'

'The Hopeful Monsters,' I said. 'Cool band name.'

Dr. Rat considered this for a moment. 'Too artsy-fartsy.'

'Whatever. But this peep cat looked pretty successful to me. I mean, it had a huge brood and was catching birds to feed them. Doesn't that sound like an adaptation for spreading the parasite?'

'That's nothing new.' Dr. Rat threw a pencil in the air and caught it. 'Cats bring their humans little offerings all the time. It's how they feed their kittens; sometimes they get confused.'

'Yeah, well, this peep cat looked healthy. Not like an evolutionary failure.'

Dr. Rat nodded, drumming her fingers on the top of PNS's cage. She'd already drawn the rat's blood and attached the test tube to a centrifuge in the corner of her lair. It had spun itself into a solid blur, rumbling like a paint mixer in a hardware store.

'That's not bad – given how many parasite mutations kill their hosts in a few days. But evolution doesn't care how strong or healthy you are, unless you *reproduce*.'

'Sure . . . but this brood was really big. Thousands of them.'

'Maybe,' she said, 'but the question is, how does this new strain get into *another cat*?'

'You're asking me?' I said. 'You're the expert.'

She shrugged. 'Well, I don't know either, Kid. And that's the deal-breaker. If the new strain doesn't have a way back into another kitty final host, then the adaptation is just a dead end. Like toxoplasma in humans, it'll never go anywhere.'

I nodded slowly, wrapping my brain around this. If this new strain couldn't find a way to infect more cats, then it would die when the peep cat died. Game over.

I looked hopefully at Dr. Rat. 'So we might not be facing a civilization-ending threat to humanity?'

'Look, cats would be a great vector for the parasite to jump from rats to humans, I'll give you that. A lot more people get bitten by cats every year than rats. But it's much more likely this is a one-off freak mutation. In fact, it's even *more* likely you just got spooked and didn't know what you were seeing.'

I thought of the rumbling basement, the awful smell – maybe *that* had been a hallucination, but the peep cat I really had seen. 'Well, thanks for the pep talk.' I stood. 'Hope you're right.'

'Me too,' Dr. Rat said softly, looking down at PNS.

I pulled the ZTM-47/74 off the printer. There would be many more forms to fill out that day; my writing hand was sore just thinking about it.

I stopped at the door. 'Still, let me know what you think about that video. It *looked* like the peep cat was being worshipped by its brood of rats. Seems like that dynamic would take a few generations to evolve.'

Dr. Rat patted the videotape I'd brought her. 'I'm going to watch it right now, Kid.' She gestured at the centrifuge. 'And I'll let you know if Possible New Strain is a relative of yours. But I have one question.'

'What?'

'Does he smell like one?'

I paused to take one last sniff of PNS, catching the little fluffs of joy the rat gave off as he consumed the lettuce she'd given him. Dr. Rat knows a lot about smells, which chemicals give each fruit and flower its distinctive aroma – but she'll never have the olfactory sense of a predator. Her nose has to live vicariously through us carriers.

'Yeah,' I admitted. 'He smells like family.'

'Well, your nose probably knows what it's smelling. But I'll call you when I get firm results. In the meantime, here's a little something that might come in handy.' She tossed me a little vial of yellow liquid. 'That's Essence of Cal Thompson. Your smell. Might be useful if that brood is related to you. Just use it carefully. You don't want to cause a rat riot.'

It looked like piss in a perfume bottle, and holding it gave me an equally unpleasant feeling. 'Gee, thanks.'

'And one more thing, Kid.'

I paused, half out the door. 'What?'

'Why did you use a spaghetti strainer? Don't they give you guys cages anymore?'

'Long story. See you later.'

Walking down the halls of the Night Watch, I started to feel guilty.

While I'd been talking to Dr. Rat, I hadn't felt so bad about my indiscretions of the night before. We were pals, and I could almost believe she'd understand if I told her about spilling the beans to Lace. But as the implacable file cabinets rose on either side of me on my way into Records, I could feel the weight of my Major Revelation Incident growing with every step. It had made sense the night before, with Lace threatening to go to the newspapers, but this morning I felt like a traitor.

On the other hand, there was no changing my mind. I still didn't want Lace to disappear.

When I reached Chip's office, he looked up at me with a gaze that seemed somehow reproachful. 'Morning, Kid.'

'Hey, Chip.' I cleared my throat and brushed away the guilty thoughts. 'I found out what happened. They added a swimming pool.'

'Who added a what?'

I pointed at the blueprints for Lace's building still spread across his desk, half obscured by stray papers and books. 'A swimming pool a few yards deep, right on the lowest level. That's how the rat reservoir came up.'

Chip stared at the blueprints, then at the yellowing plans of the PATH tunnel, his fingers finding the spot where the two intersected.

Finally, he nodded. 'Yeah. If the pool had a drain, that would do it.' He looked up at me.

'There was a big hole in the deep end,' I said. 'And I smelled something pretty bad coming from it. And felt a sort of . . . trembling. Like something big going under me.'

'Like a subway train?'

I raised an eyebrow. That explanation hadn't occurred to me. 'Maybe. But anyway, that hole is where the rats all disappeared when I cranked up my flashlight.'

'The flashlight you broke?'

'Yes, the one I broke. Who told you that?'

He shrugged. 'I hear things. Have you – ?'

'Yes, I'll file a DE-37.' I waved the growing stack of forms in my hand.

He chuckled, shaking his head. 'Man, you hunters. I break a pencil and there's hell to pay.'

'I can see how that's deeply unfair, Chip. Especially if that pencil should try to kill you with its teeth and claws, or launch its brood of a thousand deadly paper clips against you.'

Chip chuckled again, raising his hands in surrender. 'Okay, okay. Won't say another word against hunters. But don't say that Records never helped you out. We got some interesting data about your seventh-floor tenants this morning. I think you'll find it useful.'

'You know where they are?'

'Afraid not. They've disappeared completely.' He pulled out an envelope and removed five photographs. 'But this is what they look like, or did last year anyway. Probably thinner now, those of them that are still alive.'

I recognized Morgan, her dark hair and pale skin, eyebrows perfectly arched.

'Thanks.' I took the photos from him and slid them into my jacket pocket.

'And one more thing,' Chip said, unfolding a printed T-shirt across his chest. 'This is for you.'

I stared at the smiling face, the sequined guitar, the good-natured belly overlapping his belt: Garth Brooks.

'Um, Chip, am I missing something?'

'It's an anathema, Kid!' He grinned. 'We found some online posts by a couple of your missing persons – Patricia and Joseph Moore. Both big Garth Brooks fans.'

'And you went out and *bought* that thing?'

'Nope. Believe it or not, Hunt Equipment had it on file.'

My eyebrows rose. 'We had a Garth Brooks T-shirt on file?'

'Yeah. You know that big outbreak on the Upper West Side eight years ago? Couple of those guys were really into country music.' He tossed the shirt to me. 'Wear it next time you go down. Just in case our missing persons have gone subterranean.'

'Great.' I stuffed the T-shirt in my backpack. 'Anything else?'

'Nope. But don't worry, we'll keep looking.'

'You do that. And if you find out that Morgan was into Ashlee Simpson, don't worry – I've already got it covered.'

Dr. Rat had been right about the ZTM-47/74 – it was a form that made things happen. Unfortunately, they weren't the things that I'd *wanted* to happen. Instead of a well-armed extermination team heading for Lace's building that afternoon, there was only me.

I was not empty-handed, though. I had a vial of Dr. Rat's Eau de Cal, a Ziploc bag of Cornelius dander, the Garth Brooks T-shirt on under my hazmat suit, a new flashlight and some other equipment in my duffel bag, and a work order signed by the Night Mayor himself, instructing me to capture the alleged peep cat. That last one was why I was flying solo. Apparently, a big squad of poison-wielding attackers might scare kitty away, and kitty was needed for testing.

So that meant me alone.

On my way across town, I stopped at a grocery store and bought two Crunchy Tunas and a can opener. Dr. Rat's experimental Cal extract might attract the peep cat, but I prefer the classics.

Manny was back at the door; he gave me a knowing wink.

'You going upstairs or downstairs, my friend?'

'Down, unfortunately.' I slapped a fake By-Order-of-Sanitation document on his desk. Manny's eyes widened as he scanned it.

'Whoa, man. You're telling me we're getting shut *down*?'

'Just the health club. We found rats, a whole bunch.'

'Oh, that's bad.' He shook his head.

'Hey, there's no reason to make a fuss. You can say whatever you want about why it's off limits. Tell the tenants there's a gas leak or something.'

'Okay.' He exhaled through his teeth. 'But the landlords aren't going to like this.'

'Tell them the extermination won't cost anything. The city will handle it all.'

'Really?'

'Yeah, I've personally got it covered. Just one thing, though.'

He looked up from the document.

'I'll need the keys to the elevator,' I said. '*All* of them. We don't want anyone wandering around in the basement. Not even building staff.'

'Really?'

I leaned closer. 'These rats . . . *very* dangerous.'

Manny looked doubtful about surrendering his keys. But after calling the fake phone number on the fake Sanitation order, he found himself reassured by a fake city official that everything would be okay as long as he cooperated. Soon I was headed down into the darkness again.

*

First, I dealt with the security cameras, sticking a piece of black tape over each of their lenses. Easy-peasy, and some useful information might turn up for my trouble. If anyone bothered to fix the cameras, at least I'd know someone was paying attention.

Opening the locker, I stepped into the cave darkness, flicked on my new flashlight, and crept down the hidden hallway. Lace's and my footprints were still there, preserved in peanut butter, but no new ones had appeared.

I cut open the chained-up door again, and this time when I closed it behind me, I jammed wedges into the cracks, restuffing the steel wool underneath.

The site secured, I descended the stairs, flashlight in hand.

The swimming pool was almost quiet.

In the soft red glow I saw only a few dozen rats and the picked-clean skeletons of pigeons, sitting undisturbed. Apparently it wasn't feeding time. The peep cat wasn't in sight.

I found my abandoned duffel bag and I transferred a few necessary items to my new one, then stepped into the empty pool. My boots trod softly across the pigeon feathers. The few rats perching on the pool's edge watched me descend toward the deep end, mildly curious. A big fat one leaned his chin over the diving board, looking down at me.

Without a thousand panicking rodents in the way, I could see the drain much better. The concrete around it had collapsed, and through the jagged hole was a deeper darkness that offered up a damp and earthy smell. No scent of death.

The hole was big enough for a slender human body to slip through. Hunkering at the edge, I opened a can of cat food. The smell of Crunchy Tuna infused the air, and I heard little noses sniffing around me. But nothing came to investigate.

Dr. Rat has a word for what rats are: *neophobic*. In other

words, they don't like new things. Related to them or not, I was something new in their environment, and Crunchy Tuna was too.

I pushed a chunk of Crunchy Tuna down into the hole. A liquid *splat* came from below. The space down there was big; I could hear its size in the echoes.

After a few minutes of waiting, I switched off the flashlight completely. Blind in the darkness, I hoped my ears might begin to listen harder. The few rats around me continued going about their business, cleaning themselves and squabbling. A few got up the courage to dart past me and down into the hole. They sniffed the dollop of cat food below, but I heard no little teeth daring to take a bite. They were a cautious bunch.

Rats send chemical signals to one another, emotions carried by smells. One nervous individual can make a whole pack of rats anxious, fear spreading through the population like a dirty rumor. And sometimes, a pack will suddenly abandon a place all at once, collectively deciding that it has bad vibes.

I wondered if the peep cat's brood was still jittery from my flashlight blast the night before. Maybe they had left this basement forever, fleeing far down into the Underworld.

Then I heard the meow.

It reached me from a long distance, sleepy and annoyed-sounding, through a prism of echoes. The cat was still down here.

But it wasn't coming to me; I had to go to it.

The concrete was brittle – a few solid kicks opened the hole enough for me to climb through. I lowered my duffel bag as far as possible, then dropped it. The *clunk* of metal told me that the floor was about ten feet below.

Holding onto the flashlight carefully, I slipped through and let myself fall. My boots hit solid ground with a crunch of shattered concrete that echoed like a gunshot.

I switched my flashlight on low again.

A tunnel stretched away into the darkness, extending as far as I could see in both directions. Decades of dust had settled in here, filling the bottom with a loose dirt floor. It was lined with uneven stones, century-old mortar barely holding them together. They were cold and wet to the touch – the tons of dirt over my head squeezing the groundwater through them like a fist around a wet rag.

A slight breeze moved through the passage, carrying the smells of rats, earth, and fungus. Still, nothing as foul and horrible as what I had scented the day before.

The breeze felt fresh; it had to be coming from some sort of opening at the surface. I decided to move upwind. With the air blowing into my face, I could smell whatever was in front of me without it smelling me.

I've been in a lot of underground spaces in New York – subway tracks, sewers, steam pipe tunnels – but this one was different. There were no stray bits of paper, no garbage, no smells of piss. Maybe it had lain undisturbed by human beings for the century since it had been built, carrying only air, rats, and the occasional peep cat beneath the city streets. The tunnel inclined slightly as I walked, a winding stain in the center of the floor showing where rain had trickled down the slope for the last hundred years.

Then I smelled something human on the breeze. Well . . . half human.

Peeps have a subtle scent. Their feverish bodies consume almost everything they eat, leaving few smells of waste. Their dry skin exudes none of the salty sweat of a regular person. But no metabolism is perfect – my predator's nose detected a hint of rotten meat and the whiff of dead skin cells, like fresh leather hanging on a boot factory wall.

The breeze died and I froze, waiting for it to come again. I didn't want my scent to drift ahead of me. A moment later, the air moved again, and the intimate smell of family washed over me.

This peep was a relative.

As softly as I could, I laid the duffel bag on the ground and pulled a knockout injector from the zippered pocket of my hazmat suit.

I switched off the flashlight and began to crawl, a wave of nerves rushing through me. This was the first peep I'd ever hunted who was an absolute unknown. The only anathema I had was the Garth Brooks T-shirt, which somehow didn't seem equal to the task. The darkness seemed to stretch forever before me, until a hint of light played across the blackness. Gradually I was able to make out the stones in the passage walls again, and my hands in front of my face . . . and then something else.

What looked like tiny clouds were rolling along the floor, carried by the breeze. They glided toward me, silent and insubstantial, and when I waved a hand close to them, they stirred in its wake.

Feathers.

I took a pinch and held it up to my eyes. This was the soft white down from a pigeon's breast. As the light grew stronger, I saw that the whole tunnel was carpeted with downy feathers; they clung to the ceiling stones and to my hazmat suit, rolling across the floor like a slow, ghostly tide.

Somewhere ahead, there were a lot of dead birds.

Larger feathers began to appear, the dirty gray and blue of pigeon and seagull wings, trembling in the breeze. I crawled silently across the carpeted dirt floor, feeling the softness under my palms and trying not to think of pigeon mites.

Ahead I could hear breathing, slow and relaxed for a peep.

The tunnel ended at a shaft that went straight up – light

pouring down from above, a rusted iron ladder driven into the stone wall. A pile of feathers had collected at the bottom. A few whole birds lay on top of it unmoving, their necks twisted.

I froze, watching the breeze stir the feathers until a shadow moved across them. The peep was at the top of the ladder.

With the chill autumn air flowing down the shaft, it still couldn't smell me. I wondered why it was nesting up there, instead of hiding down here in the gloom. Placing my flashlight on the floor to free up my hands, I crawled to the end of the tunnel and peered up, eyes slitted against the sunlight.

He clung to the ladder twelve feet above me, staring out at the world like a prisoner at a cell window, the reddish light of late afternoon softening his emaciated face.

I lowered myself into a crouch, gripped the injector, and jumped straight up as high as I could.

He heard me at the last second, looking down just as I reached up to jam the needle into his leg. He twisted away, the injector missing completely. My hand grasped the ladder but the peep screamed and flailed his foot at me, landing a kick in my teeth. My grip loosened . . . and I was falling.

I reached out to grab a passing rung and swung inward, bouncing against the stone wall and holding on for a bare second, the breath knocked from me. Then the peep was dropping toward me, hissing, teeth bared. His body struck me broadside, wrenching my fingers from the ladder rung. We fell together, landing in a crumpled heap on the pile of pigeon feathers, his wiry muscles writhing against me.

Black fingernails raked across my face, and I scrambled free and jumped away into the tunnel, cracking my head against the low stone ceiling. Dizzy from the impact, I spun to face him, hands raised.

The peep leaped up in an explosion of feathers, his black

claws lashing through the air. I held up the injector to ward him off, and felt his flailing hand connect with it, a brief hiss sounding before the injector flew away into the darkness. The peep's next blow struck my head, knocking me to the ground.

He stood over me, silhouetted by the sunlight, swaying a little, like a drunk. I scrambled backward, crab style. He let out another scream . . .

Then tumbled heavily to the ground. The injection had knocked him out.

That good old peep metabolism, fast as lightning.

I blinked a few times, shaking my head, trying to force the pain away.

'Ow, ow, *ow*!' I said. I rubbed at a bump already rising on my scalp. 'Stupid tunnel!'

When the pain had faded a little, I checked his pulse. Slow and thready, but he was alive – for a peep, anyway. The injection would keep him out for hours, but I tagged him to be certain, handcuffing him to the lowest ladder rung and sticking an electronic bracelet around his ankle. The transport squad could follow its signal here.

Finally, I sat back and grinned happily, letting a rush of pride erase my pain. Even if he was family, this was my first peep capture outside my own ex-girlfriends. I turned him over to look at his face. Thinner than his photograph, his cheekbones high and hair wild, this was a barely recognizable Joseph Moore. He looked way too skinny for a seven-month-old peep, though, considering the pile of feathers he'd accumulated.

What had he been doing at the top of the ladder, up there in the sun?

I pulled myself up the ladder, noting how smooth the walls of the shaft were. Too slick for a cat to climb, or even a rat – only a human being could make use of it.

At the top, the afternoon light slanted through the steel-grated window. The view was the Hudson River, from only a few feet above the water level. From just overhead I heard laughter and the hum of Rollerblades.

I was *inside* the stone bulwark at the edge of the island, I realized, right below the boardwalk where people jogged and skated every day, only a few feet from the normal daylight world.

Then I saw the broken black column in front of me, a pylon from an old pier, a rotting piece of wood just big enough for a pigeon or a seagull to perch on. There was bird crap all over it, and it was just within arm's reach.

Joseph Moore had been hunting.

Then a realization swept over me, and I gripped the ladder rungs with white knuckles, remembering the picked-clean pigeon skeletons and feathers back in the swimming pool. Joseph Moore was too skinny to have eaten all those birds at the bottom of the shaft; most had been carried away. He had been hunting for the brood. With his long human arms, he had brought them food that they couldn't reach.

But unlike most human peeps, Joseph Moore wasn't at the center of the brood. He'd been stuck out here on this lonely periphery, the hated sunlight shining in to blind his eyes, forced to give up his kills for the pack to eat.

He was nothing but a servant to the brood's real master.

'The cat has people,' I said aloud.

Okay, remember those slimeballs? The ones with lancet flukes in them? It turns out that they do more than just infect cows, snails, and ants. They help save the world.

Well, okay, not the *whole* world. But they do make sure that the corner of the world where ants and cows and snails live doesn't come crashing down. Here's how it works:

When cows are looking for something to eat, they stay away from grass that's really green. Green grass is good for them, but it's green because of the cow pies fertilizing it. Now, these cow pies don't cause problems in themselves – cows are smart enough not to eat them. But cow pies have lancet flukes in them. Thus, there are fluke-infected snails nearby, which means that there must be flukey ants sitting atop stalks of green grass, waiting to be eaten.

So cows have evolved to avoid bright green grass. They don't want to get infected with lancet flukes, after all.

But a problem arises when there are too many cows and not enough grass to go around. The cows wind up eating the green grass, and getting lancet flukes in their stomachs. Less grass to go around, more sick cows. And, it turns out, sick cows have fewer calves. The cow population drops, and there's more grass for everyone.

Get the picture? The parasites control the population. They're part of nature's balance.

So what happens if you get rid of the parasites? Bad things.

Not long ago, some cattle ranchers decided to increase their herds with parasite-killing medicine. They doped every cow until all the parasites were gone. So their cattle had more and more calves, and they ate all the grass, green or not. More hamburgers for everyone!

For a while.

It turned out that those little clusters of bright green, parasite-laden grass were important. They were holding down the topsoil. Without parasites to keep the cows in check, every square inch of grass got eaten, and soon the grassland turned into a desert. New plants came in, desert shrubs that made it impossible for grass to return.

All the cows died. All the snails died. Even the ants got blown away.

Without our parasites to keep us in check, we're all in trouble.

Joseph Moore was still unconscious, snoring softly on the feathers. Maybe dreaming of his cat master.

I wondered if Dr. Rat would try to explain this new development away as just another hopeful monster. Surely a human who served a peep cat would take a few generations to evolve. Of course, people and cats have been getting along for thousands of years, since the Egyptians worshipped them as gods. Maybe this was just a new twist on that, or on the toxoplasma thing.

Whatever was going on, I had to catch this cat. The yowl I'd heard from the swimming pool must have come from the other end of the ventilation tunnel, downwind. Which meant that it would smell me coming.

'Fine,' I whispered. I was armed with one more can of Crunchy Tuna, after all.

Facing the tunnel, I realized that my night vision was gone. Glimpsing the afternoon sun across the Hudson had left me half blind, seeing only spots and traces against the darkness. I closed my eyes to let them readjust to darkness, moving slowly back down the tunnel.

Then I heard a noise, faint footfalls in the dirt.

My eyes sprang open, but the tunnel ahead remained absolutely black. The only scents came from behind me – the pile of feathers and the sleeping peep. I swore softly, no longer so proud of my hunting instincts. Just like

Joseph Moore, I had been cornered, blind and upwind. And my spare knockout injector was in my duffel bag.

I crouched in a defensive stance, listening hard.

No sound at all came from the darkness. Had I imagined the footsteps?

My stuff had to be up there somewhere, probably only a few steps away. I gritted my teeth and scuttled forward, sweeping my hands back and forth across the dirt, hunting for the cold metal of the flashlight.

I barely glimpsed her before she struck, barreling out of the darkness and crashing into me, as hard and solid as a suitcase full of books. The impact knocked my breath away and threw me to the ground. Long fingernails raked my chest, shredding my hazmat suit. I blindly swung a fist and connected with hard muscle, driving a grunt from the peep.

'Patricia!' I shouted, half guessing, and she hissed at the sound, scrambling away from the anathema of her own name. I was right – it was Joseph's wife. The light came from behind her now, igniting a shimmering halo of feathers wound into her hair and sticking to her skin. With her long fingernails and half-starved face, she looked like a human partly transformed into an awful bird of prey.

She readied herself to spring at me.

'"I've got friends in low places,"' I sang – the only Garth Brooks song that came to mind. The refrain halted her long enough for me to tear the shredded hazmat suit the rest of the way open.

Patricia Moore stared at my chest in horror; the jolly country singer stared back.

'Oh, yeah!' I said. 'She's my cowboy Cadillac!'

Her eyes widened and she screamed, spinning away to scuttle up the tunnel toward the light.

Another anathema awaited her there: her husband, faceup on the floor. I turned and scrambled deeper into the darkness, sweeping the dirt floor wildly with my palms. Where was my damn flashlight?

My racing brain wondered how long she'd been tracking me. Had she followed me from downwind since I'd dropped into the tunnel? Or maybe she always lurked near her husband, just as Sarah had stayed close to Manhattan.

Suddenly my knuckles grazed hard metal, sending the flashlight's cylinder rolling farther into the darkness. I reached out, grasping blindly, and at that moment my ears split with Patricia Moore's scream – fear for her husband and horror at the sight of his beloved face, mixed up in one terrible cry that echoed through the tunnel.

My hand closed on the flashlight.

She was already headed back, loping toward me on hands and knees, growling like a wolf.

I covered my eyes with one hand, turned the flashlight on her, and switched it to full power. Her feral grunts choked off, and the tunnel flooded with light so strong that the blood-pink veins in my eyelids were burned into my vision.

A moment later, I flicked it off and opened my eyes. Against the sunlight streaming down the shaft, I could see Patricia Moore crouching in the center of the tunnel, head pressed against the feather-strewn dirt, motionless, as if paralyzed by one too many insults to her optic nerve.

I set the flashlight on low and found my duffel bag, only a few yards down the tunnel. Pulling out the spare injector and loading it, finally thankful for all those tedious drills in Hunting 101, I whirled to face her. She still hadn't moved.

Perhaps Patricia had despaired, thinking that her husband was dead, or maybe it was too much to keep fighting in a world that included my rendition of 'Cowboy Cadillac.' But for whatever reason, she didn't move a muscle as I approached across the feathered floor.

I reached out and jabbed her in the shoulder. She winced as the needle hissed, lifted her head, and sniffed the air.

'You're one of Morgan's?' she asked.

I blinked. My vision was still spotted with tracers, but her expression seemed thoughtful, almost curious. Her voice, like Sarah's, was dry and harsh, but the way she said the words sounded so reasonable, so human.

'Yeah,' I answered.

'You're sane?'

'Um . . . I guess.'

She nodded slowly. 'Oh. I thought you'd gone bad, like Joseph.' Her eyes closed as the drug took effect. 'She says it's coming soon . . .'

'What is?' I asked.

She opened her mouth again but fell into a heap without making another sound.

Maybe I should have headed back to the surface to rest up, reload, and share my revelations about the parasite's new tricks. Maybe I should have waited right there for the transport squad, brought them in by GPS and cell phone.

Both of my captives had been so unpeeplike – Joseph facing the orange late-afternoon sun as if the light didn't faze him, Patricia speaking so clearly once she'd identified my scent.

Are you sane? she'd asked. Yeah, right. I wasn't the one living in a tunnel.

But it reminded me of the way Sarah had changed after I'd cornered her, asking about Elvis, peering into my eyes without terror. Maybe I should have mentioned this to someone right away.

Maybe I should have wondered more about *what* was coming soon.

But I didn't wait around. I still had a peep cat to catch.

After handcuffing Patricia Moore, I called the transport squad, giving them precise GPS coordinates for the captives. They wouldn't even have to disturb Manny and his tenants to collect the peeps. They could simply put on Con Edison uniforms, set up a fake construction site on the Hudson River walk, and cut their way in through the metal grate at the end of the ventilation tunnel.

They didn't need me, and with a high-priority work order from the Mayor himself in hand, it made perfect sense to follow the tunnel in the other direction: down the slope, the steady breeze at my back, toward the rumble of the huge exhaust fans.

Under the swimming pool again, I listened to the echoes bouncing down the shattered drain. The basement overhead sounded the same – still just a few dozen rats squabbling and skittering among the feathers. The brood hadn't returned, and nothing had touched the cat food I'd left behind.

I wondered how far down the tunnel the scent would travel, if floating molecules of Crunchy Tuna would tempt the peep cat out into the open. With the wind at my back, I was hardly going to catch it by surprise. I kept my flashlight on medium, not wanting to get jumped in the darkness again.

The slope grew steeper, descending as the tunnel continued. The air became chill around me, and drops of water began to plink from the ceiling. The low rumble of exhaust fans grew in the distance, throbbing like a massive heartbeat at the core of the city.

Then another sound floated up the tunnel, an impatient yowl

that cut through the low-pitched thrumming. The cat could smell me now and knew that I was coming. I wondered if it also knew two of its pet peeps had been dispatched.

Just how smart was this thing?

The echoes of the cat's cry suggested a large open space in front of me. The push of the breeze at my back had strengthened, and the pulsing beat of the exhaust fans grew more distinct.

Then I felt something, a trembling in the earth. Unlike the rumbling of the fan, it was building steadily under my feet, until it made the stones in the tunnel walls vibrate visibly. I knelt on the quivering dirt, suddenly feeling trapped in the narrow tunnel. I peered deep into the darkness, one way and then the other, searching for whatever was coming as I tried to fight off panic.

Then the rumble peaked and began to fall away, fading into the distance, just like . . . the sound of a passing train.

Chip had been right. The PATH tunnel was nearby, and the rush-hour commute was just beginning. The disturbance hadn't been some rampaging creature from the depths, just a trainload of New Jersey-ites headed home. I stood, feeling like an idiot.

But the earth-shaking passage had left something visible up ahead – strands of stirred-up dust hung illuminated in the air. Flicking the flashlight off, I saw shafts of light filtering into the tunnel. They pulsed brighter and then darker in time with the constant throbbing – I had to be close to the exhaust fans now.

The tunnel ended a little farther on, and I stepped down from its open maw into a vast cathedral of machines. Whirring turbines filled the air with the smell of grease and an electric hum. Above me I could see a huge pair of fans turning at a stately pace, the blades eighty feet across; this was Chip's ventilation system.

Between the spinning blades the sky showed through, the dark blue of early evening.

In my days searching for Morgan's apartment, I'd often seen this building from the outside, a magnificent column of brick, windowless and ten stories high, like a prison balanced on the river's edge. The inside was just as cheerless, the greasy machines layered with a slapdash coat of gray paint and bird droppings. The scant sunlight pulsed in time with the fans' rotation. The air was drawn steadily toward the fans, carrying dust and the occasional stray feather upward.

I searched the huge space nervously – my peep hearing was useless. But there was nothing unexpected in the jumble of maintenance equipment, garbage, and empty coffee cups. Whatever my quarry was – mutation or long-standing strain of the disease – its pet peeps weren't preying on the workers who kept these fans going.

But where had the cat gone? That last echoing yowl must have come from in here, but the doors to the boardwalk and piers outside were locked.

The only way out that I could find was a set of metal stairs descending into the earth. I tapped my flashlight on the handrail, sending a clanging beat into the depths. A few seconds later, the peep cat let out a long *nyeeeeow*.

The creature was leading me down.

'I'm coming,' I muttered, flicking my flashlight back on.

Below was a world of pipes and air shafts, cold water seeping through the concrete that held back the river, staining it with black bruises. The stairs kept going down, angling away from the river until the salt smell of the Hudson faded behind me and the walls were made of the granite bedrock of Manhattan. I was *under* the PATH tunnel now, in the service area that accessed its tangle of cables and shafts. Chip had a picture in his office of the huge machine that had bored this tunnel: a steam-powered drill crawling through the earth, the source of all his nightmares.

My flashlight fell on a sign hanging from chains draped across the stairs:

DANGER

Area Closed

As if answering my hesitation, the cat yowled again, the cry rising up from below like a ghost's.

I paused, sniffing the air, the hair on my neck rising. Under the dampness and grease and rat droppings, a strange scent lay, massive and unfamiliar, like a heavy hand on my chest. It wasn't the scent of peeps or of the deep earth. It was the same foul smell I'd scented the day before. Like death. Deep in my genetic memory, alarms and flashing lights were going off.

I swallowed and stepped over the sign. As my duffel bag brushed the chains, they creaked sullenly with rust.

This far down, the earth looked wounded, wet fissures splitting the granite walls. The darkness inside seemed to repulse my flashlight and sent back long echoes from my footsteps. I saw no more empty coffee cups – every piece of garbage looked smoothed down by time, half rotted away. I remembered Chip saying that PATH workers had abandoned this place, and I could see why.

Or at least, I could *feel* it: a cold presence on top of the evil smell.

Finally the stairs ended at a rupture in the rock, a fissure large enough to walk into. I stepped inside, my flashlight glinting off mica-strewn granite. The shadows around me turned jagged.

This was the deepest I had ever been.

The air had fallen still, so I smelled the brood before I heard them. They were huddled together in a ravine of stone, a few thousand rats and their peep cat. Myriad eyes glittered back at me, unafraid of the flashlight.

The cat blinked, yawning, its eyes glittering red.

Red? I thought. That was odd. Cats' eyes should be blue or green or yellow.

'What's *with* you anyway?' I asked the peep cat softly.

It just sat there.

The posse of big fat rats still surrounded it, an entourage of heavy, pale bodies, larger than any rodents I'd ever seen on the surface. All the rats were the color of dried chewing gum, their eyes pink, bred almost to albino from generations in darkness.

I carefully pulled a video camera from my duffel bag and swept it across the brood. Dr. Rat would be thrilled to have footage of these deep-dwellers in their natural habitat.

In the silence, a barely audible sound began to make itself heard.

At first, I thought it was the PATH train rumbling past again. But the noise didn't build steadily. It came and went, much slower than the sound of the fans. I felt the tiny hairs on my arms moving one way and then the other and realized that the air in the cavern was being pushed in and out, as if a slow and huge bellows was operating.

Something down here was *breathing*. Something huge.

'No,' I whispered.

In answer, a spine-melting sound washed through the cavern on a fetid breeze, like the moan of some titanic beast. It was so low-pitched that I *felt* more than heard it, like the buzz of power lines that my peep senses sometimes detect. Every nerve in my body screamed at me to stand up and run away, the sort of panic I hadn't felt since I'd become a hunter.

The sound passed away, though the air still shifted back and forth.

The peep cat winked its eyes at me in satisfaction.

Okay. I was leaving now . . . and taking the cat with me. I put the duffel bag aside. If this worked, I was going to have to run fast, carrying as little as possible.

I pulled out my second can of Crunchy Tuna and slipped my gloves on. There was no point in using my knockout injector, which would overdose the cat.

The brood stirred when they smelled the cat food. I waited, frozen, letting the scent carry to the peep cat.

The almost-human intelligence on its face faded, replaced by the same dull look that Cornelius gets when it's feeding time: pure animal desire. At least the creature wasn't some sort of diabolical genius – it was just a cat, really, and a diseased one at that. 'Come on, kitty,' I said.

It took a few steps toward me, then sat down again.

'You know you want it,' I murmured, lapsing into my kitty voice and fanning the smell toward the cat. The scent of the huge, hidden thing stirred, and a trickle of sweat coursed down my side.

The cat stood again and moved gingerly across the horde of rats, like someone stepping through a tent crowded with sleeping people. They barely stirred as it passed.

But then it stopped again, a few feet away.

'*Extra* nummies?' I nudged the Crunchy Tuna a little closer.

The peep cat just cocked its head. It wasn't budging.

Then I remembered Dr. Rat's perfume of Cal, the family scent distilled into pure essence. Perhaps smelling was believing.

I pulled out the tiny vial and opened it, waiting only a few seconds before screwing the bottle top closed again, not wanting to rile up the horde of rats.

As the smell spread throughout the room, the brood stirred like a single entity restless in its sleep. Snufflings echoed like a horde of tiny whispers around me. The rats would wake up fast once I made my move.

The cat stood up again, stretching, then took a few steps closer to the can of Crunchy Tuna. It remained only inches out of arm's reach, now staring at the can instead of me, nose quivering, suspicion and curiosity at war inside its little brain.

Of course, it was a cat, so curiosity won . . .

I snatched the creature up from the floor and squashed it to my chest. Leaping up and spinning around, I dashed back through the rough stone fissure, my flashlight bouncing maniacally off the walls.

The cat let out a disgruntled meow, and squeaks sounded from behind, a sudden panic spreading as the brood realized its master was gone. I reached the stairs and bounded upward, the metal banging like a gong under my boots. The cat fought, yowling and raking my chest, its claws catching the fabric of Garth Brooks's face in a death grip. But it couldn't escape my gloved hand.

Still struggling, it let out another scream, this one purposeful and harsh. The hum of turbines and giant fans above grew louder, but before they overwhelmed my ears I heard the rustling of a brood on the move below, like a lawn full of leaves stirred by an impatient wind.

At the last flight of stairs, I paused to peer back down. Rats streamed upward, shimmying along the handrails like tightrope walkers, bounding up the stairs, stumbling over one another in a boiling mass of fur and claws.

I dashed across the exhaust building, the image of stampeding rats spinning in my head, my senses swamped by the pulsing sunlight and mechanical sounds. We'd learned about massed rat attacks in Hunting 101, how a pack's chemical messages of panic could urge them into a state of mob hysteria. Once a horde of rats was committed to taking down prey, even a superbright burst from a Night Watch flashlight wouldn't change their minds.

And that went even for *normal* rats, without the brood bonds and hyperactive aggression of the parasite. The army pursuing me had a master to protect; this was evolutionary perfection trailing me, hungering to tear me to pieces.

The tunnel leading back to the swimming pool opened up two feet above floor level – an easy jump for me, but a climb that might take the rats a few extra moments. I would need every second of lead time to get to safety through the jammed-shut metal door.

The cat screamed again and struggled harder, and I felt something wet and warm against my chest. It was *pissing* on me as I ran! Leaving spatters of its scent on the floor, an unmistakable trail for the horde to follow.

'You little shit!' I yelled, leaping up into the exhaust tunnel.

The cat got one leg free and lashed out at my face, getting a single curved claw into my cheek, rapier-sharp and fiercely painful. I dropped the flashlight and grabbed hold of the cat with both gloved hands, pulling it away from me with a rip of skin that felt like yanking out a fishhook.

'Ow!' I screamed at it.

It hissed back at me.

The flashlight lay at my feet, but the rumble of turbines behind me was now joined by the rush of tiny claws – they'd almost reached the tunnel entrance. I dashed forward blindly, both hands clutching the squirming cat.

Then I saw something horrible ahead . . . light. Sunlight.

I stumbled to a halt.

It didn't make sense. The only light down here was at the *far* end of the tunnel, where my captured human peeps lay handcuffed, well past the swimming pool.

I swallowed. Had I gone too far already? Maybe the tunnel was shorter than it had seemed while I'd been crawling and skulking, listening between every step.

I ran a few more steps forward; then I saw them handcuffed on the sunlit ground: Patricia and Joseph Moore. This was the other end of the tunnel, a dead end.

I felt a low rumbling overhead – the transport squad in its garbage truck, getting ready to collect the peeps – and my heart leaped for a moment. Allies were only a few yards away.

But a steel grate still stood between me and them. By the time they cut through it, the horde would have torn me to pieces.

I had to get back to the swimming pool.

I turned from the light and ran, the murmur of the rats building in front of me, thousands of little claws on stone, like the sound of distant surf. The peep cat growled happily in my arms; it could smell its brood approaching.

The blackness before me began to glitter – the glow of sunlight at my back catching a swarm of reflective, night-seeing eyes. The brood filled the tunnel floor, spreading halfway up the walls like a shimmering pink smile.

I tore the remaining shreds of hazmat suit off and wrapped the cat in them to silence it, then pulled out Dr. Rat's Essence of Cal. *You don't want to cause a rat riot*, she had said.

Maybe I did.

I knelt on the ground, facing away from the horde, my body wrapped tightly around the cat. Its muffled growls rumbled like a hungry stomach.

Twisting the cap from the bottle, I hurled it spinning down the tunnel as far as I could and ducked my head to the floor.

Seconds later, they flowed over me, rat claws nicking through the Garth Brooks T-shirt like an Astroturf massage, their thin cries building as they scented what was ahead.

Rats are smart. They learn, they adapt, they know to be suspicious of free peanut butter. But these weren't rats anymore – they were a mob, whipped into a frenzy, running on instinct and chemical signals. And right in front of them was a trail of cat piss leading to a great big bottle of distilled Cal, the creature they knew had stolen their master.

When the last few had passed, I leaped to my feet, keeping the cat clutched tightly to my chest. It growled uselessly. The brood had found the bottle and fallen upon it in a churning mass.

I dashed back toward the swimming pool, half suffocating the peep cat to keep it silent, knowing they would be following me again in a few moments.

This time, I didn't miss the echoing presence of the pool overhead. I climbed up into the deep end, then headed for the stairs, grabbing the duffel bag I'd left the night before. A few rats scented their master, but they had hardly begun to stir by the time I got the heavy metal door open. From the other side, I shoved it closed again hard, stuffing steel wool back into the cracks, securing the snipped chains with a Night Watch deadbolt and squishing through the poisonous peanut butter to safety.

When the locker door slammed shut behind me, I collapsed on the floor, shaking in the darkened health club. The peep cat heaved as I loosened my grip to let it breathe again. It growled once, low and long.

You're dead meat, its eyes said.

'Oh, yeah?' I answered. 'You and what army?'

Possibly the army I'd just run from like a headless chicken.

When I'd stopped shaking, I stood up and emptied the duffel bag onto the floor. Stuffing my struggling captive into it wasn't easy, but I finally zipped the bag closed, muffling its yowls.

I was still panting, still half in shock, but as I pulled off my gloves I realized that I'd escaped. My clawed cheek felt like a pencil had been shoved through it, but the mission into the Underworld had been a success.

And the peep cat wasn't so tough after all. Maybe Dr. Rat was right, and this new mutation was no big deal, just another evolutionary experiment gone awry.

It was still pissed off, though. The bag danced, needle-sharp claw tips poking through the vinyl. Not the best confinement system, but it would do for the moment. I only had to make it to the transport squad, a few blocks away. They would have a proper cage, and in any case, I had to drop by and warn them about the loose brood rampaging in the tunnel below.

And that other thing, the big breathing thing, whatever the hell *that* was . . .

Manny's eyes widened when he saw me.

'Are you okay, man?' he said.

I shrugged. 'Yeah. But I wouldn't go down there if I were you.'

His gaze went from my shredded hazmat coveralls to my bloodied face, then fell on the struggling bulge in the duffel bag. 'What the hell is that?'

'Just one less thing for you to worry about, Manny. But be careful; there's more down there.'

'Jesus, it looks as big as a cat!' He sniffed the air, smelling the tunnel muck and pigeon feathers and feline piss all over me. 'What happened down there?'

'Just got a little ugly is all. But it's under control.'

One hand went to his face. 'Maybe you should go to a doctor, man.'

I nodded, realizing that Dr. Rat would be with the transport squad. 'Yep. That's right where I'm headed.'

I left Manny there at his desk, still wide-eyed and bemused, and headed down the river toward the entrance of the tunnel.

On the way, I spotted a stray cat lurking in the lengthening shadows. A block farther, another peered out from beneath a Dumpster full of garbage. I began to walk faster.

It's not unusual to see groups of rodents in the city, of course, but wild felines tend to stay alone. That's just predator-prey mathematics: It takes hundreds of the hunted to keep one hunter in business – there are always lots of sheep for every wolf.

The cats' smooth movements were so different from those of the scurrying rats – rather than displaying the manic wariness of lunch-meat species, predators always glide along with confidence and grace. Like they belong here and you don't.

I told myself it was just a statistical fluke, seeing two of them. Maybe it was because Lace lived so close to the meat-packing district, a place with lots of potential rat food lying around, and therefore lots of prey for feral cats. Or maybe with an angry mutant feline in my duffel bag, I was simply paying more attention than usual.

Like the cat I'd noticed the night before, these two followed my progress with cold, reflective eyes. My nerves were shot from the long day, but I got the definite feeling they knew I had a cat in my duffel bag and were not amused.

When I spotted the activity of the Night Watch across the highway, I didn't wait for the traffic lights to change.

'Well, look what the cat dragged in!' Dr. Rat called out.

'Other way around: *I'm* dragging *it*.'

Her eyes lit up as she spotted the squirming duffel bag on my shoulder. 'You caught the beastie?'

'Yeah. And its little friends are going crazy down there. You should warn the transport guys.'

'Loose brood? I'll let them know.'

As she went to talk to them, I slipped under the orange hazard tape strung around the site. The Con Ed truck was parked on the Hudson River boardwalk, its engine humming to power the work lights in the taped-off area. The sun had almost set, bleeding red into the clouds, but it was still warmer up here than down in the depths. After breathing the funk of the Underworld, a little fresh air felt good in my lungs.

The shriek of whirling metal came from the edge of the river, and showers of sparks erupted into the air. The transport guys had built a platform over the water and were cutting through the grate. As Dr. Rat spoke to the team leader, he and a few others started to get into full extermination gear; the Watch could clean out the tunnel properly now that the peep cat was in custody.

Everything was sorted out, more or less.

I wondered about the big thing under the ventilation towers, and if anyone was going to believe me about something I'd smelled and heard – and *felt* – but not seen.

'Let me put something on that.' Dr. Rat had returned with a first-aid kit, thick rubber gloves protecting her hands. She swabbed stingy stuff onto Joseph Moore's fingernail marks, then plastered a bandage over the cat scratch on my cheek. Infections don't get very far with us carriers, but it still feels weird to leave a bleeding wound untreated .

'Okay,' Dr. Rat said when my face was fixed up. 'Let's take a look at your feline friend.'

'All right. Just be careful.'

'Don't worry about me.' Through the vinyl, she squished the

cat into one corner of the bag, then unzipped the top and reached in to grab it. With any other noncarrier, I would have been nervous, but Dr. Rat handles infected rats all day.

The peep cat emerged into the sunlight, growling.

She dangled it by the scruff of its neck. 'Not too different from a regular cat.'

I took my first good look at the peep cat and frowned. Up here in the real world, it didn't seem very frightening – no strange gauntness or peeped-up musculature, no spinal ridge to show where the parasite was wound into its nervous system. Just those weirdly red-reflecting eyes.

'Maybe the parasite doesn't have much effect on felines,' Dr. Rat said.

'Maybe not on the outside,' I said. 'But it had its own brood!'

Dr. Rat shrugged, turning the cat around to look at all sides. It wailed at the indignity 'Rats may just tolerate it because it smells familiar.'

'I haven't noticed much smell from it,' I said. 'And it's related to me.'

She shrugged again. 'Well, so far I haven't gotten any positive results with PNS. I've injected some of its blood into a few test cats, and they don't show any signs of turning positive. This is an evolutionary dead end, just like I figured.' She looked closer at the peep cat, which took an angry swing at her nose with one claw, coming up short by an inch. 'Or maybe this cat is the mutant, and your strain of parasite is the same old stuff.'

'Well, now you can check for cat-to-cat transmission,' I said.

'Sure thing. Just don't get your hopes up, Kid.' She smiled. 'I know it's exciting to discover something new, and you want to feel like it's a big deal and everything. But like I keep saying, failure is the rule when it comes to evolution.'

'Maybe.' I looked up the river to where the exhaust towers stood. 'But this cat was really smart, almost like it was leading me down. And I think there was . . . something else down there.'

Dr. Rat looked at me. 'Like what?'

'Kind of a huge rumbling thing, and it was breathing.'

'Rumbling?' She laughed. 'Probably just the PATH train.'

'No, it wasn't.' I cleared my throat 'I mean, yeah, there was a train down there. But this was something else, even deeper. It smelled like nothing I ever smelled before. And it seemed like the cat was taking me along for a reason, as if it wanted to . . . *show* me what was down there.'

Dr. Rat frowned, looking at the captive cat dubiously, then her eyes swept across my sweat-matted hair, my bandaged face, and my torn Garth Brooks T-shirt. 'Cal, maybe you should get some rest.'

'Hey, I'm not being crazy here. That guy Chip in Records says that really big, old, monstery things can get woken up when tunnels get dug. And this was right under those exhaust fans.'

She chuckled. 'I know all about Records. They're always telling stories that give you hunters nightmares. They spend a lot of time reading ancient mythology, you know. But in R&D we try to focus more on the *science* side of things.'

I shook my head. 'This thing wasn't mythological. It was really big and smelled evil, and it was *breathing*.'

She lowered the struggling peep cat a bit and stared at me, trying to decide whether I was kidding or in some sort of shock or just plain bat-shit. I held her gaze steadily.

Finally, she shrugged. 'Well, you can always fill out a US-29.'

I nodded. The Unknown Subterranean form, also known as the Sasquatch Alert. 'Maybe I will.'

'But not till tomorrow, Kid. Right now you should go home and lie down.'

I started to argue, but at that moment a wave of exhaustion and hunger hit me, and I realized that I could go home to Cornelius and Lace and probably sleep for real again. The orange tape was up, the transport squad was here – the site was secured. Maybe this could wait until tomorrow.

Some more thoughts on the goodness of parasites . . .

Meet Crohn's disease, a nasty ailment of the digestive system. It gives you the runs and causes severe pain in your stomach, and there's no known way to cure it. No matter what foods you eat, the pain of Crohn's won't stop. The disease keeps its victims awake night after night and is strong enough to drive many into a deep depression.

People who get Crohn's often suffer their entire lives. The symptoms may go away for a few years but invariably return in all their destructive glory. There is no escape.

So what kind of parasite causes Crohn's?

Hah, fooled you! Unlike all the other diseases in this book, Crohn's is not caused by parasites. Quite the opposite. It is probably caused by *the absence of parasites.*

Say what now? Well, no one knows for sure, but here's what some scientists have noticed:

Crohn's disease didn't exist before the 1930s, when members of a few wealthy families in New York City got it. As time passed, the disease spread to the rest of the United States. It always started in rich neighborhoods first, only making its way into the bad parts of town much later. It took until the 1970s to reach the poorest parts of our country.

These days, Crohn's is on the march across the world. In the 1980s, it appeared in Japan, just when a lot of Japanese were starting to get really rich. Lately it's been making its way through South Korea, in the wake of that country's economic boom.

And guess what? It still doesn't exist anywhere in the third world. Poor people never get Crohn's disease. And this has led many scientists to think that Crohn's results from the most common sign of a rich society: clean water.

That's right: *clean* water.

You see, most of the invaders of our guts come from dirty water. If you drink clean water your whole life, you'll have a lot fewer parasites. But that can actually be a problem. Your immune system has evolved to expect parasites in your stomach. And when no parasites show up, your immune defenses can get kind of . . . twitchy. Sort of like a night watchman with nothing to do, drinking too much coffee and cleaning his gun again and again.

So when your twitchy, understimulated immune system detects the slightest little stomach bug, it launches into emergency mode and goes looking for a hookworm to kill. Unfortunately, there are no hookworms inside you, because your water supply is cleaner than at any time in human history. (Which you thought was a good thing.)

But your immune defenses have to do *something, so* they attack your digestive system, tearing it to pieces.

Lucky you.

*

We humans have lived with our parasites for a long time, evolving alongside them, walking hand in hand down the generations. So maybe it's not surprising that when we get rid of them all at once, strange things happen. Our bodies freak out in the absence of our little friends.

So the next time you're eating a rare steak and start worrying about parasites, just remember: All those worms and worts and other little creatures trying to wriggle down your throat can't be all bad.

They've been making us their home for a long, long time.

On the way home, I bought bacon.

The gnawing in my stomach was reaching critical proportions, my body crying out for meat to keep the parasite happy. One thing about being a carrier: Saving the world from mutant felines is no excuse for missing meals.

I put a can of tuna in front of Cornelius, then headed straight for the stove and set it alight. Then I shut the gas off, sniffing the air.

Something was different about my apartment.

Then I realized what it was – the smell of Lace all around me. She'd slept here, filling the place like a slow infusion.

My parasite growled with hunger and lust, and I hurriedly relit the stove, working until my largest dinner plate was filled with a stack of crispy strips of bacon. I carried it to the table and sat down.

The first piece was halfway into my mouth when keys jingled in the door. Lace burst through, dropping her backpack to the floor.

'Excellent smell, dude,' she said.

For a second, I forgot to eat, a piece of bacon hovering in midair. Her face was lit up with happiness, so different than it had been the night before. An almost orgasmic look of contentment came over her as she breathed in the scent of bacon.

'What?' she said, meeting my dorky stare with a raised eyebrow.

'Um, nothing. Want some?' I pushed the bacon into the center of the table, then remembered the vegetarian thing and pulled it back. 'Oh, right. Sorry.'

'Hey, no problem.' She put down her backpack. 'I'm not a vegan or anything.'

'Um, Lace, this is bacon. That's not a judgment call on the plant-or-animal issue.'

'Thanks for the biology lesson. But like I said, it smells good, and I'm going to enjoy it.' She sat down across from me.

I smiled. On the excellent-smell front, Lace's scent was much more powerful in person. I let myself breathe it in, carefully sampling it in between bites. I had expected her staying in my apartment to be torture every minute, but maybe it was worth fighting my urges, just for this simple pleasure.

Still, I ate fast to keep the beast in check.

'So,' I asked, 'are you one of those fake vegetarians?'

'No, not fake. I haven't eaten meat in, like, a year?' She frowned at the plate of seared flesh and dumped a tub of potato salad and a brand-new toothbrush onto the table from a paper bag. 'But the whole vampire thing has been very stressful, and that smell *is* comforting, like Mom cooking up a big breakfast. It takes me back.'

'That's natural. When humans were evolving, the smelling part of our monkey brains got assigned to the task of remembering stuff. So our memories get all tangled up with smells.'

'Huh,' she said. 'Is that why locker rooms make me think of high school?'

I nodded, recalling my descent under the exhaust towers, how powerfully the scent of the huge hidden thing had affected me.

Maybe I'd never smelled anything like the beast before the day before, but some fears went deeper than memory. As deep as the parasite's traces hidden in my marrow.

Evolution is a wonderful thing. Somewhere back in prehistoric time, there were probably humans who actually *liked* the smell of lions, tigers, or bears. But those humans tended to get eaten, and so did their kids. You and I are descended from folks who ran like hell when they smelled predators.

Lace had opened her tub of potato salad and was digging in with a plastic deli fork. After a few bites, she said, 'So, what's with the face?'

'Oh, this.' I touched the bandage gingerly. 'Remember how I warned you about cats?'

Lace nodded.

'Well, I went down into the Underworld through your swimming pool this afternoon. And I managed to catch . . . Um, what's wrong?'

Lace looked like she'd bitten down on a cockroach. She blinked, then shook her head. 'Sorry, Cal. But are you wearing a *Garth Brooks T-shirt?*'

I glanced down at my chest. Through the muck and puckered claw marks, his smiling face looked back at me. I'd been too hungry coming in to take a shower or even change my shirt. 'Uh, yes, it is.'

'Ashlee Simpson, and now Garth Brooks?'

'It's not what you think. It's really more sort of . . . protection.'

'From what? Getting laid?'

I coughed, bits of bacon lodging in my throat, but I managed to swallow them. 'Well, it has to do with the parasite.'

'Sure, it does, Cal. *Everything's* about the parasite.'

'No, really. There's this thing that happens to peeps: They hate all the stuff they used to love.'

She paused, a forkful of potato salad halfway to her mouth. 'They do *what*?'

'Okay, let's say you're a peep. And before you got infected you loved chocolate – the parasite changes your brain chemistry so that you can't even stand to look at a Hershey's Kiss, the way movie vampires are afraid of crucifixes.'

'What the hell is that all about?'

'It's an evolutionary strategy, so that peeps hide themselves. That's why they live underground, to escape signs of humanity, and the sun too. A lot of them really do have cruciphobia – I mean, are afraid of crosses – because they used to be religious.'

'Okay, Cal.' She nodded slowly. 'Now this is the part where you explain what this has to do with Garth Brooks.'

I grabbed a piece of bacon, which was starting to glisten as it cooled, and chewed quickly. 'Records, the department that helps us with investigations, found out that some of the folks who lived on your floor were Garth Brooks fans. So they gave me this shirt in case there was an encounter underground. Which there was.'

Her eyes widened. 'Dude! A peep did that to your face?'

'Yeah, this scratch here was a peep. But this one here was a cat – Morgan's cat, probably – that sort of put up a fight.'

'Sort of? Looks like you lost.'

'Hey, I made it home tonight. The cat didn't.'

Her expression froze. 'Cal, you didn't *kill* it, did you?'

'Of course not.' My hands went up in surrender. 'I don't kill when I can capture. No vampires were harmed in the making of this film, okay? Jeez, vegetarians.' I grabbed another strip from the plate.

'So this infected cat is where?' Lace glanced at the closet where PNS had spent the previous night.

'Elsewhere,' I said, chewing. 'I left it with the experts; they're testing to see if it can spread the disease to other cats or not. And the good news is that a Night Watch team is already cleaning up the rats under your building. It may take a few days to seal off that swimming pool, but then you can go home.'

'Really?'

'Yes. They're professionals, since 1653.'

'So you found Morgan?'

'Well, not her. But you don't have to worry about Morgan. She disappeared.'

Lace crossed her arms. 'Sure, she did.'

I shrugged. 'We can't find her, okay?'

'And it's really safe in my apartment? You're not just saying that to get rid of me?'

'Of course not.' I paused. 'I mean, of *course* it'll be safe. And of course *not* on the getting-rid-of-you part, which I wouldn't do. I mean, you can stay here as long as you want . . . which you won't need to, of course, because it's safe at home and everything.' I managed to shut up.

'That's great.' Lace reached across the table and took my hand. The contact, the first since I'd pulled her over the balcony, sent an electric shock through me. She smiled at my expression. 'Not that it's been totally horrible, dude. Except for not having any of my stuff, commuting all the way from Brooklyn, and having your heavy-ass cat lie on me all night. Other than that, it's been kind of . . . nice. So thanks.'

She let go of me, and I managed to smile back at her while scraping up the last shards of bacon from the plate. I could still feel where she'd touched me, like the flush of a sunburn coming up. 'You're welcome.'

Lace looked down at her potato salad unhappily. She dropped her fork. 'You know what? This stuff sucks, and I'm still hungry.'

'Me too. Starving.'

'You want to go somewhere?'

'Absolutely.'

Lace waited for me to shower and change, then took me over to Boerum Hill, one of the original Brooklyn neighborhoods. The elegant old mansions had been split up into apartments, and the sidewalks were cracked by ancient tree roots pushing up beneath our feet, but there were still old-school touches. Instead of numbers, the streets had Dutch family names – Wyckoff and Bergen and Boerum.

'My sister lives pretty close,' Lace said. 'I remember a couple of good places around here.'

She followed the street signs hesitantly, letting memories fall into place, but I didn't mind wandering along beside her. Moonlight lanced through the dense cover of ancient trees, and the cold air was filled with the smell of leaves rotting on the earth. Lace and I walked close, the shoulders of our jackets touching sometimes, like animals sharing warmth. Out here in the open air it wasn't so intense, being close to her.

We wound up at an Italian place, with white tablecloths and waiters wearing ties and aprons, candles on the tables. It smelled gorgeously of flesh, smoked and seared and hanging from the ceiling. Meat all over.

It was so much like a date, it was weird. Even before the parasite switched off my romantic life, taking women to fancy restaurants hadn't been my thing. I found myself thinking about the fact that everyone who saw us would assume we were dating. I pretended for a while in my head that they were right, pushing the awful truth to the back of my mind.

When the waiter came around, I ordered a pile of spicy sausage, the perfect dish to beat my parasite into overfed submission. The night before it had taken forever, but I'd finally reached a deep sleep. Maybe tonight it would be easier.

'So, dude, aren't you worried about that?' She was looking at my wounded cheek again. Dr. Rat's bandage had slipped off in the shower, and I hadn't bothered to replace it. The scar gave me a rakish doesn't-know-how-to-shave look.

'It's not bleeding, is it?' I dabbed the spot with a napkin.

'No, it doesn't look bad. But what if it got . . . infected or something?'

'Oh, right,' I said. Lace, of course, didn't know that I didn't have to worry about the parasite, having already been there and done that. I shrugged. 'You can't get the disease from scratches. Only bites.' This was more or less true.

'But what if it was licking its paws?' she said, quite sensibly.

I shrugged again. 'I've had worse.'

Lace didn't look convinced. 'I just don't want you turning all vampire on me in the middle of the night . . . Okay, that sounded weird.' She looked down, her fingers realigning the silverware on the crisp white linen.

I laughed. 'Don't worry about that. It takes at least a few weeks to go killing-and-eating-people crazy. Most strains take a lot longer.'

She looked up again, narrowing her eyes. 'You've seen it happen, haven't you?'

I paused for a moment.

'Dude, no lying to me. Remember?'

'All right, Lace. Yes, I've seen someone change.'

'A friend?'

I nodded.

A satisfied expression crept onto Lace's face. 'That's how you got into this Night Watch business, isn't it?'

'Yeah. That's right.' I looked at the other tables to see if anyone was listening, hoping that Lace didn't go much further with this line of questioning. I could hardly tell her that my first peep experience had been with a lover; she knew the parasite was sexually transmitted. 'A friend of mine got the disease. I saw her change.'

Oops. Should I have said *her*?

'So, it's like you said when you were pretending to be a health guy – you're following a chain of infection. You're tracking down all the people who caught the disease from that friend of yours. Morgan was someone who slept with someone who slept with your friend who turned, right?'

Now I was playing with my own silverware. 'More or less.'

'Makes sense,' she said softly. 'Today I was thinking that some people must find out about the disease on their own, just by accident, like I did. So the Night Watch has to recruit them to keep the whole thing a secret. And that must be where you guys get new staff. It's not like you can advertise in Help Wanted, after all.'

'No shit, Sherlock.' I tried to chuckle. 'You're not looking for a job, are you?'

She was silent for a moment, not answering my little jest, which made me extremely nervous. The waiter arrived with two steaming plates, uncovering them with a flourish. He hovered over us, grinding pepper onto Lace's pasta and pouring me more water. The smell of sausage rose up from my plate, switching my still-hungry body into a higher gear. I dug in the moment the waiter left, the taste of cooked flesh and spices making me shudder with bliss.

Hopefully, the uncomfortable questions were done with. I watched as Lace wound a big gob of spaghetti onto her fork, a process that seemed to absorb all her concentration, and as the silence stretched out and the calories entered my bloodstream, I told myself to chill.

It wasn't so surprising that Lace had spent a whole day thinking about my revelations of the night before. It was crazy to get all jumpy about a few obvious questions. As the sausage suffused my system, placating the parasite, I began to relax.

Then Lace spoke up again. 'I mean, I wouldn't want *your* job. Mucking around in tunnels and stuff. No way.'

I coughed into my fist. 'Um, Lace . . .'

'But you've got those guys who gave you the building plans, right? Records, you called them? And you have to research the history of the sewers and subways and stuff. I was thinking about that today. That's why I went into journalism, you know.'

'For the sewer research?'

'No, dude. To find out what's really going on, to get behind the scenes. I mean, there's this whole other world that no one knows about. How cool is that?'

I put my fork and knife down firmly. 'Listen, Lace. I don't know if you're serious, but it's out of the question. The people who work in Records come from old families; they grew up with this secret history. They can speak Middle English and Dutch and identify clerks who lived centuries ago by their handwriting. They've all known one another for generations. You can't just show up and ask for a job.'

'That's all very impressive,' she said, then smirked. 'But they suck at finding people.'

'Pardon me?'

Lace's grin grew wider as she wound another spindle of spaghetti onto her fork, then put it into her mouth, chewing slowly. Finally, she swallowed.

'I said they suck at finding people.'

'What do you mean?'

'Let me show you something, dude.' She pulled out a few folded photocopies from her inside jacket pocket and handed them to me. I pushed my empty plate aside and unfolded them on the white tablecloth.

They were the floor plans to a house, a big one. The labels were written by hand in a flowing script, and the photocopies had that gray tinge that meant the originals had been on old, yellowing paper.

'What is this?'

'That's Morgan Ryder's house.'

I blinked. 'Her what?'

'Her family's, actually, but she's staying there now.'

'No way.'

'Way, dude.'

I shook my head. 'Records would have found her already.'

Lace shrugged, her fork twirling, the last strands of spaghetti on her plate trailing like a satellite picture of a hurricane. 'It wasn't even that hard. All I had to do was go through the phonebook, calling all the Ryders, asking for Morgan. The first dozen said there was nobody there by that name. Then one of them got all paranoid and asked me who the hell I was.' She laughed. 'I got nervous and hung up.

'That doesn't prove anything.'

Lace pointed at the papers in my hand. 'That's the place, according to the address in the phone book. It's even in the historical register – belonged to the Ryders since it was built.'

I stared at the plans, shaking my head. There was no way this could have gotten past Records; the Mayor's office would have checked with her family directly. 'But she's not there. She's missing, like I said.'

'You said pale? Dark hair and kind of gothy?'

I opened my mouth, but it took a while for sound to come out. 'You *went* there?'

Lace nodded, beginning to wind another spindle of pasta.

'Of course, I didn't knock on the door. I'm more into investigation than confrontation. But the house has these big bay windows. And the weirdest thing is, Morgan doesn't look crazy at all. Just bored, sitting at the window and reading. Do peeps read, dude?'

I remembered the photos Chip had given me and pulled them from my jacket. Lace took one glance at Morgan's and nodded. 'That's the girl.'

'It can't be.' My head was swimming. The Night Watch couldn't have screwed up like this. If Morgan was sitting around in plain view, someone would have spotted her. 'Maybe she has a sister,' I muttered, but darker thoughts were already coursing through my mind. The Ryders were an old family. Maybe they were pulling strings, using their connections to keep her hidden. Or maybe Records was afraid to go after the Mayor's old friends.

Or maybe I'd filled out the wrong damn form.

Whatever had happened, I felt like an idiot. Everyone always joked about how we hunters were too lazy to do our own research, waiting for Records or the Health and Mental moles to tell us where the peeps were. I'd never even thought to open a phone book and look for Morgan Ryder myself.

'Don't look so bummed, dude,' Lace said. 'Morgan might not be infected, after all. I mean, she looked all normal. I thought you said peeps werc maniacs.'

Still dazed, I shook my head and answered, 'Well, she could be a carrier.'

Too late, I bit my tongue.

'A carrier?' Lace asked.

'Um, yes. Carries the disease, but without the symptoms.'

She paused, spaghetti dangling from her fork. 'You mean, like Typhoid Mary? Spreading typhus all over the place but never coming down with it?' Lace laughed at my expression. 'Don't look so surprised, dude. I've been reading about diseases all day.'

'Lace, you have to stop *doing* this!'

'What? Acting like I have a brain? Puh-lease.' She took a bite. 'So there are people who just carry the parasite? Infected but not crazy?'

'Yes,' I said, swallowing. 'But it's very rare.'

'Huh. Well, there's one way to find out. We should go over there.'

'*We?*'

'Yeah, we're practically there already.' She hooked her thumb toward the door, another satisfied grin spreading across her face. 'It's right at the end of this street.'

Ryder House filled an entire corner lot, a three-story mansion with all the trimmings: bay windows, tall corner turrets, widow's watches peering down at us with arched eyebrows. In the moonlight, the house had an intimidating look – a little too well maintained to play the part of the haunted manor, but a good headquarters for the bad guys.

I reached into my jacket pocket to heft the cold metal of my knockout injector. I'd reloaded it after taking down Patricia Moore and had decided not to hand it over to the transport squad when I'd turned in my duffel bag. However much Chip complained, sloppy equipment-keeping sometimes had its advantages.

'And you're *sure* it was her?'

'Totally, dude.' Lace pointed at a bay of three windows bulging out from the second floor. 'Right up there, sitting and reading. So what do we do? Knock on the door?'

'*We* don't do anything!' I said harshly. 'You go back to my apartment and wait.'

'I can wait here.'

'No way. She might see you.'

'Dude, it's too dark.'

'Peeps can see in the dark.' I hissed.

Lace's eyes narrowed. 'But she's like Typhoid Mary, right? No symptoms.'

I groaned. 'Okay, with typhus, that's true. But peep carriers do have some symptoms. Like night vision and good hearing.'

'And they're really strong too, aren't they?'

'Listen, just get out of here. If she – ' My voice dropped off. From the darkness beneath the Ryders' bushes, a pair of eyes had just blinked at us, glinting in the moonlight. 'Crap.'

'What is it, Cal?'

My eyes scanned the shadowed street. In the bushes, under cars, from a high window in the mansion, at least seven cats were watching us.

'Cats,' I whispered.

'Oh, yeah,' Lace said, her voice also dropping. 'I noticed that this afternoon. The whole neighborhood's crawling with them. Is that bad?'

I took a slow, deep breath, trying to channel Dr. Rat's quiet confidence. It would take generations for the parasite to adapt to new hosts, to find a path from cat to cat. The creatures watching us could be just normal felines, the brood of a crazy cat-lady, not a vampire. Maybe.

Then one of the cats' eyes caught the light of a passing car, flashing red for a fraction of a second. I tried to swallow, but my mouth was dry.

Most predators have a reflective layer behind their eyes that helps them see in the dark. But cats' eyes reflect green or blue or yellow, not red. It's *human* eyes that give off red reflections, as we've all noticed in bad photographs.

These cats were . . . special.

'Okay, Lace, I'm going to sneak in there. But you *have* to go back to my place. I'll come home and tell you everything I see.'

Lace paused for a moment, thoughts racing across her face. 'But what if you get caught? You said Morgan can hear really well.'

'Yeah, maybe. But this is my job, okay?' I felt the reassuring weight of the injector in my pocket. 'I know how to deal with peeps.'

'Sure, dude, but how about this: While I'm walking home, I could lean on a few parked cars, get some alarms going for you. Maybe that'll cover up your noise.'

'Good idea.' I took her shoulder. 'But don't stick around. It isn't safe here.'

'I'm not sticking around. Do I look stupid?'

I shook my head and smiled. 'Actually, you're pretty damn smart.'

She smiled back. 'You have no idea, dude.'

Around the corner and out of Lace's sight, I chose a four-story brownstone to climb. The outthrust stone sill of a second-floor window was an easy jump, and its chimney was pocked with missing bricks and old slapdash repairs – perfect handholds. It took about ten seconds for me to reach the top, so fast that anyone watching from a nearby window wouldn't have believed their eyes.

From the roof, I had a good view of the back side of Ryder House. As Lace's plans had indicated, a balcony jutted out from the highest floor, its wrought-iron doors closed over darkened glass. All I had to do was get to the building next door to the Ryders' and climb down.

I dropped to the next roof, leaped an eight-foot alleyway, then scaled the next building, winding up perched a few yards above the Ryders' balcony, where I took off my boots. Even after Lace got some car alarms started, I'd have to step carefully. Three-century-old houses have a way of being creaky.

The cold began to numb my feet, but my peep metabolism fought back, churning from nervousness and all that meat in my stomach. I waited, rubbing my feet to keep them warm.

A few minutes later, the first car alarm began to wail, then more, building like a chorus of demons. I shook my head as the cacophony spread, getting the distinct impression that Lace was enjoying herself.

That girl was trouble.

I dropped onto the balcony softly, its cold metal slats sending a shiver up my spine. The lock on the wrought-iron door was easy to pick.

Inside was a bedroom, the big four-poster covered with a white lace spread. It didn't smell of peep at all, just clean laundry and mothballs. I crossed the wooden floor carefully, testing every step to avoid any squeaky boards.

A strip of light showed under the door, but when I pressed my ear to it, I heard nothing except the wailing alarms down on the street. According to the plans Lace had copied, the next room had been a small servants' kitchen back in the olden days.

The door opened without creaking, and I slipped through. So far, the house looked very normal – the kitchen counters were crowded with the usual pots and pans. There wasn't anything weird, like sides of raw beef hung up and dripping blood into the sink.

But then my nose caught the scents wafting from the floor.

Fourteen mismatched bowls stood in a row, licked clean but smelling of canned cat food – salmon and chicken and beef tallow, malted barley flour and brewer's rice, the tang of phosphoric acid.

Fourteen – one peep cat was a hopeful monster; fourteen were an epidemic.

Voices filtered up through the shrieking alarms, and the house creaked as people walked across one of the floors below me. I crossed the kitchen carefully, taking advantage of the car alarms while I still could. One by one, they were being switched off, replaced by a chorus of dogs barking in retaliation. Soon enough, the neighborhood would return to peace and quiet.

I crept into the hallway and leaned over the banister, trying to distinguish words amid the chatter downstairs. Then recognition shivered through me . . . I heard Morgan's voice. Lace had been right. My progenitor was really here.

My hands tightened on the banister, and I shut my eyes, all my certainties falling away. Had Records really screwed up, or was someone in the Night Watch helping Morgan hide?

The last car alarms had been silenced, so I decided to crawl down the stairs on my stomach. I crept forward in inches, moving only during bursts of laughter or loud conversation below.

There were at least three other voices besides Morgan's – another woman and two men. The four of them were laughing and telling stories, flirting and drinking, the clink of ice rattling in their glasses. I could smell an open bottle of rum, the alcohol molecules wafting up the stairs. One of the men began to sweat nervously as he told a long joke. They all laughed too hard at the punch line, with the anxious sound of people who've just met one another.

I couldn't smell Morgan, which hopefully meant she couldn't smell me. In any case, I'd just showered, and although my jacket still carried a whiff of the Italian place, the rum and aftershave of the two men downstairs would drown it out.

The last car alarm choked off into silence outside.

I inched forward on my belly, oozing down the steps like a big slug, and soon I could see their shadows moving on the floor. Just one more step down and I would be able to peer into the parlor.

Through the slats of the banister, I finally saw her – Morgan Ryder, dressed in coal black against pale skin, swirling a drink in her hand. Her eyes glittered, her whole attention focused on the man sitting next to her. The four of them had broken into two conversations, two couples.

Then I realized who the other woman was: Angela Dreyfus, the final missing person from the seventh floor. Her eyes were wide with perpetual surprise, set in a face as thin as a *Vogue* model's. And her voice sounded dry and harsh, even though she kept sipping from her drink. She had to be parasite-positive. And yet Angela Dreyfus was sane, cogent, flirting coolly with the man sitting beside her on the overstuffed couch.

Another carrier.

My head spun. That made three of us: Morgan, Angela, and me, out of the people who'd been infected in Lace's building. But only one percent of humans has natural immunity, so it should take a population of hundreds to make three carriers. But here we had three out of five.

That was one hell of a statistical fluke.

Then I remembered Patricia Moore talking to me almost coherently after the knockout drugs had hit her, just as Sarah had. And how Joseph Moore had braved the sunlight, hunting with such determination. None of them had been your standard wild-eyed vampire.

Cats, carriers, and non-crazy peeps. My strain of the parasite was more than just a hopeful monster; this was a pattern of adaptations.

But what did they all add up to?

Something stirred the air behind me, and my muscles stiffened. Soft footsteps fell on the stairs above, so light that the centuries-old boards didn't complain. A sleek flank brushed against my legs, and tiny clawed feet strode across my back.

A cat was walking over me.

It stepped from my shoulders, then sat on the step below my head, looking directly into my eyes, perhaps a bit puzzled as to why I was snaking down the stairs. I blew on it to make it go away. It blinked its eyes in annoyance but didn't budge.

I stole a glance at Morgan, but she was still focused on her man, touching his shoulder softly as he made them all more drinks. At the sight, a surge of random jealousy moved through me, and my heart began to beat faster.

Morgan and Angela were seducing these men, I realized, just as Morgan had seduced me; they were spreading the strain.

Did they *know* what they were doing?

The cat licked my nose. I suppressed a curse and tried to give the creature a shove down the stairs. It just rubbed its head against my fingers, demanding to be scratched.

Giving up, I began to stroke its scalp, sniffing its dander. Just like the cat beneath Lace's building, it had no particular smell. But I watched its eyes, until they glimmered in the light from below. Bloodred.

I lay there, unable to move, still nervously petting the peep cat as Angela and Morgan flirted and joked and drank, readying the unknowing men to be infected. Or eaten? Were they pretty enough? The cat purred beneath my fingers, unconcerned.

How many more peep cats were out there? And how had this all happened here in Brooklyn, right under the nose of the Night Watch?

After an interminable time, the peep cat stretched and padded the rest of the way downstairs. I started to think about slinking back up to the servants' kitchen and escaping. But as the cat crossed the floor toward Morgan, my heart rose into my throat.

It jumped into her lap, and she began to stroke its head.

No, I mouthed silently.

A troubled look crossed Morgan's face. She fell silent, bringing her hand up and sniffing it. A look of recognition crossed her face.

She peered at the stairs, and I saw her eyes find me through the banister.

'Cal?' she called. 'Is that *you*?'

We carriers never forget a scent.

I scrambled to get upright, dizzy from the blood gathered in my head.

'Cal from *Texas*?' Morgan had crossed to the bottom of the stairs, her drink still in her hand.

'There's someone up there?' one of the men asked, rising to his feet.

As I stumbled backward up the stairs, Angela Dreyfus joined Morgan at the bottom. My knockout injector only carried one load, and these women weren't wild-eyed peeps; they were not only as strong and fast as me, they were as smart.

'Wait a second, Cal,' Morgan said. She put one foot on the bottom step.

I turned and bolted up the stairs, racing through the kitchen and the bedroom. Footsteps followed, floorboards creaking indignantly, the old house exploding with the sounds of a chase.

Bursting out onto the balcony, I leaped up and grabbed the edge of the next roof, pulling myself over and snatching up my boots. Still in my socks, I took the one-story drop that followed, sending a stunning jolt up my spine. I stumbled and fell, rolling onto my back as I yanked my boots back on.

Springing to my feet, I jumped across the eight-foot alleyway and scrambled up onto the roof of the brownstone. I paused for a moment, looking back at Ryder House.

Morgan stood on the balcony, shaking her head in disappointment.

'Cal,' she called, her voice not too loud – perfectly pitched for my peep hearing. 'You don't know what's going on.'

'Damn right I don't!' I said.

'Wait there.' She slipped off her high-heeled shoes.

A door slammed somewhere below me, and I took a step back toward the front edge of the brownstone, glancing over my shoulder. A flicker of movement on the street caught my eye. Angela Dreyfus was moving through the shadows, a squad of small, black forms slinking along beside her.

They had me surrounded.

'Crap,' I said, and ran. I leaped to the next building and raced across it, meeting a dead end: an alley fifteen feet across. If I didn't make the jump, I'd be sliding down a windowless brick wall to the asphalt, four stories below.

A fire escape snaked down the back of the building, where a high fence surrounded a small yard. I pounded down the metal stairs, taking each flight with two quick jumps, my thudding footsteps making the whole fire escape ring. Once on the ground I scrambled across the grass and over the fence into another yard.

I kept moving, jumping fences, stumbling over stored bicycles and tarp-covered barbecue sets. At the opposite corner from Ryder House, a narrow alley full of garbage bags led out to the street – only a ten-foot-high iron fence and a spiral of razor wire between me and freedom.

I tossed my jacket over the wire, then climbed the wet plastic bags, sending rats scurrying in all directions. The mountain of garbage swaying beneath me, I jumped, rolling over the fence, feeling the razor wire compress like giant springs through the jacket.

Then the street rushed up to meet me like an asphalt fist.

Bruised and gasping for breath, I rolled over, listening for the sounds of Morgan following me. There was nothing except the footsteps of the still-scattering rats. I scanned the streets, but Angela was nowhere to be seen.

A single cat was watching me, however, peering out from underneath a parked car. Its eyes flashed red.

Scrambling to my feet, I tried to pull my jacket off the razor wire, but it stayed caught. Abandoning it, I started limping hurriedly in the opposite direction from Ryder House, the wind cutting through my T-shirt, my right elbow bleeding from the fall.

One block later, a cab stopped for my raised hand and I jumped in, shivering like a wet dog.

An epidemic was loose in Brooklyn.

My apartment was dark. I flipped the light switch but nothing happened.

I stood there shivering for a moment, my eyes adjusting to the gloom.

'Hello?' I called.

In the glow of the DVD-player clock, I saw a human form sitting at the kitchen table. The smell of jasmine was in the air.

'Lace? Why are the lights – ?'

Something zoomed through the air at me.

My hands shot up and caught the missile, plastic and soft. I looked at it, dumbfounded – my spatula, generally used for flipping pancakes.

'Um, Lace? What are you doing?'

'You can see in the dark,' she said.

'I . . . oh.'

She hissed out a breath. 'You dumb-ass. Did you think I'd forgotten about when you swung me across to Freddie's balcony?'

'Well – '

'Or that I didn't notice when you *sniffed* that thing on my wall? Or that you eat nothing but meat?'

'I had some bread tonight.'

'Or that I wouldn't bother to follow you for half a block, and watch you climb up a fucking *building*?'

Her voice cracked at the last word, and I smelled her anger in the room. Even Cornelius had been quieted by its force.

'We had a deal, Cal. You weren't supposed to lie to me.'

'I didn't lie,' I said firmly.

'That is such *crap*!' she shouted. 'You're a carrier, and you didn't even tell me there *was* such a thing until tonight!'

'But – '

'And what did you say to me? "A *friend* of mine slept with Morgan." I can't believe I didn't see through that. A friend, my ass. You got it from her, didn't you?'

I sighed. 'Yeah, I did. But I never lied to you. I just didn't bring it up.'

'Listen, Cal, there are certain things you're supposed to mention without being asked. Being infected with vampirism is one.'

'No, Lace,' I said. 'It's one of those things I have to hide every day of my life. From everyone.'

She was silent for a moment, and we sat in the darkness, glaring at each other.

'When were you going to tell me?' she finally asked.

'Never,' I said. 'Don't you get it? Having this disease means never telling anyone.'

'But what if . . .' she started, then shook her head slowly, her voice dropping to a whisper. 'What if you want to sleep with someone, Cal? You'd have to tell them.'

'I can't sleep with anyone,' I said.

'Jesus, Cal, even people with HIV have sex. They just wear a condom.'

My heart was pounding as I repeated the bleak dogma of Peeps 101. 'The parasite's spores are viable even in saliva, and they're small enough to penetrate latex. *Any* kind of sex is dangerous, Lace.'

'But you . . .' She trailed off.

'In other words, Lace, it just can't happen. I can't even kiss anyone!' I spat these last words at her, furious that I was having to say this all out loud, making it real and inescapable again. I remembered my pathetic little fantasy at the restaurant, hoping someone might mistake us for a couple, confusing me for a normal human being.

She shook her head again. 'And you didn't think this would be important to me?'

My pounding head reverberated with this question for a while, remembering the sound of her breath filling the room the night before. 'Important to you?'

'Yeah.' She stood and dragged her chair under the overhead light, climbed up onto it, and screwed the bulb back in. It flickered once in her hand, then stayed on.

I squinted against the glare. 'I guess *everything's* important to you. Do you want to read my diary now? Go through my closet? I told you practically everything!'

Lace stepped down from the chair and crossed to the door. Her backpack lay there, already full. She was leaving.

'Practically everything wasn't enough, Cal,' she said. 'You should have told me. You should have *known* I'd want to know.' She took a step closer, placed a folded piece of paper on the table, and kissed me on the forehead. 'I'm really sorry you're sick, Cal. I'll be at my sister's.'

My mind was racing, trapped in one of those nightmarish hamster wheels when you know it *really matters* what you say next, but you can't even get your mouth open.

Finally, a flicker of will broke through the chaos. 'Why? Why do you care if I'm sick?'

'Christ, Cal! Because I thought we had something.' She shrugged. 'The way you keep looking at me. From the first time we saw each other in that elevator.'

'That's because . . . I *do* like you.' I felt my throat swelling, my eyes stinging, but I was not going to cry. 'But there's nothing I can do about it.'

'You could have told me. It's like you were playing a game with me.'

I opened my mouth to protest but realized that she was right. Except I'd been mostly playing the game with myself, not admitting how much I liked her, trying to forget the fact that it was bound to come to this – her feeling disappointed and betrayed, me caught in my deception, sputtering hopelessly.

But I didn't know how to say all that, so I didn't say anything at all.

Lace opened the door and left.

I sat there for a while, trying not to cry, clinging to that minuscule place inside me that somehow managed to be quietly pleased: Lace had liked me too. Yay.

Some time later I fed Cornelius and got ready for a long night awake in the throes of optimum virulence. I unhid my spore-ridden toothbrush and got out all the Night Watch books I'd secreted away, returning the apartment to how it had been before Lace had arrived. I even sprayed the couch with window cleaner, trying to erase her scent.

But before I went to sleep I looked at the folded piece of paper she'd left behind. It was a cell-phone number.

So I could call and tell her when her building was safe? Or when I was ready to send a replacement spaghetti strainer? Or was it an invitation to a *really* frustrating friendship?

I lay down on the futon and let Cornelius sit on my chest, comforting me with all his fourteen pounds, and getting ready to relish these questions and others as they danced behind my eyelids for the next eight hours.

Wait, did I say eight hours?

I meant four hundred years.

Imagine dying from a mosquito bite.

About two million people every year do just that, thanks to a parasite called plasmodium. Here's how it works:

When an infected mosquito bites you, plasmodium is injected into your bloodstream. It moves through your body until it reaches your liver, where it stays for about a week. During that time it changes into a new form — sort of like a caterpillar turning into a butterfly.

Did I say butterfly? Actually, it's more like a microscopic tank. Plasmodium grows treads that allow it to crawl along your blood vessel walls, and it develops a sort of missile launcher on its head. This launcher helps the parasite blast its way into one of your red blood cells.

Inside the blood cell, plasmodium is safe, hidden from your immune system. But it stays busy. It consumes the insides of the cell and uses them to build sixteen copies of itself. Those burst forth and go on to invade more of your blood cells, where they each make sixteen *more* copies of themselves . . .

You can see where this might become a problem. This problem is called malaria.

Getting malaria sucks. As your blood cells are

consumed by plasmodium, you get chills, then a high fever that comes back every few days. Your liver and spleen expand, and your urine turns black with dead blood cells.

It gets worse. All those blood cells are supposed to be carrying oxygen through your body. As they get turned into plasmodium-breeding factories, the oxygen stops flowing. Your skin turns yellow, and you become delirious. If your malaria remains untreated, you'll eventually go into a coma and die.

But why is plasmodium so nasty? Why would a parasite want to kill you, when that means that it too will die? This seems to go against the law of optimum virulence.

Here's the thing: Humans can't give one another malaria, because most people don't bite each other. So to infect other humans, plasmodium needs to get back into a mosquito.

This is trickier than it sounds, because when a mosquito bites you, it only sucks a tiny, mosquito-size drop of blood. But plasmodium doesn't know *which* drop of blood will get sucked, so it has to be *everywhere* in your bloodstream, even if that winds up killing you.

In this case, optimum virulence means total domination.

But plasmodium isn't completely lacking in subtlety. Sometimes it takes a break from killing you.

Why? Because if too many humans in one place get malaria at the same time, it might wind up killing them all. This would be very bad for plasmodium; it needs a human population to keep breeding. So every once in a while, plasmodium plays it cool. In fact, one strain can hang around inside you for as long as thirty years before it makes its move.

It lets you think that you're okay, but it's still there, hiding in your liver, waiting for the right moment to unleash its engines of destruction.

Clever, huh?

I woke up in a foul mood, ready to kick some ass.

I started with Chip in Records.

'Hey, Kid.'

'Okay, first thing: *Don't* call me Kid!'

'Jeez, Cal.' Chip's big brown eyes looked hurt. 'What's with you? Didn't get enough sleep last night?'

'No, I didn't. Something about Morgan Ryder living half a mile away kept me awake.'

He blinked. 'You did what now?'

I sighed as I sat down in his visitor's chair. I'd been practicing that dramatic line all the way here, and Chip was looking at me like I was speaking Middle Dutch. 'Okay, Chip. Listen carefully. I found Morgan Ryder, my progenitor, the high-priority peep that you guys have been looking for since the day before yesterday. In the *phone book*!'

'Huh. Well, don't look at me.'

'Um, Chip, I *am* looking at you.' It was true. I was looking at him. 'This is Records, is it not? You guys do have phone books down here, don't you?'

'Sure, but – '

'But you've been messing with me, haven't you?'

He raised his hands. 'No one's messing with you, Cal.' Then he leaned forward, lowering his voice a bit. 'At least, no one in Records is. I can tell you that.'

I stopped, mouth already loaded with my next

sarcastic remark. It took me a moment to switch gears. 'What do you mean, no one in Records?'

He looked over his shoulder. 'No one *in Records* is messing with you.'

The ceiling fan squeaked overhead.

'Who?' I whispered.

Chip took a breath and gestured me closer. 'All I can say is, that case got lifted from us.'

'Define *lifted*.'

'Transferred to a higher level. High priority, like you said. After you found out her last name, certain individuals told us to track down the other three missing persons but to leave Morgan Ryder alone. They wanted to handle her special.'

A little shudder went through me. 'The Mayor's office?'

Chip said nothing, which said everything.

'Um, does that happen a lot?'

Chip shrugged unconvincingly. 'Well . . .' He chewed his lower lip. 'Actually, it doesn't happen that much. Especially not this way.'

'Which way?'

He leaned even closer, his whisper barely audible above the squeaking of the ceiling fan. 'With no one telling you about it, Cal. You see, we were supposed to be copied on any info that the Mayor's office found and then pass it along to you. But you weren't supposed to know that we'd been pulled off the case. And I'm not supposed to be telling you this *now*, in case you haven't figured that out yet.'

'Oh.' I leaned back heavily in Chip's spare chair, my righteous anger turning to mush. Yelling at Chip was one thing, but busting in to raise hell with the Night Mayor was something I couldn't visualize. Four-hundred-year-old vampires have that effect on me.

So this *was* a conspiracy. But the Night Mayor? He was the head guy, the big cheese. Who would he even be conspiring against?

All of us? The whole Night Watch?

Humanity?

I leaned over the desk again. 'Um, Chip? Seeing as how you weren't supposed to tell me this, maybe we should pretend that you didn't?'

Chip didn't say a word, just pointed to the biggest of the many signs on his bulletin board – even bigger than the WE DO NOT HAVE PENS sign – and I knew absolutely that our secret was safe.

In large block letters were the words WHEN IN DOUBT, COVER YOUR ASS.

Next, I went to see Dr. Rat.

If I could trust anyone at the Watch, it would be her. Unlike the Shrink and the Mayor, she wasn't a carrier. She hadn't been alive for centuries and didn't give a rat's ass about the old families. She was a scientist – her only loyalty was to the truth.

Still, I decided to proceed a little more cautiously than I had with Chip.

''Morning, Dr. Rat.'

''Morning, Kid!' She smiled. 'Just the guy I wanted to see.'

'Oh, yeah?' I forced a smile onto my face. 'Why's that?'

She leaned back in her chair. 'Those peeps you brought in yesterday – did you know they can *talk*?'

I raised an eyebrow. 'Sure, of course. Patricia Moore spoke to me.'

'I've never seen anything like it before.'

'What about Sarah? She talked to me.'

Dr. Rat shook her head. 'No, Cal, this is different. I mean, a lot

x

of peeps become lucid for a few moments after you hit them with knockout drugs. But those two you caught yesterday have been having flat-out *conversations*.'

I sat down heavily. 'But they're husband and wife. What about the anathema? Shouldn't they start screaming at the mere thought of each other?'

'That's what you'd think.' She shrugged. 'But they've been calling from one holding pen to another. As long as they don't actually *see* each other, they're fine.'

'Is it the drugs?'

Dr. Rat pursed her lips. 'After one night? No way. And as far as I can tell, this isn't the first time they've had these conversations. I think they were *living together* down in that tunnel – sharing the hunting duties, talking to each other in the darkness. Damnedest thing I've ever seen. They're practically . . .' She trailed off.

'Sane?' I said softly.

'Yeah. Almost.'

'Um, except for the cannibals-living-in-a-tunnel part?'

Dr. Rat shook her head again. 'We didn't find any human remains in that tunnel, Cal. They were just eating pigeons. Come to think of it, those skulls in Sarah's lair dated at more than six months old. That's why it took so long to find her – she'd stopped preying on people, had switched over to eating rats.'

'Eww. Ex-boyfriend sitting right here.'

She flashed her don't-be-a-wuss look at me. 'Yeah, well, rat consumption is a lot better than eating people. I think your strain is . . . different.'

'What about, "So pretty I had to *eat him*"?'

Dr. Rat sat back down at her desk, spreading her hands. 'Well, maybe the onset symptoms of the strain are just as bad as a normal peep's. But eventually the parasite settles down. It doesn't seem to turn people into raving monsters . . . not forever anyway.'

I nodded. That theory fit with what I'd seen of Morgan and Angela Dreyfus the night before.

'Maybe we caused this,' Dr. Rat said softly.

'Huh? We who?'

'The Night Watch. It's hard for crazed peeps to run amok in a modern city, especially with us on the case. So this could be an adaptation to the Night Watch. Maybe you're part of a whole new strain, Cal, one that has a lower level of optimum virulence – the peeps are less violent and insane, the transmission usually sexual. It's more likely to survive in a city organized to catch maniacs.'

'So more than one in a hundred people would be immune?'

'Sure.' Dr. Rat nodded slowly. 'Makes sense, really. Except for the cat-worshipping.' She noticed the change in my expression and frowned. 'You okay, Cal?'

'Um, I'm great. But did you just say "cat-worshipping"?'

'Yeah, I did.' Dr. Rat smiled and rolled her eyes. 'Those two you caught yesterday will *not* shut up about the peep cat. Is kitty okay? Can they see it? Is it getting enough food?' She laughed. 'It's like the anathema in reverse; like maybe they used to hate cats and now they love them – I don't know. Weird mutation, huh?'

'*Mutation?* A cat-worshipping mutation? One that appears at exactly the same time as a cat-infecting mutation?' I groaned. 'Doesn't that seem like too much of a coincidence to you, Doctor?'

'But it's still just a coincidence, Kid.'

'How can you be so sure?'

'Because the peep cat isn't viable.' She stood and walked to the far wall, where a pile of cages were filled with various cats, all of whom had the scruffy, streetwise look of strays. 'See these little guys? Since yesterday I've been trying to produce transmission from the peep cat to one of them . . . and *nothing*. Doesn't matter if they lick each other, eat from the same bowl. Zilch. It's like trying to force two mosquitoes to give each other malaria; it's hopeless.'

'But what about transmission through rats?'

She shook her head. 'I've been testing that too. I've tried biting, ingestion, even blood transfusion, and I haven't gotten the parasite to move to a single rat, much less from rat to cat. That peep cat is a dead end.'

I had to bite my lip to keep from arguing. The peep cat *wasn't* a dead end; I knew about a dozen others. But how could I explain about them to Dr. Rat without telling her everything I'd seen the night before? If I told her about Ryder House, I'd have to mention Morgan and Angela, and how I'd found them . . . which would mean bringing up what Chip had told me about the Mayor's office. And once I admitted my suspicions about the Night Mayor, I'd have to start my own counterconspiracy.

Suddenly my racing mind was halted by the smell of Dr. Rat's lair, a scent that had been conspicuously absent the night before: rats. Ryder House had been so clean. No piles of garbage, no reeking decay. No sign at all of a brood of rodents.

'What if rats don't matter?' I said softly.

She snorted. 'You found a huge brood down in the tunnel, Cal.'

'No, that's not what I mean. Those rats carry the parasite, sure. They were the reservoir. But what if they weren't the vector for the peep cat getting infected?'

'But I told you, it doesn't travel from cat to cat. So what else is left?'

'Humans.'

She frowned.

'What if this strain really is like malaria?' I continued. 'Except with cats instead of mosquitoes? Maybe it just bounces back and forth between felines and people.'

Dr. Rat smiled. 'Interesting theory, Kid, but there's one problem.' She crossed to the cage where the peep cat lay calmly watching us and stuck a finger in through the bars.

'Um, Dr. Rat, I wouldn't do that . . .'

She chuckled; the cat was sniffing her finger, its whiskers vibrating. 'This cat isn't violent. It doesn't bite.'

My hand went to my cheek. 'Are you forgetting what it did to my face?'

Dr. Rat gave a snort. '*Any* cat will attack if you get it mad enough. And anyway, that's a scratch, not a bite.' She turned back to the cat, rubbing its forehead through the wires of the cage. It closed its eyes and began to purr.

'But the cats are important somehow!' I shouted. 'I know they are!"

She turned to face me. 'The *cats*? Plural?'

'Oh.' I cleared my throat. 'Well, potentially plural.'

Dr. Rat narrowed her eyes. 'Cal, is there something you're not telling me?'

There were lots of things I hadn't told her. But at that moment a horrible thought crossed my mind . . .

'Wait a second,'I said. 'What if the strain spreads between cats and humans *without* biting? How would that work?'

Dr. Rat's suspicious expression didn't waver, but she answered me. 'Well, it could happen in a few ways. Remember toxoplasma?'

'Who could forget toxoplasma? It's in my brain.'

She nodded. 'Mine too. Toxoplasma spores are airborne. Cats leave them in the litter box, then they go up your nose. But that would only work from cat to human, not the other way around. For two-way transmission, you and a cat would have to breathe on each other a lot at short range . . .'

I remembered something Dr. Rat had said the day before, and my stomach did a back flip. 'You mean, if the cat stole your breath?'

She smiled. 'Like in those old legends where cats were demons? Yeah. That might work.' A frown crossed her face. 'And you know, those old stories date from around the time of the plague.'

'Yeah. Plague.'

Dr. Rat's eyes widened. My face must have been turning odd colors. 'What did I say, Cal?'

I didn't answer. A small but horrible memory had drifted through my mind, something Lace had said the night before.

'Yeah,' I said softly, 'really nice.'

'What's really nice?' said Dr. Rat.

'I have to go now.'

'What's wrong, Cal?'

'Nothing.' I stood shakily. 'I have to go home is all.'

She raised an eyebrow. 'Feeling sick?'

'No, I'm fine. This conversation just reminded me, though . . . My cat is, um, unwell.'

'Oh.' She frowned. 'Nothing serious, I hope.'

I shrugged, dizzy from standing up too fast. My throat was dry. What I was thinking could not be true. 'Probably not too serious. You know how cats are.'

The cab ride back to Brooklyn was the most unpleasant twenty dollars I'd ever spent. I stared out the window as we soared across the Williamsburg Bridge, wondering if I'd gone insane. Wondering if Cornelius had really contracted the disease from me.

The old cat had never bitten me, hadn't even scratched me in the last year

Airborne, Dr. Rat had said.

That had to be nuts. Diseases transmitted by fluids didn't just suddenly become airborne. If they did, we'd all die from Ebola, we'd all get rabies from a walk in the woods, we'd all be carrying HIV . . .

We'd all be vampires.

Of course, diseases change. Evolution never sleeps. But my strain was too well developed to be brand-new. It infected cats, turned its victims into feline-worshippers and carriers, created smarter and saner peeps. A whole raft of adaptations.

And those ancient legends about cats stealing breath – those stories were seven hundred years old. If this strain had been around for seven hundred years, where had it been hiding?

Then I remembered the pale rats below the surface, buried deep until the reservoir had bubbled up beneath the PATH train. Could they have been down there in the darkness for centuries, keeping an ancient strain of the parasite hidden?

And the foul thing I'd smelled but not encountered down there. What did a hidden strain of the parasite have to do with that unseen subterranean creature?

The ride took forever, my sweating palms leaving hand-prints on the vinyl seats, the sunlight flashing through the struts of the bridge, the taxi meter ticking like a time bomb, and the memory that had struck me in Dr. Rat's office replaying, Lace's voice saying again and again: 'Except for not having any of my stuff, commuting all the way from Brooklyn, and *having your heavy-ass cat lie on me all night*. Other than that, it's been kind of . . . nice.'

'Yeah. Really nice,' I whispered again.

*

I picked up a flashlight at the dollar store on the way home.

'Here, kitty, kitty!' I called as the door swung open. 'It's nummy-time.'

For a moment I heard nothing and wondered if Cornelius had somehow figured out that I knew his secret and had escaped my apartment for the wider world. But then he padded out from the bathroom to greet me.

I switched on the flashlight, shining it straight into his eyes . . .

They flashed bloodred. He blinked at me and cocked his head.

I crumpled to the floor, dropping the flashlight. In addition to all my girlfriends, I'd infected my own cat. How much did that suck? 'Oh, Corny.'

He meowed.

After a whole year, how had I not noticed his eyes? Of course, with my night vision, I almost never kept the lights on. Cornelius came to rest his head on my knee and let out a soft meow. I rubbed him, stoking up a good purr.

'How long?' I wondered aloud.

Probably for most of the last year. Cornelius always slept with me on the futon, and I couldn't count the number of times I'd woken up with him perched on my chest, bathing me in Crunchy Tuna breath. He could have contracted the parasite even before I'd noticed the changes in myself.

Maybe it had been through him that Sarah had been infected. She'd always complained of his bladder-crushing weight in the morning.

Maybe the sex had been irrelevant. Maybe she'd been his peep, not mine. Maybe Lace was already . . .

I stood up and fed Cornelius, going through the motions on autopilot, fighting off panic. She'd only spent one night here, after all. And even if she'd been infected, it wouldn't be as bad as

Sarah. This was an early diagnosis. I just had to get her into treatment as soon as possible.

Of course, getting her into treatment meant going to the Night Watch and admitting that I'd committed a Major Revelation Incident. And telling them everything I'd seen out in Brooklyn, and that the Mayor's office was covering something up. And trusting them with Lace's life, when I didn't even trust them to use the phone book anymore.

I began to realize just how badly everything was about to crumble. The Night Watch had been corrupted and the parasite had gone airborne, helped along by Morgan Ryder – a new Typhoid Mary, with the added bonus of feline familiars.

Even if Lace wasn't already infected, I had to warn her. No matter how nonviolent Patricia and Joseph Moore might seem at the moment, someone had eaten the guy in 701 and turned his guts into graffiti.

I remembered the motivational computer simulations Dr. Rat had shown in Peep Hunting 101 – showing how we were help-ing to save the world. On their way to being epidemics, diseases reach something called *critical mass*, the point at which chaos begins to feed upon itself – roving peeps in the streets, garbage-men afraid to go to work, garbage piling up, rats breeding and biting – more peeps. Except that this strain would include nerv-ous people getting cats to save them from the rats, and the cats making more peeps . . .

You get the picture. In the days and weeks ahead, the time bombs set by Morgan and Angela would begin to explode into temporary cannibals. New York City was going to get nasty.

I took a deep breath. I couldn't think about all that yet. The first thing I had to do was find Lace and test her for early signs of infection. I took her cell-phone number from where it lay on the table and dialed.

She answered on the first ring. 'Lace here.'

I swallowed. 'Hey. It's me, Cal.'

'Oh. Hi, Cal.' Her tone sounded flat. 'That was fast.'

'Um, what was fast?'

'What do you think? You calling me was fast, dumb-ass.'

'Oh, right,' I said. 'Well, I had to.'

'You did?' Her voice gave a hint of interest.

'Yeah . . . something's come up.'

'Like what, dude?'

'Like . . .' *You have contracted a deadly disease. Soon, you may begin to eat your neighbors – but don't worry, you will eventually switch to pigeons, or perhaps rats.* 'Um, I can't really talk about it on the phone.'

She groaned. 'Still with the top secret, huh? Need-to-know basis?'

'Yeah. But this is something you *really* need to know.'

There was a long pause, then a sigh. 'Okay. I was kind of hoping you'd call. I mean, maybe I was a little bit hard on you last night. But I was kind of angry with . . . the way things are.'

'Oh. Right.' I had the feeling she was about to get angrier.

'Okay. So where and when?'

'Right now. Except I'm out in Brooklyn. Twenty minutes?'

'Okay. I'm hungry anyway. How about that diner where we ate before? Where was that?'

'Bob's? Broadway and Eleventh. See you there. And thanks.'

'For what?'

'Not hanging up on me.'

A pause. 'We'll see.'

We said good-bye and disconnected. Lace had sounded so normal, I thought, allowing myself to hope. Maybe it took a peep cat more than one night to spread the parasite. Or maybe I was grasping at straws. If she'd been infected the night before last, the only symptom Lace would display so far would be a slight increase in night vision.

I headed for the door.

'*Meow*,' Cornelius cried. He was lying in my way.

'Sorry, Corny. Can't stay.'

He yowled again, louder.

I slid him away from the door with my foot. 'Move. I have to go.'

He scrambled over my boot and back to the door, still yowling.

'You can't go out, okay?' I yelled and picked him up, planning to step out and then toss him back through from the other side. He started to struggle.

'What's your *problem*?' I said, pulling open the door.

Morgan and Angela stood there, grinning from ear to ear.

'How did you find me?' I finally managed.

'*I* don't forget the names of people I sleep with, Cal Thompson,' Morgan said.

'Oh.'

'And I thought that looked like you on the tapes, monkeying around in the basement of my old building, being all brave and daring.' Morgan laughed and turned to Angela. 'Cal's from Texas.'

'Yeah, you told me,' Angela said.

'And look, he has a *kitty*!' Morgan said, reaching out to tickle Cornelius's chin. 'Isn't it cute?'

'Yes, he is,' I answered, and threw Cornelius in her face.

I followed the yowling ball of cat through the door, whipping the knockout injector from my pocket. Angela's hands went up to defend herself, the injector hissing as the needle sank into her forearm.

'You Texas butt-head!' she shouted, then crumpled to the floor.

I ignored the squawling mass of cat and Morgan and headed for the stairs.

Halfway down, Morgan's voice echoed through the stairwell. 'Stop, Cal! You're being a pain!'

I kept running, taking each flight of stairs with a single, bone-jarring leap.

'Your Night Watch isn't going to help you now, you know!' she called, her sneakers squeaking on the concrete steps behind me.

I'd already figured that much was true; I didn't trust the Night Watch anymore. But I wasn't about to trust the person who'd infected me either. From now on, I was on my own.

Reaching the last flights of stairs, I ran through the lobby and burst out the front doors of my building, hoping that by some miracle a cab would be waiting there. The street, of course, was empty of cabs.

But not of cats.

There were dozens of them, maybe a hundred, perched on postboxes and garbage bags, crowding the stoops across the street, all watching me with the same expression of mild amusement.

My knees grew weak, and the world went dizzy; I almost fell to the concrete. But Morgan was right behind me. I pulled my belt from around my waist and cinched it through the curving handles of the front door. Then I took a few deep breaths until the faintness passed.

The cats around me hadn't moved. Maybe Dr. Rat was right – they were nonviolent.

Seconds later, Morgan approached the other side of the glass door, grabbed the inside handles, and pulled. The belt held tight.

It would take her a while to wear down the leather, or for some random passerby to let her out.

I stumbled back from the door.

'Cal!' she called, her voice muffled through the glass. 'Stop!'

I shook my head and turned to walk down the street, ignoring her cries.

'Cal!' The sound faded behind me.

The cats watched placidly, no concern in their expressions. But somehow their collective gaze kept me from running – some threat implicit in their eyes suggested that if I disturbed the quiet street, they would turn into an angry horde and devour me.

So I walked slowly, feeling their red-flickering eyes with every step.

Another two blocks up was Flatbush Avenue, busy and normal and not overrun with cats. I stuck out my shaking arm and hailed a taxi to Manhattan.

Halfway across the bridge, my phone rang. It was the Shrink.

'Kid, we need to talk.'

'*Don't* call me Kid!'

There was a long silence on the other end. Evidently, the words had surprised the Shrink just as much as they had me.

'Um, if you don't mind?' I added lamely.

'Certainly. . . Cal.'

I frowned. 'Hey, wait a second. I thought you didn't like talking on phones.'

'I don't, but the world is changing, Cal. And one must adapt.'

I wanted to point out that telephones were *so* 1881 – not exactly cutting edge – but the Shrink's choice of words froze the remark in my mouth.

'The world is changing?' I said hoarsely.

'You hadn't noticed?'

'Um, I'd say there's been some weird stuff going on.' I cleared my throat. 'And I'm starting to feel like nobody's keeping me in the loop.'

'Well, perhaps you're right. Perhaps we haven't been fair to you.'

The cab slowed as the bridge descended into Chinatown, and a few moments of reception crackle interrupted the conversation. Ahead of me were crowds of workday pedestrians – all within arm's length of one another – a perfect breeding ground for infection and for sudden violence spinning out of control.

When the rattle in my ear subsided, I said, 'And you're going to tell me what's going on?'

'Of course. I, for one, have always wanted you to know what's going on. I've always trusted you, Cal. But you see, you're so very young compared to the rest of us.'

'The rest of the Night Watch?'

'Not the Watch. We carriers, Cal, with all those centuries behind us. And those of us in the old families. Some thought you wouldn't understand the way things were changing.' She sighed. 'I'm afraid we've been treating you as a bit of a human.'

'Um, last time I checked, I was one.'

The Shrink laughed. 'No, Cal, you're one of us.'

I groaned, not wanting to get into some weird semantic argument. 'Could you just tell me what's going on!'

'I'll let her tell you.'

'Her who?'

'Just get where you're going. Don't worry. She'll be there.' *Click*. She'd hung up.

How did the Shrink know where I was going? I couldn't imagine the Mayor's office having tapped my phone. That was *way* too high-tech for them. Then I remembered Cornelius sitting by the door, yowling. He'd smelled Morgan out there, which meant that Morgan could have heard my conversation with Lace. I replayed it in my mind . . . Bob's on Broadway and Eleventh, I had helpfully said aloud.

She would be waiting? But who was *she*?

I dialed Lace's number on my cell, but there was no answer. *Out of service*, the recorded voice said. We were approaching Houston, the cars around us slowing to a walking pace. I paid, jumped out, and ran toward Broadway and Eleventh, trying to untangle the meaning of the Shrink's call.

The Shrink knew that I knew. My first thought was that Chip had broken his promise and talked to the Mayor's office, but then Morgan's words at my door came back to me: '*I* don't forget the names of people I sleep with, Cal Thompson.'

Morgan knew that I had forgotten her last name, something the Shrink had always chided me about. But how would Morgan have known that, unless someone had told her?

They were all in it together – Morgan Ryder, the Shrink, and the Night Mayor, along with the other carriers and the old families of New York – all of them knew something about my strain of the parasite and what it meant. They had kept me in the dark from the beginning.

And if it hadn't been for Lace's detective work, I would *still* be in the dark.

Lace . . . I thought, speeding up.

Rebecky greeted me at the door. 'Hey, Cal! Hungry again already?'

I tried not to pant. 'Yeah. Meeting someone.'

'So I noticed.' Rebecky winked. 'I never forget a face. She's right back there.'

I nodded and headed toward the rear corner table, still breathing heavily, still dizzy, still trying to put together everything I had to explain to Lace, so harried and distracted that it wasn't until I'd *thunk*ed myself down into the booth that I realized the girl sitting across from me wasn't Lace.

It was Sarah.

20. THE PARASITE OF MY PARASITE IS MY FRIEND

Here is the story of how parasitic wasps saved twenty million lives.

But to tell the tale, first you get to hear about mealworms, a kind of insect that's just as unpleasant as its name. Mealworms aren't very big – a cluster of thousands looks like a tiny white speck. But this single speck can devastate whole continents. Here's how:

The average mealworm has eight hundred kids, almost all of which are female. Each of these offspring can have eight hundred *more* kids. Do the math: One mealworm can produce five hundred million great-grandchildren. And they aren't really worms at all; the young ones can fly, carried from plant to plant on the wind, spreading infection as they go.

Thirty years ago, a species of mealworm rampaged through Africa, attacking a staple crop called cassava and almost starving twenty million people. That's a pretty big death toll for a microscopic parasite. Fortunately, however, cassava mealworms have their own parasite, a species of wasp from South America.

A word about parasitic wasps: *nasty.*

Instead of a stinger, they kill with something called an *ovipositor*, which injects eggs instead of venom. And, believe me, these eggs are much worse than poison. At least with poison, you die fast.

Here's what wasp eggs do to their unlucky hosts: Some hatch into 'soldiers,' which have big teeth and hooked tails. They roam around in the victim's bloodstream, sucking out the guts of any children left by other wasps. (Parasitic wasps are very territorial.) Other eggs hatch into wasp larvae, which are basically big bloated stomachs with mouths. Protected by their soldier siblings, they ravenously consume the host from within, sucking away its juices as they grow into wasps themselves. Once they're big enough to grow wings, the larvae eat their way out into the world and fly off to lay more eggs. The soldiers don't leave, they just stay behind with the dried-up, dying host, having done their duty for their waspy brothers and sisters. (Isn't that sweet?)

So what happened in Africa? Long story short: The crops were saved.

Once the right species of wasp was let loose, the mealworms were dead meat. Mealworms may spread as fast as the wind, but wherever they go, the wasps can follow. Wasps can fly too, after all, and they're pretty much psychic when it comes to finding mealworms. If a single plant in a huge field is infected, the wasps will find the mealworms and inject them with their eggs. No one really knows how wasps track down microscopic mealworms, but some scientists have an intriguing theory:

The infected plant asks for help.

That's right: When a cassava plant is attacked by

mealworms, it begins to send out signals to any wasps in the area. Some unknown chemical rises up and draws the wasps toward it, like a big red highway flare saying, *Help me! Help me!*

Of course, another way to translate the message is: *Mealworms! Get your hot delicious mealworms!*

You could say that the cassava and the parasitic wasp have an evolutionary deal: 'I'll tell you when I'm infected with mealworms, and you come and deposit your deadly eggs in them.'

It's a great relationship, because the parasite of your parasite is your friend.

'Hiya, darling,' Sarah said. 'You're looking good.'

I didn't say anything, paralyzed by the sight of her. Sarah was utterly transformed from my last glimpse before the transport squad had taken her away. Her hair was clean, her fingernails pink and neatly trimmed; there was no demented gleam in her eye. As her familiar scent reached me through the smell of grease and frying eggs, Bob's Diner seemed to shudder, as if time were snapping backward.

She was even wearing a thick black leather wristband, a definite reference to Elvis's 1968 Comeback Special. Very appropriate.

Rebecky slapped down a cup of coffee in front of me, breaking the spell. 'Thought I recognized you,' she said to Sarah. 'It's been a while since you've been in here, right?'

'Been out of town. Hoboken mostly, then a few days in Montana, of all places,' Sarah said, shaking her head. 'But I'm back to stay.'

'Well, good. Looks like Cal here sure missed you.' She patted me on the shoulder, chuckling at my blank expression. 'The usual, Cal?'

I nodded. When Rebecky had gone away, I found my voice. 'You're looking good too, Sarah.'

'Been putting on some weight, actually,' she said, shrugging and taking a huge bite of the hamburger in front of her.

'It suits you,' I said. 'Makes you look more . . .'

'Human?' Sarah grinned.

'Yeah, I guess.' My mind started to struggle for a better word, but an alarm was going off deep in my brain. 'Where's Lace?'

'Lace, huh?' Sarah frowned. 'What kind of name is that?'

'Short for Lacey. Where is she? You guys didn't . . .' I looked around for the Shrink's minders, sniffed the air for other predators. All I smelled was Bob's: potatoes and meat and onions, all turning brown on the grill – and Sarah, who smelled of family.

She shrugged. 'Look, Cal, I don't know who you're meeting here. Dr. Prolix just called me ten minutes ago and told me to come here and talk to you. She thought you'd listen to someone your own age. She said maybe you needed a jolt.'

'Well, mission accomplished on that.'

'And she figured it wouldn't hurt if you saw how well I was doing.'

'Yeah. You look . . . so sane.'

'Am sane. Feels good.'

I shook my head, trying to think straight through the tangle of memories welling up in me. Lace would get here any moment now. Maybe I could run and try to catch her on the way. If Lace said the wrong thing in front of Sarah, the Watch might figure out that she knew too much.

I looked out the window, searching the street for Lace's face among the lunchtime crowds. But my gaze kept coming back to the girl in front of me – Sarah, alive and well and *human*.

I couldn't run yet; I had to know . . . 'What *happened*?'

Sarah chewed a bite of burger thoughtfully, then swallowed. 'Well, first this total *dickhead* gave me a disease.'

'Oh, yeah.' I drank some coffee, frowned at its bitterness. 'I never had a chance to say sorry about that. I didn't know – '

'Yeah, yeah. I guess we're both to blame. Safe sex, blah, blah,

blah.' Sarah sighed. 'Then there was my little . . . breakdown. But you saw most of that.'

I nodded. 'Until you disappeared.'

Sarah took a long breath, staring out the window. 'Well, the parts you missed out on are kind of hazy for me, too. Sort of like a long, bad dream. About being hungry.' She shuddered. 'And eating. Then there you were again, rescuing me.' She smiled tiredly, then took another bite.

'Rescuing you?' I swallowed, never having thought of it that way myself. 'It was the least I could do. But, Sarah, how did you get so normal? So *fast*?'

'Good question, which reminds me.' She pulled out a bottle of pills, dumped two into her palm, and swallowed. 'Two with every meal.'

I blinked. 'There's a cure?'

'Sure. They had me straightened out about six hours after I got to Montana.'

'When did that happen? The cure, I mean.'

'At least seven hundred years ago.'

There it was again, that seven-hundred-year thing. 'The plague? This doesn't make any sense, Sarah.'

'It will, Cal. Just listen up. I'm here to tell you everything. Doctor's orders.' She bit deep into her burger, hurrying now that she was only a few swallows from the end.

'Which doctor? Prolix?'

'Yep, the Shrink. She's been telling me all about what's coming.' Sarah looked out at the crowds on the sidewalk. 'They figured I could take it, because of my personal eating habits lately.' She looked down at her hamburger with momentary suspicion, then took another bite. 'And because they don't have time to mess with me. Or with you, anymore. Time to face facts, Cal.'

Suddenly, the restaurant felt overcrowded, claustrophobic. I could smell the people in the booth behind me, the pressure of the passersby on the street. 'The disease is out of control, isn't it? We're going to wake up one day in one of those zombie-apocalypse movies, the parasite spreading faster than anyone can stop it.'

'No, Cal. Don't be silly. The disease is *in control*, the way it should be. The parasite's calling the shots now.'

'It's doing *what*?'

'It's in charge, making things happen. The way it's supposed to. The Night Watch was always just a holding pattern, keeping down the mutation while waiting for the old strain to come back.'

I shook my head. 'Wait. What?'

Sarah held up her fork and knife, looking from one to the other. 'Okay. There's two versions of the parasite. The new kind and the old kind. Right?'

'Two strains, I know.' I nodded. 'And we've got the new one, you and me.'

Sarah sighed. 'No, dickhead, we have the *old* kind. The original.' She rattled her pill bottle. 'This is mandrake and garlic, mostly. Totally old-school. Until seven hundred years ago, people used to totally control this disease.'

'Until the plague?'

'Bingo. That's when the new strain showed up.' Sarah shook her head. 'You've got to blame the Inquisition for that. You know, when Christians got it into their heads that cats were evil and started killing loads of them? That was bad for the old version of the parasite, seeing as how it jumps back and forth between felines and humans.'

'Right . . . I know about that. But that's the *old* version?'

'Yes. Pay attention, Cal. *As* I was saying, it's 1300 A.D. and everyone's killing cats. So with hardly any cats around, the rat population grows like crazy. More human-to-rat contact, evolution of various diseases, fleas and ticks, blah, blah, blah.' She waved her hand. 'Plague.'

'Um, I think you're skipping over something there.'

She snorted. '*I'm* not the one going for a biology degree. I'm just a philosophy major who eats people. But here's the bio-for-philosophers version: A new strain of the parasite appeared, one that moved back and forth between rats and humans, *without* cats. Of course, as with any new strain, the optimum virulence was a mess; the peeps were much more violent and difficult to control. A total zombie movie, like you said.'

'And the old strain went underground.'

'Very good.' Sarah smiled. 'They told me you'd understand.'

'But that was Europe. This is New York.'

'Rats go everywhere, Cal. They love ships, so of course the new parasites made it to the New World. Even here, the old strain was pushed down into the deep.'

'But now it's coming back up,' I said. 'Why aren't we doing something about it? Why are the old carriers hiding it from the rest of the Watch?'

'Excellent questions.' She nodded slowly, chewing the last bite of her hamburger. 'That's what you scientists never seem to understand: The *whys* are always more important than the *hows.*'

'Sarah, just tell me!'

'Okay.' She placed her palms on the table. 'Feel that?'

I looked at the surface of my coffee; its black mirror reflected the lights overhead with a pulsing shimmer. 'You mean the subway going by?'

She shook her head, her eyes closed. 'Feel deeper.'

I placed my hands on the table, and as the train faded, I felt another, more subtle shudder in its wake. Like something disturbed in its sleep, turning over. Like the trembling I'd felt through my cowboy boots, the first time I'd seen the peep cat.

Sarah opened her eyes. 'Our strain is coming up because it's being *pushed* up.'

I remembered the unseen thing I'd smelled in the Underworld, and the shudder in my hands took over my whole body for a moment. 'By what?'

Sarah lifted her palms from the table, sighed, then shrugged. 'There are a lot of things down there, Cal, things human beings haven't seen in a long time. We lost a lot of knowledge during the plague. But the old guys do know one thing: When the ground starts to tremble, the old strain will rise up. They need us.'

'Wait a second. Who needs *who*?'

'They' – she looked out the window at the passing crowds – 'need us. We're the immune system for our species, Cal. Like those kick-ass T-cells and B-cells you always told me about, we get activated by an invasion. New-strainers are just zombies, vampires. But those of us with the old disease, the carrier strain, we're *soldiers*.'

My mind spun, trying to reconcile what Sarah was saying with what I'd seen Morgan doing, spreading the disease haphazardly, enlisting hordes of cats. 'But why is this a secret? I mean, why didn't this come up in my Night Watch courses? Does Dr. Rat know about it? Or Records?'

'It's older than Records. Older than science. Even older than New York. So the carriers kept it a secret from the Night Watch humans, Cal. It's not going to be pleasant for them, the next few months. But we need all the soldiers we can get. Fast.'

'So you're spreading the disease on *purpose*?' I asked, but Sarah's eyes had left mine, looking over my right shoulder, a pleasant smile filling her face.

A hand fell on me. 'Uh, hey, Cal. Sorry I'm late.'

I looked up. Lace was staring down at Sarah, a little unsure.

'Oh, hi.' I cleared my throat, realizing I'd waited too long; the inevitable collision had happened. 'This is Sarah. My ex.'

'And you must be Lacey.' Sarah extended her hand.

'Uh, yeah. Lace, actually.' They shook.

'Hot stuff, coming through!' said Rebecky, sliding a plate of pepper steak in front of me. Lace sat down next to me, wary of the woman across from her. Rebecky's gaze moved among us, intrigued by the obvious discomfort of it all.

'Coffee, honey?' she asked Lace.

'Yeah, please.'

'Me too,' I said.

'Me three,' Sarah added. 'And another hamburger.'

'And one of those.' Lace pointed at my pepper steak. 'I'm starving.'

'Pepper steak?' I said. 'Oh, crap.'

'Hey, it's not against the law, dude,' Lace muttered as Rebecky walked away.

'What isn't against the law?' Sarah asked, licking her fingers.

'Eating meat,' Lace said. 'Sometimes people change, you know?'

Sarah smiled. 'Oh. Used to be a vegetarian, did you?'

I started in ravenously on my own pepper steak. Otherwise, I was going to faint. 'She was. Until recently.'

Sarah looked from Lace to me, then giggled. 'You've been very naughty, haven't you, Cal?'

'It was Cornelius.'

'Could someone please tell me what's going on?' Lace asked.

Sarah sighed. 'Well, Lacey, things are about to get complicated.'

Lace raised her hands. 'Don't look at me, girl. I never. even kissed this guy. In fact, I'm really pissed at him right now.'

'Oh, poor Cal!' Sarah said. Then she added in a cruel baby voice, 'Did kitty beat you to it?'

'What the *hell* are you guys talking about?' Lace said.

I dropped my fork to the table. Things were spinning out of control, and I had to do something to unspin them. Most important, I had to get Lace out of here, or she would wind up in Montana.

Sweeping Sarah's bottle of pills into my pocket, I pushed Lace out of the booth and dragged her toward the door.

'What the hell!' she shouted.

'Cal,' Sarah called. 'Wait a second!'

'We have to leave,' I hissed to Lace. 'She's one of *them*.'

'What, an old girlfriend? I could tell that.' Lace paused, looking back at Sarah. 'Oh, you mean . . .?'

'Yes!'

'Whoa, dude.'

As we reached the door, I glanced back. Sarah wasn't following us, just watching our retreat with an amused expression. She pulled out a cell phone but paused to wave it at me: *shoo*. For some reason – old loyalty? lingering insanity? – she was giving us time to get away.

The street in front of us was thronged with pedestrians, but I didn't smell any predators among the crowd – just lots of humans crammed together, ready for infection and slaughter. I kept us moving, tugging Lace along in one random direction after another.

'Where are we going, Cal?'

'I don't know,' I said. 'But we have to get out of here. They know about you.'

'Know *what* about me? That you told me all your Night Watch stuff?'

I didn't answer for a moment, trying to think, but Lace pulled me to a stop. 'Cal? Tell me the truth, or I'll have to kill you.'

I glanced behind her – still no signs of pursuit. 'They sent Sarah to find me.'

'And you told her about me?'

'No! *You* did. When you ordered that pepper steak!' I tried to get Lace moving again, but she pulled me to a stop.

'What the hell? What's pepper steak got to do with this?'

'You're starving, right? Feeling faint? And you've been craving meat all day . . .'

She didn't answer, just stood there with eyes narrowed, my words finally sinking in. 'Um, earth to Cal: You and I *didn't sleep together.*'

'Believe me, I know. But you see, there's this new strain . . . I mean, turns out it's an old strain, and it has to do with cats. They're the vectors we have to worry about now.'

Unsurprisingly, this explanation didn't alter Lace's perplexed expression. She just stood there staring back at me. A few passersby bumped into her, but the contact didn't register. Finally, after ten long seconds, she spoke slowly and clearly. 'Are you saying that your fat-ass cat has turned me into a vampire?'

'Um, maybe?' I coughed. 'But I can test you, and we'll know for sure.'

'Dude, you are so dead.'

'Fine, but wait until we find someplace to test you.'

'Someplace like where?'

'Someplace dark.'

Finding pitch blackness in Manhattan isn't easy at noon. In fact, finding pitch blackness in Manhattan isn't easy anytime.

I considered going to Lace's apartment, but if the Watch was looking for us, they were as likely to start there as anywhere. I also thought about renting a hotel room and yanking the curtains closed, but if Lace was infected, there was no point throwing away money. We might be on the run for a while.

The pills were still clutched in my hand; even if Lace was infected, we could control the parasite. I could analyze the garlic-and-mandrake compound and keep her human. We could escape whatever the old carriers had planned for the end of civilization.

'What about a movie theater?' Lace asked.

'Not dark enough.' The light from exit signs always drives me crazy during movies. 'We need cave darkness, Lace.'

'*Cave* darkness? Not a lot of caves in Manhattan, Cal.'

'You'd be surprised.' My nerves twitched as a trembling came through the soles of my boots. We were standing on the sidewalk grates over Union Square station. I pulled her toward an entrance.

I swiped us through a turnstile and tugged Lace down the stairs and to the very end of the platform, pointing into the darkness ahead. 'That way.'

'On the tracks? Are you kidding?'

'There's an old abandoned station at Eighteenth. I've been there before. Plenty dark.'

She leaned over the tracks; a small and scampering thing darted among discarded coffee cups.

'The rats won't bite you,' I said. 'Promise.'

'Forget it.'

'Lace, we subway-hacked all the time in Peep Hunting 101 .'

She pulled away, glanced at the couple on the platform watching us, and hissed, 'Yeah, well, I didn't sign up for that class.'

'No, you didn't. You didn't sign up for any of this. But we have to know if you're infected.'

Lace stared at me, her eyes gleaming darkly, like wet ink. 'What happens if I am a vampire? Do you, like, vanquish me or something?'

'You're not a vampire, Lace, just sick, maybe. And this strain is easy to control. Look.' I pulled the pills from my pocket and rattled them. 'We'll get out of the city. Otherwise, they'll put you into treatment. In Montana.'

'*Montana?*'

I nodded, pointing down the dark tunnel. 'The choice is yours.'

The 6 train rattled into view, and we waited as the platform cleared. I tugged Lace into the security camera blind spot, just next to the access ladder down to the tracks.

She looked down the tunnel. 'And you can cure me?'

'Not cure. Control the parasite. Make you like me.'

'What, all superstrong and stuff?'

'Yeah. It'll be great!' After the cannibal stage was over.

'But the disease will kill me eventually, right?'

I shrugged. 'Yeah. After a few hundred years.'

Lace blinked. 'Dude. Major consolation prize.'

We ran down the middle of the tracks.

'Don't touch that,' I said, pointing down at the wood-covered rail running between our track and the next one over. 'Unless you want to get fried.'

'The famous third rail?' Lace said. 'No problem. I'm a lot more worried about trains.'

'The local just passed. We've got a few minutes.'

'A *few*!'

'The abandoned station's only four blocks away, Lace. I'll know if the rails start rumbling. Supersenses and everything.' I pointed between the columns that held up the streets over our heads, the safe spots. 'And if a train does come, just stand there.'

'Oh, yeah, that looks *totally* safe.'

We charged down the tunnel, and I tried not to notice that Lace wasn't stumbling over the tracks and rubbish, as if the darkness didn't bother her. But it wasn't cave dark yet. Work lights dangled around us, casting our manic and fractured shadows against the tracks.

The express train swerved into view ahead, taking the slow curve with one long screaming complaint. The cold white eyes of its headlights flickered through the steel columns like the light of an old movie projector. In the strobing light, I saw that Lace had come to a halt. The train was on the express track; it wouldn't hit us, but the approaching shriek of metal wheels had paralyzed her.

The wall of metal flew past, whipping Lace's hair around her face and throwing sparks at our feet. Light from the passing windows flickered madly around us, and a few passengers' faces shot by, looking down with astonished expressions. I put my arm around Lace, the rhythm of the train's passage shuddering through our bodies. Its roar battered the air, loud enough to force my eyelids shut.

When the sound had faded into the distance, I asked, 'Are you okay?'

She blinked. 'Dude, that was loud!'

Lace's voice sounded thin in my ringing ears. 'No kidding. Come on, before another train comes.'

She nodded dumbly, and I pulled her the rest of the way to the abandoned station.

The Eighteenth Street station opened up in 1904, the same time as the rest of the 6; part of that turn-of-the-century dig-fest, I suppose.

Back then, all subway trains were five cars long. In the

1940s, with the city's population booming, they were doubled up to ten, which left the old subway platforms a couple hundred feet too short. During the station-stretching project, a few in-between stations like Eighteenth were deemed not worth the trouble and shut down.

The Transit Authority may have forgotten these underground vaults, but they are remembered by a host of urban adventurers, graffiti artists, and other assorted spelunkers. For the next sixty years, the abandoned stations were spray-painted, vandalized, and made the subject of drunken dares, urban myths, and fannish Web sites. They are tourist stops for amateur subterraneans, training grounds for the Night Watch – the twilight zone between the human habitat and the Underworld.

I pulled Lace up onto the dark and empty platform. Six decades of graffiti swirled around us, the once-bright spray paint darkened by accumulated grime. Crumbling mosaic signs spelled out the street number and pointed toward exits that had been sealed for decades. As Lace steadied herself at the platform's edge, she looked around with wide eyes, and my heart sank. It was awfully close to cave darkness here; a normal person should have been waving a hand in front of her face.

'So what now?' she said.

'This way.' Deciding to give her a real test, I led her to the door of the men's bathroom, a relic of sixty years ago. The broken remains of a sink clung to one wall, and the broken wooden doors of the stalls leaned at haphazard angles. The last smells of disinfectant had faded; all that remained was warmish subway air filled with the scent of rats and mold and decay. Distant work lights reflected dimly from the grimy tiles. Even with my fully formed peep vision, I could hardly see.

I pointed into the last stall. 'Can you read that?'

She peered unerringly at the one legible line among the tangled layers of graffiti. For a moment, she was silent, then said softly, 'This is how it all started. Reading something written on a wall.'

'Can you see it?'

'It says, "Take a shit, Linus."'

I closed my eyes. Lace was infected. The parasite must have been working overtime, gathering reflective cells behind her corneas, readying her for a life of nocturnal hunting, of hiding from the sun.

'Who's Linus?' Lace asked.

'Who knows? That's been there for a while.'

'Oh. So what happens now?' she said. 'I mean, Cal, did you bring me down here to . . . get rid of me or something?'

'Get rid – ? Of course not!' I pulled the pills from my pocket. 'Here, take two of these, right now.'

She shook out two and swallowed them, the pills catching for a moment in her dry throat. She coughed once, then said, 'Is it really that dark down here? This isn't some trick you're pulling? I can really see in the dark?'

'Yeah, a normal person would be totally blind.'

'And I got this from your cat?'

'I'm afraid so.'

'You know, Cal, it's not like I had sex with your cat either.'

'But he sat on your chest while you slept and . . . exchanged breath with you, or something. Apparently that's the way the old strain spreads, but nobody ever told me about it. Things are really screwed up right now at the Watch. In fact, things are about to go nuts in general.' I turned her to face me. 'We'll have to get out of the city. There's going to be a lot of trouble as the infections set in.'

'Like you said when you first told me about the Watch?

Everyone biting one another, a total zombie movie? So why not give everyone the pills?'

I chewed my lip. 'Because they want the disease to spread, for some reason. But maybe they'll eventually use the pills, and things will settle down, but until then . . .'

She looked at the bottle, squinting at its label. 'And these really work?'

'You saw Sarah – she's normal now. When I captured her, she was eating rats and hiding from the sun and living in Hoboken.'

'Oh, great, dude,' Lace said. 'So that's what I have to look forward to?'

'I hope not,' I said softly, reaching for her hand. She didn't pull away. 'Sarah didn't have any pills at first. Maybe you'll just go straight to the superpowers. I mean, you'll be really strong and have great hearing, and a great sense of smell, too.'

'But Cal, what about the Garth Brooks thing?'

'Garth Brooks? Oh, the anathema.'

'It makes you start hating your old life, right?'

'Yeah.' I nodded. 'But Sarah's over that too. She was even wearing an Elvis armband.'

'Elvis? What *is* it with your girlfriends?' Lace sighed. 'But the anathema won't happen to me?'

I paused, realizing I didn't know anything for sure. None of my classes had covered the cat-borne strain or the ancient garlic-and-mandrake cure – it had all been kept secret from me. I didn't know what symptoms to look for, or how to adjust the dosage if Lace started to grow long black fingernails or fear her own reflection.

I cleared my throat. 'Well, we'll have to watch for symptoms. Is there anything in particular you really like? Potato salad?' I wracked my brain, realizing how little I knew about

Lace. 'Hip-hop? Heavy metal? Oh, yeah, the smell of bacon. Anything else I should worry about if you start despising it?'

She sighed. 'I thought we covered this already.'

'What? Potato salad?'

'No, stupid.' And then she kissed me.

Her mouth was warm against mine, her heart still beating hard from our dash through the darkness, from the creepiness of the abandoned station, from the news that she would soon turn into a vampire. Or maybe just from kissing me – I could feel it pounding in her lips, full of blood. My own heartbeat seemed to rush into my head, strong enough to pulse red at the corners of my vision.

A predator's kiss: endless, insistent, and my first in six long months.

When we finally parted, Lace whispered, 'You feel like you've got a fever.'

Still dizzy, I smiled. 'All the time. Supermetabolism.'

'And you've got supersmell too?'

'Oh, yeah.'

'Dude.' She sniffed the air and frowned. 'So what do I smell like?'

I inhaled softly, letting Lace's scent claim me, the familiar jasmine of her shampoo somehow settling the chaos of the past twenty-four hours. We could kiss again, I realized, do anything we wanted. It was safe now, even with the parasite's spores in my blood and saliva, because she was infected, just like me.

'Butterflies,' I said after a moment of thought.

'*Butterflies?*'

'Yeah. You use some kind of jasmine-scented shampoo, right? Smells like butterflies.'

'Wait a second. Butterflies have a smell? And it's *jasmine*?'

My body was still humming from the kiss, my mind still

reeling from all the revelations of the day, and there was something comforting about being asked a question I knew the answer to. I let the wonders of biology flow forth. 'It's the other way around. Flowers imitate insects – patterning their petals after wings, stealing their smells. Jasmine tricks butterflies into landing on it, so they carry pollen from one flower to another. That's how jasmine flowers have sex with each other.'

'Dude. Jasmine has sex? Using butterflies?'

'Yeah. How about that?'

'Huh.' She was silent for a moment, still holding me, thinking about all those flowers having butterfly-mediated sex. Finally, she said, 'So when butterflies land on my hair, do they think they're having jasmine-sex with it?'

'Probably.' I leaned closer, burying my nose in her smell. Maybe the natural world wasn't so jaw-droppingly horrible – appalling, nasty, vile. Sometimes nature could be quite sweet, really, as delicate as a confused and horny butterfly.

The subway platform trembled under us again, another train coming. Eventually, we'd have to return to the surface, to face the sunlight and the coming crumbling of civilization, to ride out whatever tumult the old carriers had planned now that the old strain was surging into daylight. But for the moment I was content to stand there, the thought of an apocalyptic future suddenly less panicking. I had something that I'd thought lost forever: another person warm in my arms. Whatever happened next seemed bearable.

'Will the disease make me hate you, Cal?' she asked again. 'Even if I take the pills?'

I started to say I wasn't sure, but in that moment the rumbling underfoot shifted, no longer building steadily. Then it shifted again, like something winding toward us, and among the false butterflies of Lace's hair I caught another scent, ancient and dire.

'Cal?'

'Wait a second,' I said, and took a deeper breath.

The foul smell redoubled, sweeping over us like air pushed up through subway grates by a passing train. And I knew something as thoroughly as my ancestors had known the scents of lions and tigers and bears . . .

A bad thing was on its way.

The next time you go to the doctor, check out the plaques on the wall. One of them, usually the biggest, will be decorated with an intriguing symbol: two snakes climbing up a winged staff.

Ask your doctor what this symbol means, and you'll probably get this line: The staff is called the *caduceus*. It's the sign of Hermes, god of alchemists, and the symbol of the American Medical Association.

But that is only half the truth.

Meet the guinea worm. It hangs around in ponds, too small to see with the naked eye. If you drink guinea-worm-infected water, one of these beasties may find its way into your stomach. From there, it will make its way to one of your legs, working chemical magic to hide from your immune system. It will grow much bigger, as long as two feet.

And it will have babies.

Adult guinea worms may be invisible to your immune system, but their kids have a different strategy – they set off every alarm they can.

Why? Well, overexcited immune defenses are tricky, painful, dangerous things. With all those baby guinea worms raising a ruckus, your infected leg becomes inflamed. Huge blisters appear, which makes you run screaming to the nearest pond to cool them down.

Very clever. The young guinea worms smell the water and pop out of the blisters. Then they settle down to begin their wait for the next unwary drinker of pond water.

Ew, yuck, repeat.

Guinea worms have been pulling this trick for a long time. In fact, it was *thousands* of years ago that ancient healers found out how to cure them. The procedure is simple, in theory. Just pull the adult worms out of the victim's leg. But there's a trick: If you pull too quickly, the worm breaks in half, and the part left inside rots away, causing a terrible infection. The patient usually dies.

Here's how the doctors of the ancient world did it:

Carefully draw one end of the worm out, and wrap it around a stick. Then, over the next seven days or so, wind the guinea worm outward, like reeling in a fish in *very* slow motion. That's right: It takes seven days. Don't rush! It won't be the most enjoyable week you ever spent, but at the end you'll have your body back in good working order. And you'll also have a stick with a wormy thing wrapped around it.

And this icky leftover will become the symbol of medicine.

Ew.

But maybe it's not such a weird symbol. Historians figure that guinea-worm removal was the first-ever form of surgery. Back then, it was probably a pretty amazing feat, pulling a snake out of a human body. Maybe the doctors hung the snake-wrapped stick on their walls afterward, just to show that they could get the job done.

So the next time you're at the doctor's office, be on the lookout for this heartwarming symbol of the ancient healing arts. (And don't believe all that crap about the great god Hermes; it's all about the guinea worms.)

'Stay here,' I said.

'What's up?'

'I smell something.'

Lace frowned. 'Dude. It's not me, is it?'

'No! Hush.' I squatted, pressing my palms flat against the trembling platform. The shudder in the graffitied concrete built, then gradually faded again, tacking toward us, back and forth through the warrens of the Underworld. The hairs on the back of my neck pricked up, sensing a low and shuddering note hanging in the air, the same vast moan I'd heard below the exhaust towers.

'Cal? What the hell?'

'I think something's coming.'

'Some*thing*? Not a train?'

'I don't know what it is, except that it's part of all this craziness. And it's old and big, and . . . getting closer.'

A crumbling exit sign pointed up a set of stairs, but I knew from Hunting 101 that it had been long since paved over. We would have to run back to Union Square along the tracks.

But first I needed a weapon.

I brushed past Lace and through the bathroom stall, kicking away the last pieces of wood clinging to one corner of its metal frame. I wrenched the seven feet of rust-caked iron from the crumbling cement and weighed it in my hands. Brutal and straightforward.

'What about me?' Lace said from the doorway.

'What about you?'

'Don't I get a club-thingy?'

'Lace, you couldn't even pick this up. You don't have super-powers *yet*.'

She scowled at me and lifted a fragment of rusty iron from the floor. 'Well, whatever's coming, it's not catching me empty-handed. It smells like death.'

'You can smell it? *Already?*'

'Duh.' She sniffed and made a face. 'Dead rat on steroids.'

I blinked. Lace was changing faster than any peep I'd ever seen, as if the new strain was mutating at some hyped-up pace, changing as it moved from host to host. Or maybe the beastie simply smelled bad. The stench was overpowering now, sending signals of alarm and fury coursing through my body. Though my mind screamed *run*, my muscles were itching for a fight.

And somehow, I was certain they were going to get one. My instincts sang to me that the creature knew we were here; it was hunting us.

'Let's go,' I said.

We jumped from the platform, landing with a crunch on the gravel bed. As we dashed headlong up the tracks, the lights of the next station glimmered along the curved rails, seeming to pull away from us as we ran. It was only four blocks; and I told myself we were going to make it.

Then I saw – through one of the bolt holes that workers jump into if they get caught by an approaching train – a blackness deeper than the subway tunnel's gloom. A hole in the earth. A few yards closer, a cold draft hit us, goose-pimpling my flesh and carrying another wave of the beast's smell.

'It's coming,' Lace said, nose in the air. She had come to a halt, holding her foot-long piece of iron high, as if she were going to stake a vampire. But this was bigger than any peep, and I was fairly sure that it didn't have a heart.

'Stay behind me,' I said. I pointed toward the opening. 'It'll come out of there.'

Her eyes peered into the blacker-than-black space for a moment. 'So what is this thing again?'

'Like I said, I don't . . .' My voice trailed off, an answer dawning on me. Not so much words or images, but *a feeling* – a generations-forgotten dread, an enemy long buried, a warning never to lose the old knowledge, because the sun can't always protect us from what lives in the lower depths. I felt again the shuddering revelation from my first biology courses, that the natural world is less concerned with our survival than we ever admit. As individuals, even as a species – we are here on borrowed time, and death is as cold and dark and permanent as the deepest fissures in the stones we walk on.

'What is it, Cal?' Lace asked again.

'It's the reason we're here.' I swallowed. The words came from my mouth unbidden. 'Why peeps are here.'

She nodded gravely. 'Is that why I want to kill it so much?'

I might have answered her, but I didn't get a chance, because the thing finally showed its face – if you could call it that. The white-pale, squirming shape emerged into the tunnel without eyes or nose, or discernible top or bottom, just a mouth – a ring of spikes set in a glistening hole, like the maw of some mutant and predatory earthworm, adapted to chew through rock as easily as flesh.

Segments ran down its length, like a rat's tail, and I wondered for a moment if this was just a part of a much greater monster. This white, gelatinous mass emerging from the tunnel might have been its head, or a clawed tentacle, or a bulbous and spiny tongue; I couldn't tell. All I knew was what the parasite inside me wanted: My constant hunger had turned suddenly to boundless energy – *attack*, the parasite demanded.

In a blind fury, I ran toward the beast, the rusty iron in my hands hissing through the air like ancient hatred.

The eyeless beast sensed me coming, its body flinching away, and the tip of my swinging iron barely scraped its flesh, tearing a stringy tendril from its side, which unraveled like a thread pulled from a garment. The tendril flailed angrily, but no blood gushed – all that flowed from the wound was another wave of the beast's smell.

While I teetered off balance, it struck back, the mouth shooting toward me on a column of pale flesh. I stumbled backward, and the teeth reached their limit a few short inches from my leg, gnashing wetly at the air before snapping back into the beast.

I swung again, striking home in the monster's flank and squishing to a halt as if I'd hit a wall of jelly, the impact ringing dully in my hands. The huge pale body wrapped itself around the staff, like a human doubling over from a blow to the stomach.

I tried to pull away, but the iron was firmly stuck, and the toothed maw shot out toward me again. The extended mouth slashed past my legs, one stray tooth catching and ripping my jeans. I jumped straight into the air, stomping down on the appendage with one cowboy boot. My weight forced it to the ground, but its slick hide slipped out from under my foot, toppling me backward onto the tracks. The whole beast uncurled over me, rolling more of itself out from the tunnel to crush me.

Then Lace flashed into view, her iron stake slashing through the air and straight into the ring of teeth. At this contact the creature let out an earsplitting screech. The noise was metallic and grinding, like a sack of nails dumped into a wood-chipper. The beast twisted back, crashing against the subway wall, its bulk dislodging a shower of grit.

Lace pulled me to my feet as I yanked the iron staff free, both of us stumbling backward, certain we'd hurt the thing. But the grinding turned to a violent hissing, and a spray of metal shards shot out from its maw, battering us. The creature's ring of teeth had rendered the iron into shrapnel, which it spat out like a rain of rusty coins. We fell to our knees, and I saw it rearing up again, a new set of teeth jumping out from its hide.

I raised up the iron staff and felt Lace's hands join mine on the weapon.

'The rail!' she shouted in my ear, tugging at the iron. I didn't have breath to answer, but I understood, and let her slide the butt of the weapon toward the edge of the track as the monstrous mass descended, impaling itself. Lace jumped away from the pole; I knew I should let go, but the murderous imperative that had filled me from the moment I'd smelled the creature kept my hands on the weapon, guiding it backward until it lodged firmly against the third rail.

A shower of sparks cascaded from the point of contact, the mad buzz of electrocution sweeping across my body, every muscle locked fast by the wild energies moving through me – enough juice to power a subway train. And yet, despite the pain, all I felt was the satisfaction that the worm, my age-old enemy, was feeling it too, glowing from inside, spiderwebs of red veins pulsing inside its glistening skin.

That pleasure lasted half a second; then Lace was pulling me away by my jacket, breaking my mortal grip on the iron staff. More sparks flew, but the beast didn't make a sound; it just flailed randomly, like some giant, exposed muscle struck with a doctor's hammer again and again. Finally, it pulled itself free, retreating back into its tunnel, leaving behind a burned scent of injury and defeat.

But it wasn't fatally wounded, I somehow knew; it was tougher than that. I swore and fell back on the tracks, shivering.

Lace wrapped her arms around me. 'Are you okay? You smell . . . totally toasted.' She opened my palms, which were black with charred flesh. 'Jesus, Cal. You were supposed to let go.'

'Had to kill it!' I managed through electrocution-lockjaw.

'Chill, dude. It's gone.' She peered up the tunnel. '*And* there's a local coming.'

That focused my mind, and we scrambled into the mouth of the thing's tunnel, pulling out of sight just as the headlights flared around the corner. The train roared past as we cowered together.

'So this is what you feel?' she yelled over the noise. 'When you fight those things?'

'Never saw one before,' I said.

'Really? But it felt . . .' She was breathing deep, her brown eyes wide and gleaming. 'It felt like something we were *supposed* to do. Like that strength you were talking about, when mothers save their kids.'

I nodded. It seemed too soon for Lace, but I couldn't deny how well she'd fought. The worm and the parasite were connected; maybe seeing the beast had accelerated her change.

Since my first sight of the creature, the puzzles of the last few days had begun to solve themselves in the back of my brain. This invasion, these ancient creatures rising up through the century-old cracks in the city's sinews – halting it was what the old, cat-vector strain was *for*. This was why peeps had been created.

There were *more* of those things down here, I could tell – a plague of worms that humanity had faced before. Lace and Sarah and Morgan and I were only the vanguard; we needed lots of help.

Now I understood what Morgan was doing, spreading the old strain of the parasite, massing a new army to face the coming days. And suddenly I could feel a similar imperative surging through my own body – every bit as strong as the six hundred and twenty-five volts from the third rail – something I had suppressed for six long months.

I took Lace's hand. 'Are you feeling what I'm feeling? A sort of post-battle . . .'

'Horniness?' she finished. 'Yeah. Weird, isn't it?'

'Maybe not.' Our lips met again, a kiss as intense as the passing train's thunder in our ears.

24. PARASITES R US
Let us recap:

Parasites are bad.

They suck your blood out of the lining of your stomach. They grow into two-foot-long snakes and roost in the skin of your leg. They infect your cat and then jump up your nose to live in cysts inside your brain, turning you feline-centric and irresponsible. They take over your blood cells in hopes of infecting passing mosquitoes, leaving your liver and brain crumbling from lack of oxygen. They incense your immune system, causing it to destroy your eyeballs. They take terrible advantage of snails and birds and ants and monkeys and cows, stealing their bodies and their food and their evolutionary futures. They almost starved twenty million people in Africa to death.

Basically, they want to rule the world and will crumple whole species like balls of paper and then reshape them in order to carry out their plans. They turn us into walking undead, ravaged hosts that serve only their reproduction.

That's bad. But . . .

Parasites are also good.

They have bred howler monkeys to live in peace with one another. Their lousy genes help track the history of the human species. They prevent cows from overgrazing grasslands into windblown deserts. They tame your immune system so it doesn't destroy your own stomach lining. Then they go and *save* those twenty million people in Africa, by laying their eggs in those *other* parasites, the ones trying to starve them.

Which is all quite good, really.

So parasites are bad and good. We depend on them, like all the other checks and balances of the natural world; predators and prey, vegetarians and carnivores, parasites and hosts all need one another to survive.

Here's the thing: They're part of the *system*. Like government bureaucracies with all those forms that have to be filled out in triplicate, they may be a pain, but we're stuck with them. If every parasite suddenly disappeared from the earth one day, it would be a much bigger disaster than you'd think. The natural order would crumble.

In short, parasites are here to stay, which is a good thing, really. We are what we eat, and we consume them every day, the worms lodged in slices of rare beef or the toxoplasma spores floating up our noses from boxes of cat litter. And they eat us every day too, from ticks sucking our blood to microscopic invaders reshaping our cells. The exchange goes on unendingly, as certain as the earth traveling around the sun.

In a manner of speaking, parasites are us.

Deal with it.

When we pulled ourselves back up onto the subway platform, everyone gave us a wide berth.

You could hardly blame them. We were covered in dust and sweat, our palms reddened with rust, our expressions crazed. And the funny thing was, we were all over each other. Fighting the worm had redoubled my usual implacable desires, and somehow Lace was affected too. We kept stopping just to smell each other, to hold hands tightly, to taste each other's lips.

'This is weird,' she said.

'Yeah. But good.'

'Mmm. Let's go somewhere a little more private.'

I nodded. 'Where?'

'*Any*where.'

We ran up the stairs and into Union Square, crossing the park, walking without a plan. The city seemed weirdly blurry around us. My connection with Lace was so intense, everyone else seemed faded and remote. The parasite's imperative mixed with six months of celibacy screaming inside me, heady and insistent.

I thought about risking her apartment – after all, she'd have to pick up some clothes *some* time – and started to draw Lace toward the Hudson. But then my eyes began to catch glimpses of them. Their smells grew under the current of humanity in the streets.

Predators.

They were spread out across the crowd, walking not much faster than normal humans, but somehow completely different. They moved like leopards through high grass, leaving only the faintest stir behind them. Maybe a dozen, all more or less my age.

No one else seemed to notice them, but their uncanny movements made my head pound. I'd never seen so many carriers in one place before. Night Watch hunters always work alone, but this was a pack.

And the funny thing was, they were really *sexy*.

'Cal . . .?' Lace said softly.

'Yeah. I see them.'

'What are they?'

'They're like us. Infected.'

'The Night Watch?'

'No. Something else.'

By the time I spotted Morgan Ryder, she was already standing in front of us, blocking our path, wearing all black and an amused expression.

'What do we do?' Lace asked, squeezing my hand hard.

I sighed, bringing her to a halt.

'I guess we talk to them.'

'How did you find us?'

Morgan smiled, taking a drink of water before she answered. She'd taken us to a hotel bar on Union Square. The others had kept moving, except for one waiting at the door of the place and cradling a cell phone. Occasionally, he glanced back at her and signaled.

Even with Lace beside me, I was having trouble not staring at Morgan. Memories of the night I'd been infected were rushing back into me. Her eyes were green, I finally recalled. And her black hair set such a contrast, gathered in locks as thick as shoelaces against her pale skin.

'We didn't find you,' she said. 'That is, we weren't looking for you. We were after something else. Something underneath.'

'The worm,' Lace said.

Morgan nodded. 'You smelled it?'

'We *saw* it,' Lace said. 'Took a big chunk out of it too.'

'It was in the old Eighteenth Street station,' I said.

Morgan nodded and made a hand gesture to the carrier in front, and he spoke into his cell phone.

Our beers arrived, and Morgan raised hers into the air. 'Well done, then.'

'What's going on?' I said.

'What? Are you finally going to listen to me, Cal? Not going to run away?'

'I'm listening. And we already know about the old strain and the new, and that we're meant to fight the worms. But what you're doing is crazy – infecting people at random is no way to go about this.'

'It's not as random as you think, Cal.' She leaned back into the plush couch. 'Immune systems are tricky things. They can do a lot of damage.'

I nodded, thinking about wolbachia driving T- and B-cells crazy, your immune defenses eating your own eyeballs.

But Lace hadn't benefited from six months of parasitology. 'How do you mean?'

Morgan held the cold beer against her cheek. 'Let's say you've got a deadly fever – your body temperature is climbing past the limit, high enough to damage your brain. That's your immune system hoping that your illness will fry before you do. Killing the invader is worth losing a few brain cells.'

Lace blinked. 'Dude. What does that have to do with monsters?'

'We're our species' immune system, Lace. Humanity needs a lot of us, and soon. The worms are a lot worse than a few more peeps, and chaos is a fair trade for our protection. It's like losing those brain cells when you get a fever.' Morgan turned to me. 'And it's hardly random, Cal. It's quite elegant, really. As the worms push closer to the surface, they create panic in the Underworld broods; a nervous reaction spreads through the rat reservoirs that carry the old strain. The rats come up through the sewers and PATH tunnels and swimming pool drains. Then a few lucky people, like me, get bitten and we begin to spread the strain. It's happening all over the world, right now.'

'So where's the Night Watch in all this? I mean, who elected *you* the carrier queen? Or whatever?'

'I'm in charge because my family knew what to do, once they saw what I had become. Once I felt the basement calling me, drawing me down.' Her eyelids half closed, fluttering, and she took a slow, deep breath. 'I knew the whole planet was in trouble . . . I was so *horny*.'

Lace and I exchanged a glance.

'As for the Night Watch' – Morgan rolled her eyes – 'they were never more than a temporary measure. I mean, come on, Cal. If you were really fighting to save the world from vampires, you wouldn't keep it a secret, would you?'

'Yeah, that's what I said.' Lace spread her hands. 'You don't hide diseases, you publicize them. And eventually someone comes up with a cure.'

Morgan nodded. 'Which is exactly what the old carriers were afraid of: *science*. A cure for the parasite would erase both peeps and carriers. Meaning that the next time the worms rose up from the Underworld, humanity wouldn't have anyone to protect it –

like switching off your own immune system.' She laughed and took a long drink of beer. 'There's only one logical reason you'd have a secret government organization hunt vampires – if you *wanted the vampires to survive.'*

'Oh.' I gripped my beer glass, certainties falling away all around me. I saw the rows of dusty file cabinets, the ancient pneumatic tubes, the stacks of endless forms. Inefficiency perfected. 'So I've been working for a big joke?'

'Don't be whiny, Cal. The Watch had its uses. By keeping a lid on the new strain, it allowed that to happen.' Morgan pointed out the window at the crowded streets. 'Big old cities are like houses of cards, giant cauldrons of infection waiting to happen. This was always the plan, huge reservoirs of humans, a potential *army* of carriers to take on the ancient enemy.' Morgan's eyes were bright as she downed the rest of her beer, her throat working to empty it. 'We're just the beginning.'

She thumped her glass on the table, laughing, proud that *she* was one chosen to be the harbinger of doom. And I could smell the parasite humming in her, making every man and woman in the room glance in our direction, making their palms sweat. Without knowing it, everyone wanted to join Morgan's army.

The whole thing was madness, but amid all the insanity, one thing kept bugging me. 'Why was I kept in the dark? I'm an old-strain carrier, after all.'

For a moment, Morgan looked sheepish. 'You were. . . um, an accident.'

'A *what*?'

'A little indiscretion of mine. It's not easy, you know, being a sexual vector.'

'Tell me about it. But I was an *accident*?'

She sighed. 'We didn't want the science types at the Night Watch catching on, not until we'd reached critical mass. So we started in a controlled way at first, with our house cats and a few kids from the old families. Except for you, Cal.' Morgan sighed. 'I only wanted a drink that night. But your accent is just so *cute*.'

'So you just infected me?' I closed my eyes, realizing how much this sucked. 'God, you mean I lost my virginity *to the apocalypse*?'

Morgan sighed again. 'The whole thing was really embarrassing; my parents sent me to Brooklyn when they found out.' She shrugged. 'I thought I'd be safe in a gay bar, okay? What were you *doing* in there anyway?'

Lace looked at me sidelong. 'You were where?'

I took a sip of beer, swallowed it. 'I, uh, hadn't been in the city . . . very long. I didn't know.'

'Hmph. Freshmen. Thank God you turned out to be a natural carrier.' Morgan smiled and patted my knee. 'So no harm done.'

'Sure, easy for you to say,' I grumbled. 'Couldn't you have at least told me the truth a little sooner?'

'When those geeks at the Night Watch found you before I did, we *couldn't* tell you right away. It just would have confused your pretty head.'

'So when *were* you going to tell me?' I cried.

'Uh, Cal? Did you miss the last two days? I kept trying. But *you* kept running away.'

'Oh. Right.'

'A freshman?' Lace said, frowning. 'How old are you anyway?'

'Oh, I'm sure he's much more grown up now,' Morgan said, patting my knee again. 'Aren't you, Cal?'

Hoping to move the conversation along, I said, 'So what happens now?'

Morgan shrugged. 'You two can do whatever you want. Run. Stay. Get laid all over town. But you should probably join up.'

'Join up . . . with you?'

'Sure. The New Watch could use you.' She waved for the waitress. 'And I could use another beer. We've been chasing that stupid worm all day.'

I looked at Lace, and she looked back at me. As usual, I didn't know what to say, but the thought of us fighting together, the exhilaration we'd shared down in the tunnel, sure beat the idea of running off to Montana. This was our city, after all, our species.

'What do you want to do, Cal?' Lace said softly.

I took a deep breath, wondering if I was saying too much, too soon, but saying it anyway. 'I want to stay here, with you.'

She nodded slowly, her eyes locked with mine. 'Me too.'

'God, you two,' Morgan said. 'Just get a room.'

I realized that this was in fact a hotel bar, and that Brooklyn or the West Side seemed much too far away right now. I raised an eyebrow.

Lace smiled. 'Dude. Why not?'

The orange was fading from the sky, but through my binoculars, the waters of the Hudson sparkled like teeth capped with gold, the river's choppy surface holding the last dregs of the pollution sunset, which was turning bloodred as it disappeared behind the spiked jaw of New Jersey's skyline.

A warm, insistent body pushed against my ankles, making noises under its breath. I looked down. 'What's the matter, Corny? I thought you liked it up here.'

He looked up with hungry eyes, assuring me that his annoyance had nothing to do with a fear of heights. Just impatience: It was taking the promised nummies too long to arrive.

At first, bringing Cornelius up to the roof had made me nervous, but Dr. Rat says that peep cats have an improved sense of self-preservation. She also talks a lot about feline high-rise syndrome, the magical ability of cats to survive a fall from any height. In fact, with all the time Dr. Rat spends talking about cats these days, she may need a new nickname.

'Don't worry, Corny. She'll be back soon.'

On cue, I heard the scrape of cowboy boots on concrete. A hand reached over the edge of the roof, then another, and Lace pulled herself into view, her face faintly red from the effort.

I frowned. 'Don't you think it's a little light out to be climbing buildings?'

'You should talk, dude!' Lace said. 'At least I wasn't on the street side.'

'Like there aren't a million people on the piers?'

She snorted. 'They're all watching the sunset.'

Cornelius yowled, sensing that our argument was delaying nummies.

'Yes, Corny, I love you too,' Lace muttered, slipping off her backpack and unzipping it. She pulled out a paper bag, which gave off the mouthwatering scent of rare hamburgers.

Cornelius began to purr as Lace opened one of the foil-wrapped burgers for him, laying to one side the pointless bun and wilted leaf of lettuce. He liked the mayo, though, and licked it off her fingers as she placed the hamburger on the black-tar roof. Then he dug noisily into the main event.

Lace looked at her cat-spittled fingers. 'Great. Now I'm supposed to eat with these?'

I laughed, pulling my burger from the bag. 'Relax. Corny doesn't have any diseases. Nothing you haven't already got anyway.'

'Tell me about it,' she said, glancing over the roof's edge. 'What's Dr. Rat always saying? About how cats can fall from any distance?'

'Hey!' I knelt and protectively stroked his flank. He munched away, paying no attention to her threats.

'You're right anyway,' Lace said. 'A fat-ass cat like him would probably leave a crack in the sidewalk, big enough for monsters to get through. Manny wouldn't like that.'

Manny did like Corny, though. Pets weren't officially allowed in Lace's building, but he and the staff had started to make exceptions. With so many people complaining about rat noises in their walls, we'd been lending Cornelius out overnight. A lot of Lace's fellow tenants took us up on the offer, after we'd explained how once a cat gets its dander inside your apartment, rodents will give you a wide berth. You just had to get used to waking up with him sitting on your chest.

This building was on the front line, after all; Lace and I had made it something of a personal project.

Plus, Lace still had that apartment with the cheap rent and the good views. Once Health and Mental had fired off a few nasty memos to her landlords about the rat issue, they'd extended those seventh-floor leases indefinitely. These particular landlords had plenty of money already, having been New York City landowners for almost four hundred years.

Of course, we know that staying in town won't be a cake-walk. New York City can be very stressful. There are rough days ahead, right around the corner. It takes some getting used to, going to Bob's Diner for pepper steak, innocently chatting with Rebecky while fully aware of what's coming next – the melt-down, the crumbling of civilization, the zombie apocalypse.

Or, as they call it in the New Watch these days, the Inflammation.

When the burgers were eaten, I said, 'We should get back to work.'

Lace rolled her eyes, always ready to demonstrate her incredulity that I officially outranked her in the New Watch. But she lifted her binoculars, training them on the red-tinged river. 'So what are we looking for again?'

'Worm signs,' I said.

'No duh. But no one ever tells me, what in fact *are* the signs of a worm?'

I shrugged. 'Worminess?'

She turned from her vigil long enough to stick her tongue out at me.

I smiled and raised my own binoculars. 'You'll know them when you see them. We always do.'

'Sure. But do they even *like* water?'

'Another good question. After all, the PATH tunnel doesn't actually go *through* the water, just under it.' I swept my amplified gaze across to the exhaust towers, the dynamos of subterranean fresh air that had caused this whole turn of the worm. Above the windowless column of bricks, shapes circled in the fading light, their white feathers toasted a dull orange by the sunset. This was a new thing, the wheeling cloud of seagulls that perpetually hovered over the towers. No one knew what it meant.

Some new airborne vector? Mere coincidence? Scavengers sensing a coming kill?

I sighed. 'Sometimes I don't think we actually know anything.'

'Don't worry, Cal,' she said. 'It's still early days.'

The whoop of a siren filtered up from the street, and we ran to the other side of the building, peering down into the darkness. The flash of police-car lights filled the cavern between our building and the one across the street, the pop of radios echoing up. Definitely an arrest.

'Got your badge?' I asked.

'Always. Best part of the job.'

We sometimes have to intervene, when the police are about to take a confused and violent newbie off to jail. We flash our Homeland Security badges and talk some biowarfare crap, and everyone backs off real quick. Ten hours later, the peep is in Montana, hooked up to an intravenous garlic drip and getting the lowdown way too fast.

Of course, newbies take a lot less convincing, these days. The signs are everywhere.

I focused my binoculars, training them on the crowd gathered around the police car. The cops were putting handcuffs on some guy, and a woman was yelling at him, shaking her purse by its broken strap. A wallet and some other stuff lay scattered across the sidewalk. A backup police car rolled down the block at a leisurely speed.

I sighed, lowering the binoculars. 'Looks like a purse-snatching. Just a perp, not a peep.'

One thing you can say for them, peeps don't steal, except for maybe the occasional chunk of meat. They can't think far enough ahead to go for the cash. And it's interesting how, even with the Inflammation going on, regular crime still happens. Maybe more so. End of the world or not, people aren't going to change *that* much.

'Yeah,' Lace sighed, lowering her binoculars. 'This sucks.' Her teeth chewed at her lower lip.

'Don't worry,' I reassured her. 'We'll get some action tonight. We always do.'

'Yeah, whatever.' She shook her head. 'I'm just bummed.'

'Why?'

She let out a long breath. 'Side effects.'

My eyebrows raised. 'From the pills?'

'No, the disease.' Lace turned to me and made a face. 'I don't like potato salad anymore.'

I had to laugh. 'Don't worry. Carbs just don't do it for the parasite.'

'Sure, but what if it's . . . you know, the anathema. What if I'm starting to hate stuff?'

'Is that what you're worried about?' I nodded sagely. 'Well, maybe we should do a little testing, just to make sure.'

I drew her closer, and we kissed. The chill wind kicked up, and Corny padded over to slide figure eights between our ankles, but our mouths stayed locked, warm and unbreakable. So much was changing around us, it was good how this feeling stayed the same.

She still smelled wonderful.

'Hating me yet?' I asked after a while.

'No. In fact . . .' She stopped. 'Whoa. Did you feel that?'

I knelt and placed a palm on the black tar. The slightest rumble filtered up through the fourteen stories of the building. 'Two big ones, fading now.'

'I'll call them in,' Lace said, pulling out her phone, her thumbs darting out a text message to the tracking office.

I sniffed the air, smelling traces of the beasts. Impressive how the scent reached all the way up here, as if the earth were growing more porous every day.

But all I wanted to do was hold Lace again.

'Funny how that happens,' I said. 'How we're always kissing, or about to, when they come around?'

She pressed send, looked up from the tiny screen, and smiled. 'You've noticed that too?'

I nodded slowly. 'Remember, Morgan said she could feel something here, after she'd been infected. She'd sneak down into the basement and the darkness would turn her on. Drive her crazy.'

'That's parasite mind control, right? Making carriers horny so the disease spreads fastest where it's needed most?' Lace smiled, pleased at her own analysis; she was starting to get the biology down.

'Sure, mind control.' I frowned. 'But you and I are already both infected. Why does it care what we do?'

'Maybe it just likes us, dude,' Lace said.

She pulled me close again, and our mouths met. The scent of the worms began to fade, overwhelmed by Lace's jasmine and the salt of the Hudson. We stayed there on the roof for a while, letting the warmth between us build, moved by nothing more than what our bodies wanted from each other. The monsters had passed for now.

Still, part of me is always waiting for the tremors in the earth to come again.

And they will, soon.

You may have seen the signs where you live. Garbage piling higher and higher on the streets. Pale rats scurrying along the subway tracks. Strangers in black trying to pick you up in bars. A red flash in the eyes of your cat, or its weight heavy on your chest in the morning.

But that's nothing. When the epidemic really starts to roll, civilization will crumble, blood will run in the streets, and some of your neighbors may try to eat you. But resist the temptation to buy a shotgun and start blowing their heads off. Just feed them garlic and plenty of sausage, and eventually they'll calm down. You see, they're not the real enemy. Compared to the monsters coming next, those ravening cannibals aren't so bad. In fact, they're on your side.

The real enemy will be close behind, though, and that shotgun won't help you one bit. Nothing in the arsenal of science will avail against these creatures. A lot of us will die.

Don't panic, though. Nature has provided. There has always been a defense against the worms, a disease hidden in the sewers and deep cracks, coursing through the veins of a few old families, waiting for its time to bubble up.

So stock up on some bottled water and a few cans of pasta sauce, maybe the kind with extra garlic. Set aside a few good books and DVDs, and buy a decent lock for your door. Try not to watch TV for a few months – it will only upset you. Don't take the subway.

And leave the rest to us vampires. We've got your back.

THE END

Find out what happens next in the world of *Parasite Positive* in

THE LAST DAYS

by

Scott Westerfeld

About the Author

Scott Westerfeld is a software designer, composer and writer. He lives with his partner, writer Justine Larbalestier, and they divide their time between New York City and Sydney. Visit his website at www.scottwesterfeld.com

For more info about Scott and other Atom authors visit www.atombooks.co.uk

twilight

STEPHENIE MEYER

About three things I was absolutely positive. First, Edward was a vampire. Second, there was part of him – and I didn't know how potent that part might be – that thirsted for my blood. And third, I was unconditionally and irrevocably in love with him.

*

Edward in the sunlight was shocking. I couldn't get used to it, though I'd been staring at him all afternoon. His skin, white despite the faint flush from yesterday's hunting trip, literally sparkled, like thousands of tiny diamonds were embedded in the surface. He lay perfectly still in the grass, his shirt open over his sculpted, incandescent chest, his scintillating arms bare. His glistening, pale lavender lids were shut, though of course he didn't sleep. A perfect statue, carved in some unknown stone, smooth like marble, glittering like crystal.

Now and then, his lips would move, so fast it looked like they were trembling. But, when I asked, he told me he was singing to himself; it was too low for me to hear.

I enjoyed the sun, too, though the air wasn't quite dry enough for my taste. I would have liked to lie back, as he did, and let the sun warm my face. But I stayed curled up, my chin resting on my knees, unwilling to take my eyes off him. The wind was gentle; it tangled my hair and ruffled the grass that swayed around his motionless form.

The meadow, so spectacular to me at first, paled next to his magnificence.

Hesitantly, always afraid, even now, that he would disappear like a mirage, too beautiful to be real ... hesitantly, I reached out one finger and stroked the back of his shimmering hand, where it lay within my reach. I marveled again at the perfect texture, satin smooth, cool as stone. When I looked up again, his eyes were open, watching me. Butterscotch today, lighter, warmer after hunting. His quick smile turned up the corners of his flawless lips.

"I don't scare you?" he asked playfully, but I could hear the real curiosity in his soft voice.

"No more than usual."

He smiled wider; his teeth flashed in the sun.

I inched closer, stretched out my whole hand now to trace the contours of his forearm with my fingertips. I saw that my fingers trembled, and knew it wouldn't escape his notice.

"Do you mind?" I asked, for he had closed his eyes again.

"No," he said without opening his eyes. "You can't imagine how that feels." He sighed.

I lightly trailed my hand over the perfect muscles of his arm, followed the faint pattern of bluish veins inside the crease at his elbow. With my other hand, I reached to turn his hand over. Realizing what I wished, he flipped his palm up in one of those blindingly fast, disconcerting movements of his. It startled me; my fingers froze on his arm for a brief second.

"Sorry," he murmured. I looked up in time to see his golden eyes close again. "It's too easy to be myself with you."

I lifted his hand, turning it this way and that as I watched the sun glitter on his palm. I held it closer to my face, trying to see the hidden facets in his skin.

"Tell me what you're thinking," he whispered. I looked to see his eyes watching me, suddenly intent. "It's still so strange for me, not knowing."

"You know, the rest of us feel that way all the time."

"It's a hard life." Did I imagine the hint of regret in his tone? "But you didn't tell me."

"I *was* wishing I could know what you were thinking . . ." I hesitated.

"And?"

"I was wishing that I could believe that you were real. And I was wishing that I wasn't afraid."

"I don't want you to be afraid." His voice was just a soft murmur. I heard what he couldn't truthfully say, that I didn't need to be afraid, that there was nothing to fear.

"Well, that's not exactly the fear I meant, though that's certainly something to think about."

So quickly that I missed his movement, he was half sitting, propped up on his right arm, his left palm still in my hands. His angel's face was only a few inches from mine. I might have – should have – flinched away from his unexpected closeness, but I was unable to move. His golden eyes mesmerized me.

"What are you afraid of, then?" he whispered intently.

But I couldn't answer. As I had just that once before, I smelled his cool breath in my face. Sweet, delicious, the scent made my mouth water. It was unlike anything else. Instinctively, unthinkingly, I leaned closer, inhaling.

And he was gone, his hand ripped from mine. In the time it took my eyes to focus, he was twenty feet away, standing at the edge of the small meadow, in the deep shade of a huge fir tree. He stared at me, his eyes dark in the shadows, his expression unreadable.

I could feel the hurt and shock on my face. My empty hands stung.

"I'm . . . sorry . . . Edward," I whispered. I knew he could hear.

"Give me a moment," he called, just loud enough for my less sensitive ears. I sat very still.

After ten incredibly long seconds, he walked back, slowly for him. He stopped, still several feet away, and sank gracefully to the ground, crossing his legs. His eyes never left mine. He took two deep breaths, and then smiled in apology.

"I am so very sorry." He hesitated. "Would you understand what I meant if I said I was only human?"

I nodded once, not quite able to smile at his joke. Adrenaline pulsed through my veins as the realization of danger slowly sank in. He could smell that from where he sat. His smile turned mocking.

"I'm the world's best predator, aren't I? Everything about me invites you in – my voice, my face, even my *smell*. As if I need any of that!" Unexpectedly, he was on his feet, bounding away, instantly out of sight, only to appear beneath the same tree as before, having circled the meadow in half a second.

"As if you could outrun me," he laughed bitterly.

He reached up with one hand and, with a deafening crack, effortlessly ripped a two-foot-thick branch from the trunk of the spruce. He balanced it in that hand for a moment, and then threw it with blinding speed, shattering it against another huge tree, which shook and trembled at the blow.

And he was in front of me again, standing two feet away, still as a stone.

"As if you could fight me off," he said gently.

I sat without moving, more frightened of him than I had ever been. I'd never seen him so completely freed of that carefully cultivated façade. He'd never been less human . . . or more beautiful. Face ashen, eyes wide, I sat like a bird locked in the eyes of a snake.